Seven Day Wife

Mia Faye

Mia Faye

ISBN: 9798640189155

Author's note: This is a work of fiction. Some of the names and geographical locations in this book are products of the author's imagination, and do not necessarily correspond with reality.

For all romantics out there

TABLE OF CONTENTS

Chapter 1

Yvette

I knew I had made a mistake.

I let the box drop from my hands and sank onto the pavement. I took a quick peek into the back of the truck and let out an exasperated sigh. I was nowhere close to being done. Moving always seemed so easy in the movies; a quick montage with music and the whole apartment was transplanted magically into the new house. Turns out it wasn't so easy; there was the whole process of actually grabbing boxes and carrying them up to three flights of stairs, again and again, until your arms turned into spaghetti.

The mistake was not getting a professional moving company to do the whole thing for me. It's not that I didn't want to, really. Hiring professional movers would have cost an arm and a leg, and I was fresh out of body parts after spending all my money on rent and the move to Bend. Then there was the fact that Tyler, my best friend, had offered to help me move and volunteered his own van. So, at the time, it seemed like a reasonable plan.

It didn't seem so reasonable anymore. Tyler emerged from the apartment complex, and I could tell from his face he was thinking the exact same thing as me.

"We're right on track," he said. "Only about 600 boxes to go."

He sat down next to me on the pavement, patted himself down, and extracted a cigarette from one of his pockets. He put it between his lips but didn't light it; it just sat there, dangling idly in his mouth.

"Can't we take a break?" I asked him. "I just want to lie down here and let the feeling return to my fingers."

"Bad idea," Tyler said. "If we take a break, we won't be able to get back to work. Trust me."

1

"I'm starving. Are you starving?"

"Oh, I'm famished. But I know what you're thinking, and the answer is no. We can't get a quick bite."

"Why not!" I whined, swayed slightly, and laid my head on his shoulder.

"Well, because one of us was adamant that we finish moving you in before we go exploring the city, and it wasn't me."

"Why do you always have to be the voice of reason? Just once, support me! You're supposed to be my best friend!"

"I *am* your best friend. I've been lifting these heavy ass boxes all morning, haven't I? What is all this shit anyway? How can one person own so much useless stuff?"

"It's not useless; how dare you?" I lifted my head from his shoulder and gave him a withering glare.

"No?"Tyler got up and walked over to the back of the van. He opened the nearest box and pulled out a battered-looking record.

"Vinyl," he said smirking. "In the year of our Lord 2019. Pretty unusual for a 25-year-old woman."

"You know that's my dad's old collection. What was I supposed to do, leave it behind?"

"That's exactly what you were supposed to do. Donate them, chuck them into a river… anything."

I got up and went over to the truck as well.

"More lifting and carrying, less complaining. Come on."

Tyler shook his head, but his eyes were twinkling with mirth. He pulled the cigarette from his mouth and stuffed it back into his pocket. It was an odd little habit of his; I don't think I'd ever seen him actually smoke. He grabbed the box of records and gave me a playful shove with his hips, and then he set off toward the apartment.

I let out a long sigh and shook my head to spur my reluctant body into action. I reached for the next box and flipped it open. It contained part of my extensive shoe collection, and from the way it settled heavily into my arms, a few bricks too.

I only made it a few steps away from the truck. The apartment block seemed so far away, and the box was beginning to cut into my fingers. I tried to adjust my body, sinking low to transfer the weight onto my legs as I shifted the box so that I had a better grip. It was a bad idea. The movement only made me more aware of how tenuous my grip was in the first place, and when I tried to go back to the way I had been holding it, I felt it start to slip.

I froze, muttered a quick prayer, but knew it was pointless. My fingers got slicker and slicker, and I sank lower and lower, and then I lost my grip altogether, and suddenly the box was falling. I heard myself curse, letting out a string of choice expletives.

But the box did not make it to the ground.

I didn't see or hear him approaching. He seemed to come out of thin air; one minute I was alone, the next he was just there. I saw his hand shoot out, and the alarm caused me to let go of the box completely.

"Careful!" he said, reaching out with both hands and grabbing it, securing it inches from the ground.

I took a stunned step back to examine the stranger. It might have been the exhaustion, or the sun, or maybe even the fact that little stars were popping up in my vision. But it occurred to me that this was, without a doubt, the most beautiful man I had ever laid eyes on.

He towered over me, so I had to look up at him, into the sun. It created a sort of halo around his face, making him look even more beautiful.

He had the bluest eyes, soft pools of shimmering aqua that burned with intensity, the corners of which were crinkled from smiling. His hair was blond, long and wavy, falling into his face and around his ears. He had a strong square jaw with a hint of stubble, and a mouth that seemed to curve naturally into a permanent smile. But that wasn't the most remarkable thing about him. He was imposing enough, physically, but there was an air of masculinity about him that I couldn't describe. It was everything about him; his scent, the way his muscles tensed as he held on to the box, and the way he looked at me, his eyes assessing, caressing, and—I was sure I was imagining it—undressing me.

I was suddenly aware of the old, oversized shirt I was wearing, the wildness of my hair, and the complete lack of make-up on my face. I was dressed for a lazy afternoon on the couch, not a chance encounter with a gorgeous man. I felt simultaneously shy and bold. I wanted to reach up and pull the errant strands from his forehead, that slick little clump of blond hair that was clinging to his face. And I wanted to melt and disappear into the earth.

"You can let go; I've got it," the man said, and I forced my mind back to the present. I didn't have as much luck with my heart, though, which I hadn't even noticed was hammering at top speed.

I did as I was told, letting go and stepping back.

The man readjusted his grip on the box. It didn't seem as heavy in his hands, somehow. I noticed the grey T-shirt for the first time, the grey slacks and running shoes. Going for a run in the middle of the day?

"Where are we going?" he asked me.

I opened my mouth, then closed it. It seemed to take a long time for my brain to put two and two together. Was he asking if he could carry it up for me? As in up the stairs, to my tiny one-bedroom apartment? Where I would no doubt die from shame?

"No, that's okay," I said, my voice feeble. "I think I can manage."

"Are you sure?" He was beaming now, and I knew it was from the irony of the situation. I hadn't been managing too well 10 seconds ago.

"Oh, yeah. I just lost my grip a little, but I'm sure I'll make it."

"What's your name?" he asked me, his eyebrows knitting together.

"Yvette," I said. "What's yours?"

"I'm Cameron. Cam. Listen, Yvette, I'm sure you're perfectly capable of carrying this and any other boxes up to your apartment. I'm simply offering to help. You can grab one of the others, ideally not as heavy as this, and we'll get going, how about that?"

He must have been in his mid-thirties and had a natural charm I was sure had left a string of broken hearts in his wake. Despite myself, I found myself nodding. I *did* need some help with the boxes; at the pace Tyler and I were working, it would take us most of the day to finish, so I mumbled my agreement, trooped back to the truck and picked out a much lighter box, this one containing some of my old clothes.

Cameron made a 'shall we' motion with his head, and I pointed with my chin in the direction of the building. He stepped aside, indicating that I should go first, and I obliged. We set off walking slowly, and I promptly realized the problem with the formation. It seemed silly to even worry about it, but I was suddenly very conscious of my walk. An ex-boyfriend used to make fun of the way I walked, calling it 'my adorable waddle'. Worse, though, I was treating him to an unrestricted view of my ass.

It got especially pronounced when we got to the stairs. I could almost feel the heat from his gaze, and even though I was sure it wasn't really the case, it felt like his eyes were on my ass. My cheeks felt like they were under a microscope, as though there were two white-hot beams burning holes into the seat of my pants. It went on and on. Three flights of stairs had never seemed so long; I wasn't even aware of the box in my hands, or the increasing raggedness of my breathing, or the way my legs were starting to get heavy. All I knew was that this handsome stranger was ogling me, and it pushed me faster up the stairs.

I emerged into the third-floor hallway with a sigh of relief. I sped into apartment 23, pressing myself into the wall when the door swung open before I could reach for it. Tyler stepped out, saw me, and opened his mouth to say something. But then he saw Cameron, and I felt a flush of pleasure at seeing him react to Cameron the exact same way I had.

"Hey!" Cameron greeted him cheerily. "Where do I put this?"

Tyler stepped aside, kicking the door with his foot. He shook his head like he was just coming out of stupor. "My God!" he said, looking from me to the back of Cameron.

"I know, dude," I said. "I know. Go get more boxes. Cam said he'll help."

"Oh, he can definitely help. Maybe he can help you set up your bed."

"Boxes, Tyler." I blushed and shouldered my way into the apartment after Cameron.

"This is a lovely place," Cameron said. He was standing in the middle of the room, hands-on-hips.

"It's a dump," I said. "But it will do."

"Oh, I wouldn't call it a dump. It has an excellent view."

He beckoned me over to the window, and I reluctantly walked over. I had looked out the window several times since getting here; there was nothing outside but a long stretch of a boring brown wall, and on the other side of it, a far more luxurious apartment complex.

"Spectacular," I said, trying and failing to conceal my sarcasm.

Cameron laughed. "Look over there," he said, pointing to one of the windows on the apartment building. "The same floor, a little over on the right. See that window?"

"Yeah?"

"That's my bedroom window."

My head snapped around to him. "Wha… what do you mean?" I asked.

"I live there," he said. "Right across from you. I think that makes us neighbors."

He flashed me a cheeky smile. This time there was no mistaking the innuendo, or the twinkle in his eyes.

"Welcome to the neighborhood, Yvette."

Chapter 2

Yvette

For people who lived in two separate buildings, Cameron and I bumped into each other a lot. Chance encounters unless they weren't. I was beginning to get the impression he was planning these random meetups, that he had figured out my schedule and was availing himself at crucial points so he could make me hyperventilate.

It made sense because the first time it happened, I was leaving the apartment to go to the grocery store, and I literally walked into him outside the building.

"You never look where you're going, do you?" he asked me.

I blinked up at his sweaty face. "I try, but there's this lump of a guy who keeps crossing my path."

"Or is it you who keeps crossing his?"

"Hmm. Let's see." I looked from left to right and then back to the entrance of the building. "I may be wrong, but don't you live in that building over there?"

Cameron smiled his annoyingly charming smile. "Hmm. You may have a point."

"And why are you always out running?" I asked. "It's the middle of the day!"

"Who says I'm out running?" Cameron said, adopting what he imagined to be a mischievous expression. "Maybe I just wanted to arrange an accidental run-in with the cute new neighbor." He said it with such casual confidence, in an almost throwaway fashion. Right away, I felt my cheeks start to heat up.

"And what would be the objective of this run-in?" I asked him in a low voice. I hadn't even noticed it, but we were very close to each other. I could feel the heat coming off his body, could smell his aftershave, and the slightest hint of sweat. It was incredibly intoxicating.

"Oh, you know how it goes," he said. "A couple of accidental meetings and who knows where things could lead."

"Right."

"Besides, if she happens to be clumsy and prone to dropping things, I figure I should be there to help her out, you know?"

"Surely there's an easier way to keep tabs on her," I said, feeling bold and a bit reckless.

"Oh? Do tell?"

"You could get her number, for example, and any time she's heading out, she would notify you, and you could time your run-ins a bit better."

"Excellent idea." He pulled his phone from his sweatpants and handed it to me. I typed my number in with trembling fingers and gave it back to him.

"Alright, then," Cam said, pocketing the phone and giving me a genial pat on the shoulder. "See you next time."

Next time happened to be a few days later.

I knew it was him even before I heard the knock on my door. I was new in the neighborhood; I didn't have any friends to visit. I had just finished unpacking my bedroom, the last step to moving in completely. I was panting, a sheen of sweat glistening on my forehead when I went to get the door.

Cameron was hidden behind a medium-sized white box. He looked me over with the laser-focused intensity I had come to expect from him, and I felt the way I always did when he looked at me; like he was seeing right through my clothes. Not that he needed any help to do so. My top was sticking to my skin thanks to the sweat, and I had on the smallest short shorts I owned.

Cam hesitated, his eyes doing a little flick down to my legs and then traveling slowly upward. It was quite the rush, knowing I had at least stunned him, even if only for a moment.

"Hey, neighbor," I said.

"Hey," he said, shaking his head slightly. "I uh… I brought you a cake. Welcome gift, you know. I wanted to go with the traditional home-cooked meal, but I'm not much of a cook." He flipped the box open, and I stood on tiptoe to see inside.

"I hope you like blueberry."

"Thanks," I said. I took the cake and stepped aside to let him in.

He walked into the apartment and started to look around. It was a small space, probably much smaller than his own place, but I had done my best to maximize the space. My couch was in one corner of the room, across from the small TV Tyler had gotten me as a going-away present, and which I was still trying to figure out how to mount. The rest of the room was filled with a random assortment of things; a small bookshelf, another shelf with records, the entirety of my painting collection, still lined against the walls while I decided how and where to put them up, and my little makeshift office in the far corner of the room.

"I like what you've done with the place," Cameron commented, nodding his approval. I couldn't figure out whether he was being sarcastic.

"Uh, thanks. I was just finishing up unpacking if you can believe it."

Cameron shrugged. "Moving is tedious."

"So tedious. I don't know why I thought it would be simple."

"Movies?"

"Right. And sitcoms."

"Do you need some help?"

"Oh." Why did I always blush in front of the man? "I

was… I mean, I don't want to keep you."

"No, no, it won't be a problem. So, what are we unpacking? Kitchen? Bathroom?"

"Bedroom," I said.

Cameron's lip twitched, and his tone immediately turned flirty. "I wouldn't mind helping you out in the bedroom."

"It's mostly just clothes, to be honest," I said. I didn't know what I was playing at; I was not ready for that man to see my bedroom.

"Are you sure?"

"Yeah. It's just a bunch of clothes I need to fold. But thanks for offering."

Cam nodded. He took a few steps toward me and leaned in to whisper into my ear. "You have stunning legs, Yvette. They're quite the distraction."

I blinked and swallowed hard, unsure how to react to that. But I didn't get a chance to. Cam sidestepped me and made for the door, and he was gone before I could even thank him for the cake.

I thought about his comment a lot for the rest of the day. And his behavior toward me. I hadn't known what to make of it that first time we met, but now I was sure of it. We seemed to have a playful banter, one that had apparently evolved into outright flirting. I didn't mind that one bit. Cam was a great-looking guy. The thing I had trouble with was how much he seemed to affect me.

I had always been shy and introverted. Mousy, almost. But with Cam, I found myself bolder, more willing to say and do things I would otherwise never have considered.

Several times I found myself thinking of him; random thoughts that would just pop up in my head. I found myself remembering his stare and the silent promise in his eyes when he looked at me. Or his sweatpants, which were always just tight enough that I could see the outline of his strong legs, and much more. I thought about his voice, low and intimate and manly, and his lips, whispering compliments right against my ear.

It was a very long day. I finally finished unpacking late at night and sat down to admire my handiwork. I wasn't going for a replica of my old apartment, but it came pretty close. It didn't feel like home yet, but it looked like it. I could definitely get used to living here.

My eyes fell on the cake, still on the coffee table where Cam had left it. I got up and went into the kitchen, picked out a plate and some cutlery. I stacked the plate with a generous slice, and then on a whim, pulled a chair up to the window and drew the curtains aside slightly.

I had no difficulty locating Cam's apartment. I had been looking out every day, trying to catch him doing something I could then make fun of. But I had only seen him once, for a brief moment in the morning, before he closed the window.

I bit into a forkful of the cake and let out an involuntary sigh. It was creamy and soft and full of flavor. I made a mental note to ask Cam where he got it.

My wait was rewarded after about ten minutes. I saw a flash of motion, and then the curtains to Cam's bedroom window flew open. My heart leaped into my mouth, and I instinctively drew my own curtains back, terrified that he had seen me. I waited for a few breathless seconds, and then I stuck my head back around the sheer fabric. I couldn't see into his bedroom too clearly, but I could make him out, or at least his body. He was topless, and from the way he was sitting up and then lowering himself out of sight, I gathered that he was working out.

His body was exactly as I had imagined it would be. Chiseled, athletic, extremely easy on the eye. I stared at him so absentmindedly that I didn't notice the fork slip out of my hand. The sound of it clattering to the floor brought me back to earth, and at the same moment, I felt my phone begin to vibrate in my pocket.

I smiled when I saw his name on the screen. "Hello?" I

said.

"I know a spot with a much better view," Cam said. I looked out the window at his apartment; he had stopped working out and was leaning against the window, looking right in my direction.

"I don't know what you mean," I said.

"You might want to get your eyes checked. You shouldn't have to squint, you know. It's not good for your eyes."

"Oh, you think I was watching you? From my window?"

"I'm fairly certain, yes."

"You're mistaken, sir. I was actually watching the old lady a few windows down from yours. I didn't even notice you."

"Is that so?"

"Yeah."

"So, you wouldn't notice if I did... this?"

As I watched, he reached down and tugged at the strings securing his sweatpants. My breath caught in my throat. He pushed the pants off slowly, letting them roll off his hips and drop to the floor, then stepping out of them one leg at a time. He was left with nothing but boxers, tiny, perfectly fitted boxers that left nothing to the imagination. I pressed my thighs together, suddenly very hot.

"You know, I think you're right. I can't see anything from this far out. You mentioned something about a spot with a better view?"

"I did. I could show it to you if you want?"

"Show me the spot, you mean?"

"That too, yes." He paused while I was still trying to get my brain to formulate words. "Ah, well," Cam said. "I guess it doesn't matter since you were really looking at old Mrs. Witten in the apartment below."

"But if I wasn't..."

"Then I would ask you to come over, in that sexy little slip you're wearing, and I'll give you a tour of my bedroom. Views and all."

There was something so sexy about how cocky he sounded, how assured he was. He knew I was attracted to him. He knew that there was no way I was going to say no. A delicious tingle was spreading from between my legs, pulsing outward to every nerve in my body. I stood at that window, staring out at the half-naked man across from me, and I knew the decision had been made long before he even asked.

I dropped the plate on the table and left the house right as I was. Partly because I was afraid if I hesitated, I would change my mind, but mostly because of the anxiety that was slowly starting to creep in. Or was that excitement?

The wind billowed against me as I crossed to the other side, and my nightgown danced merrily around my ankles. Yet the chill never really registered.

By the time I got to his door, the panic had grown tenfold, and I considered for the first time that this was a bad idea. I lifted my hand to knock, paused, then let it drop. This was definitely a bad idea. I wrapped the nightgown around my body, shook my head, and started to turn away.

The door swung open before I could leave, however. And there he was. He hadn't bothered to put anything else on; he was still in those impossibly sexy boxers and nothing else. He had been right, I thought. The view was way better up close.

I meant to say something, was going to protest somehow. But he stepped forward, and his hand snaked around my waist, and the next thing I knew, I was being pulled into the apartment. My legs left the ground, and I was being lifted, and then Cameron's lips were crushed against mine.

Chapter 3

Cameron

She smelled of lavender and rich perfume, something with heady notes of vanilla which I knew would linger in the air long after she was gone. It seemed to come from everywhere all at once; her hair, as it flayed out on the wall I had pinned her to, the crook of her neck, where I buried my head and— moments later— my teeth, and the silk gown she was wearing, soft and light and easily brushed aside.

I let my hands trace the contours of her figure, exploring first the lovely swell of her hips, then letting my fingers lazily draw patterns all the way to her lower back. From there, it was a short journey to her bottom, and I grabbed her and lifted her so that her legs wrapped around my back.

She tasted of cake and fruit, and perhaps wine. I kissed her passionately, fiercely, letting the full extent of my desire pour out of my lips and onto hers. She responded with an abandon that drove me insane; her mouth on mine was urgent, challenging, and dancing along with mine, sweet and slick and wonderful.

But it was her body that really set me on fire. She felt incredible, crushed as she was against the wall. I pressed myself onto her, feeling the wall behind her and pushing her still, wanting to get even closer to her. She was warm and soft everywhere my skin came into contact with her. I fit right alongside her, my body on hers and hers around mine.

I deepened the kiss, letting my hand slide up her body, all the way to her chin and tilting it up so I could ravish her properly. My tongue lashed out, probing the slight resistance of her lips and then delving into her mouth. Just like she had before, she matched the zeal and intensity. Her own tongue slipped out, and now we were wrestling, tangling, my head swimming in a heady mix of lust and excitement.

A cold draft blew past us, and I remembered that the door was still open.

I pulled away with some effort, breaking the kiss and stepping back so that Yvette's feet slowly hit the floor. Her eyes slid open, heavy and drowsy and beautiful. Green eyes. I hadn't noticed.

I licked my lips, and they tasted just like hers.

I reached out and swung the door shut, then turned my attention back to her. I put my hands on either side of her and leaned down. She was standing on tiptoe, but she was still about a head shorter than me. She lifted her face to me and closed her eyes. Her lips were pursed, an invitation to resume the kiss.

"Welcome to my lovely home," I announced.

She opened her eyes again. Her eyebrows came together, confused. "What?"

"Welcome," I said again. "I promised you a tour, right?"

"Of your bedroom, right."

"Then let's get to it, shall we?"

I could tell she didn't want the tour, and I didn't either unless it involved my fingers touring her body. But I needed to slow down, get myself under control first. Things were moving a bit too quickly. I made a sweeping gesture around the living room, and Yvette followed it with mild interest.

"Living room," I said. "Over there, kitchen, and beyond that, pantry. Over here, we have a hallway, which leads to the bedrooms, my office, bathrooms, and TV room."

"Let's start with the bedroom," Yvette said, and I couldn't help smiling.

I reached over and found her hand, interlocking her fingers in mine. I led her into the first room on the left, my bedroom, and flicked the light on.

"Whoa," she gasped, letting my hand go and stepping into the room. She turned around almost full circle, taking in everything. My own eyes were fixed on her; I couldn't help it. She looked radiant, the way her face was lit up, and her eyes were like bright bulbs, and her cheeks were rosy from the kiss. Her gown had come open at some point, though she wasn't aware of it. I could see the pale skin just beyond the open folds of the gown, the rise of her breasts, and down below, the adorable lace panties she was wearing.

She went over to the window and peered out, no doubt looking to see if she could spot her apartment. I followed her there and pointed over her shoulder.

"My God, those curtains are practically see-through," she commented, shaking her head. "Why didn't you tell me?"

"Why would I? The view is incredible."

I could tell she understood exactly what she meant. And that was my favorite thing about Yvette so far; she could pick up on all my subtle flirtations and respond in kind.

"My view isn't so bad either," she said, turning her body to me. I could feel the heat from her body, electrifying the space between us.

I reached out with a finger and slipped it into the edge of her gown. Keeping my eyes on her, I pulled it in and outward, so that the gown came away slowly until it slipped off her shoulder and rustled to the floor.

She stood in front of me, her breasts jutting out proudly, screaming for my touch.

"I think you're sexy as fuck," I told her, and I meant it.

She wasn't tall, Yvette, but she had the body of a model. She had a cute, petite face in which large green eyes were the standout feature. Soft brown hair had been tied in a neat bun on top of her head, but a few strands were dangling on her forehead. She had a long, graceful neck, curving beautifully into a pair of elegant shoulders and long arms. Her breasts were ample and perky. She had an almost pear-like shape because her body curved at the hip into a wide, round ass that was only topped by her shapely legs.

I knew I was staring, but I couldn't help it.

Yvette stepped up to me, smiling as if she understood exactly what was going on in my head.

"So," she said.

It was invitation enough.

I grabbed her once more, finding her lips with ease. Her arms went around my neck, and when I grabbed around her waist, she leaned into my body and lifted herself, wrapping her legs around me once more.

I turned around with her in my arms and led her to the bed. I doubted I could restrain myself this time, but I didn't care. We fell in together, our kiss unbroken, a messy tangle of limbs. I felt her fumble with the front of my boxers. The brush of her fingers so close to my cock drew a startled gasp from me, and I could feel her smiling even as I kissed her.

Encouraged, she ventured in, letting her fingers slide past the fabric and into the boxers. Long, warm fingers wrapped around my girth, and I gasped again. In an attempt to pay her back for the sweet agony she was subjecting me to, I reached my hand between our tussling bodies and caressed her torso, working my way up until I cupped a heavy breast.

Now we were both moaning. I flicked at her nipple, pinched it ever so softly, and massaged her breast. She squeezed my cock, rubbed it from within the boxers, and ran her finger along the slit of the head. It was more than I could take. I shifted my body, pulled it away from her. She protested, but I was already traveling south, trailing kisses along her body as I went.

She fell silent the minute I got to her navel. And she started to jerk and buckle when I spread her thighs and dove in. She had thick thighs, as I had seen and expected. Her fragrance was richer down there, a combination of her scent and the essence of her womanhood. It was there that I buried my head, and with a few tentative flicks of my tongue, I found her swollen lips.

I thought she had been moaning before, but it was nothing compared to what was happening now. The room was filled with sounds of her harried breathing, her groans, and moans coming through gritted teeth.

I kept the pressure up, enjoying the way her body was twisting and her hips grinding against my hands. I alternated between kissing her lips to push them apart, licking along and beyond them to the center of her heat, and flicking my tongue at the swollen hood of her clitoris. Several times she tried to twist away from me, and I had to grab her thighs and keep them open.

"Please," she whispered after some time. Her voice was barely audible, raspy, and breathless. "Please." I knew what she was saying. Funny, how I understood even the subtlest little hints she was giving me.

I gave her lips one final kiss, then retreated from between her legs and straightened up. I rolled away, reaching for the bedside drawer, and fumbling around for a condom. I looked over at Yvette as I slipped it on, at her heaving bosom, and the way her body was laid out on my bed, waiting for me. My cock pulsed and throbbed.

She was so wet by the time I repositioned myself on top of her that I had no difficulty finding and driving into her. It was a single, long thrust, and I buried myself all the way. Yvette gasped then held her breath. Her leg coiled around my back, and with it, she pulled me down and deeper inside her.

I reached for her chin again, and she understood the touch to be a plea, a request. I wanted to see her, to look into her eyes as I took her. She obliged, opening her eyes, and looking at me just as I was starting to move.

It was slow at first; I withdrew slowly, pulling my hips all the way back, and then driving back into her with a sure stroke. Each time she moaned a little louder, and with each thrust, I got more frenzied. Soon, our bodies were mashing together as I pounded harder and faster. A thin film of sweat materialized between us as we both writhed and contorted our bodies. Her hands were on my back, and her fingers were starting to dig painfully into my skin. I fell onto my elbows, bringing my ears right next to her lips.

The sounds coming from her were enough to tip me over the edge. Not yet, though. I closed my eyes and willed myself to wait for her.

I didn't have to wait long.

Her whole body froze, and I thought for a second, I had somehow hurt her. Then she started to shudder, from the tips of her fingers all the way down to her toes, her body rocking and trembling uncontrollably. She clasped the shaft of my cock tighter than ever; her hands were like bars of steel on my back, and her hips wouldn't stop grinding against me.

I couldn't make sense of any of the things she was saying. With one final guttural grunt, she tensed up one last time, and then her body went completely still.

Without missing a beat, I slipped out and turned her over. She lifted her ass to me, and I reached over and pushed her head down into the mattress. I guided myself back into her, grabbing her by the hips to find purchase.

I think I meant to be gentle, slow. But Yvette wouldn't let me. She rocked back and forth on her knees, meeting my forward thrusts with backward thrusts of her own, and in seconds I was panting, hanging on for dear life. I grabbed a handful of the bedding and ground mercilessly into her, feeling her second orgasm start to tear through her.

And then I was coming too. I roared, and she cried out loudly, and our bodies collapsed in shared bliss. I fell forward onto her back, where I stayed until my breathing returned to normal.

I heard her voice as if from miles away. It was all indecipherable, but I was sure I knew the gist of it, and I mumbled something back. Yvette lowered herself to the bed, and I rolled off her and onto my back.

I thought that was a proper welcome-to-the-neighborhood gift.

Chapter 4

Cameron

I had been at Penguin Publishers for over 10 years, and I still got nervous going in for management meetings. Every single time. Even when I knew the agenda of the meeting, I would still feel that tense anxiety that I first experienced on my first day of work. I remember it like it was yesterday; I was a young, awkward kid just out of school, walking into a boardroom full of dark suits and even darker expressions. It was terrifying. And I had to walk up to Wyatt Banks, the owner of the company, and introduce myself. I remember just being grateful that I waited until *after* the meeting to puke my guts out.

Things had changed since then, but not by much. I was walking into a meeting with representatives of the board and other important suits. I was nervous, although not nearly as much as I had been the first time. And, I would have to introduce myself to Wyatt again, even though we had known each other for ten years and worked closely for more than half of those.

It was an open secret by now; Wyatt, the man who had dragged a struggling publishing company kicking and screaming into the future and given it an enviable reputation across the country, a man who had been renowned for his brilliance, was in the moderate stages of dementia. He had done a good job of keeping the diagnosis under wraps, but people talk, and those closest to him had always known about it. The real problem was that it was getting harder and harder for him to run the company. His wife Meredith had sensibly taken over much of the workload, but Wyatt was a stubborn man, and he insisted on going about his day as he always did and working the way he always had. It was his work that had gotten the company to where it was, after all.

It was with all this in mind that I walked into the boardroom that morning. I didn't know what to expect. It was supposed to be our quarterly planning meeting, but these meetings never went the way you expected them to. Plus, something about the way Meredith had sounded on the phone when she called to confirm my attendance struck me as odd.

There was no one in the boardroom when I got there. I glanced at my watch, wondering if I was early, but I was right on time. After confirming that I was in the right room and checking that I had the right date and time, I let myself in and sat down in one of the chairs.

Minutes ticked by silently. I looked out the large transparent wall on one side of the room and busied myself watching the other employees go about their duties. A smartly dressed young woman filed past the room, her head buried in a thick folder, and I froze, convinced that I knew her. In the Biblical sense, that is, I was almost certain Yvette Matthews had just walked past the room. But that was impossible. My mind must have been playing tricks on me, picking out residual memories, and projecting them to the fore.

The door opened, and I looked up to see Meredith Banks walking in. She was alone. "Cam," she said, walking over to my chair and shaking my hand. "I hope I didn't keep you waiting?"

"Not at all," I said. I looked over her shoulder, still expecting to see men in suits filling in.

"Oh, the quarterly meeting has been postponed," Meredith said, sitting down next to me. "At least for the time being."

"Is everything okay?" I asked.

Meredith sighed. She took her glasses from her face and rubbed her eyes. At that moment, she looked older than I had ever seen her look. "No," she said. "It's Wyatt."

I had to make a conscious effort to stay calm. "What happened?"

"Nothing happened. Well, not really. I know everyone is already talking about it, so it isn't much of a secret. But I know you, at the very least, are aware of Wyatt's Alzheimer's?"

I nodded.

"Well, he's been getting worse every day. His memory is completely shot. He has trouble even remembering where he is, who he is. It used to be random spells that would last minutes, once or twice a week, but now he can barely make it through the day without one of his episodes. I don't know what to do. This morning, he didn't even recognize me, and I had to force him back in bed because he was adamant that he had to attend an important meeting at work." Her voice cracked at the end, and she trailed off.

"I'm so sorry, Meredith. I know Alzheimer's can be a bitch."

"Thanks, Cam. I just wish I knew what to do. I feel powerless like I'm supposed to sit there and watch my husband just waste away in front of my very eyes."

"What do the doctors say?"

Meredith shook her head. "At this point, all they talk about is keeping Wyatt comfortable. And I know exactly what that means."

I tried to picture Wyatt in a home. It wasn't a very pretty picture.

"Anyway, that's not why I wanted to see you, Cam."

"Okay?"

"As you know, Wyatt has personally handled a lot of things in the company over the years, most of which he should have delegated. Now, I'm trying to get him to stay at home, so we're going to have to take on some of his duties ourselves."

"Of course, yeah."

"As you know, the annual company retreat is in just over a week. Wyatt was actually very fond of it. He used to say it was the most important event in the year, because it helped motivate the staff, and if the staff was happy, the company would always be successful."

It was true; over the years, the company retreat had gone

from the little team-building exercise we had to endure once a year to this huge event everyone looked forward to. Its theme changed every year, but it was always fun, and Wyatt usually spared no expense on it.

"I need you to take over for him this year," Meredith went on. "I know it's short notice, and I really wish we had planned this earlier, but here we are. You're just going to have to do your best in the time left."

"Had he worked on it at all?" I asked.

"Even if he had, it would be almost impossible to get it out of him. It's probably best to assume you're working from a blank slate."

"Okay. I'll see what I can do."

"Good. I knew I could count on you. There's one more thing I need your help with before you go."

"Yeah?"

"This one is more personal. As you know, I usually handle the new hires in the department, and I'm supposed to be meeting a young lady we just hired. You know, show her around, take her through a brief orientation, get her settled in… But I have to get back home and take care of Wyatt, so I need you to handle this for me, too."

"Uh, I don't know, Meredith, I've never really…"

"You were new once, right? Just remember your own orientation, and then do just that. All you really have to do is take her through the company policies, show her to her office, and then HR will take it from there. I would reschedule, but she was supposed to report at nine, and I don't think I can."

"Who is this, anyway?" I asked. "I didn't know we were hiring."

"She is part of the new editorial team I'm putting together. We're hoping to create an entirely new digital archive, and she was one of the first people who interviewed. Brilliant woman, I think she'll fit in perfectly."

"Okay," I said. "Orientation. Got it. Is there anything else? Someone you want me to fire for you, perhaps?"

Meredith smiled, but only for a second. The stress lines returned to her face almost instantly."As a matter of fact, there is. I'm telling you this in confidence, Cam, because I trust you, okay? This whole thing with Wyatt means there's going to be a shake-up in the company. I can't reveal any details yet, but the board is looking to fill Wyatt's position with someone from within the company, someone who knows how we run, someone who has the potential to carry out Wyatt's vision. Nothing is set in stone, of course, but I want you to know that I've recommended you for the job."

I stared at her for a long time, waiting for the other shoe to drop."What?"

"I think you'd be perfect for it. You've been with us for over ten years. You know the company in and out, and everyone loves you. Personally, I think it's a no-brainer. So, this company retreat, it isn't just any old event; it's also a chance for you to show your leadership, get the staff behind you."

"I don't know what to say, Meredith, really."

"Then don't say anything," she said, getting up and gathering her things. "Just knock the damn thing out of the park, and we'll see what happens."She picked out a folder from the pile she was clutching and handed it to me."Don't forget. New hire. Probably waiting in the lobby."She gave me a final wink, and then she turned and left.

I checked my watch and cursed under my breath. It was five minutes past nine. I got to my feet and rushed out the door. I shouldered past several people, leaving a trail of angry protests along the way. I tried to remember my own orientation, but it was mostly hazy. I couldn't even recall who had received me, but I knew it was a surly old man with wobbly chins and a less-than-sunny disposition.

Keep it simple, I told myself. Just give her a quick tour, dump her at her desk, and be on your way. I had a lot of work to do if the retreat was to have a chance of success. I stepped into the lobby and looked around, then realized I had no idea who I was looking for. I flipped the folder open and scanned the first page. The name jumped out at me first. I read and reread it, wondering if this was my brain playing more tricks on me. I looked up, my eyes scanning the room. And then I saw her. Her hair was different; the wild curls straightened out and slicked back neatly. But it was definitely her. Big green eyes. Charming smile. It was Yvette.

Chapter 5

Yvette

"What are you doing here?" I asked getting to my feet and walking over to him. He looked like he had seen a ghost. I was pretty sure I had the exact same expression.

"Uh, I would ask you the same question, but seeing as I've been sent to welcome our newest employee…"

"*Our* employee? As in you work here?"

"Yeah."

"You can't be serious."

"You're right," Cam said, adopting his sarcastic persona. "This is all part of an elaborate prank I'm playing on you. Next, I'm going to give you a tour of the office, then show you to your desk."

The minute he said the word 'tour,' my mind went into overdrive, and I was suddenly back in his living room, pinned to the wall next to his door while he shoved his tongue down my throat. That was supposed to have been a tour, too.

"Seriously, though," I said. "You work here?"

Cam shook his head in disbelief. He reached into his pocket and pulled out his wallet, from which he drew out a card and handed it to me.

Cameron Palmer

Managing Editor

Penguin Publishing

"That is such a wild coincidence," I said.

"You're telling me," he said. "I mean, what are the chances? You move in next to me, and then a few days later, you start a job at my company?"

27

"Dear God, I hope you're not my boss," I said without thinking. I flinched, but Cam only laughed.

"What's the problem?" he asked. "You're worried I'll ride you too hard?"

I couldn't believe his audacity. I couldn't believe he would do that here. And I couldn't believe how fast the blood rushed to my labia.

"Stop!" I admonished him, looking around for any spectators.

Cam grinned. "Again, that is. Ride you too hard *again*."

Now I was positively blushing. I took a step back from him, worried that he would grab me and kiss me again because that was exactly the kind of impulsive thing Cameron would do. And I wasn't sure I would hate it too much if he did.

"Okay, okay," he said, clearly noticing my discomfort. "I'm just trying to wrap my head around all this. When did you apply for this job?"

"A couple of weeks ago."

"Wait, is that why you moved here?"

"Yeah, I'm from Rockford. I saw this job posting, and I applied with the usual skepticism. I've always wanted to work in publishing, so when I was told I got the job, it was a dream come true. I had to move."

"Wow."

I knew what he was thinking because I was thinking about it too. How had we seen each other naked but not had a basic conversation about ourselves and our lives? But I knew the answer as soon as the question popped into my head; it was the same reason Cam could flirt with me in a public lobby, and my body responded immediately.

A tall, skinny man walked past us, and Cam greeted him. It seemed to jog his senses, reminding him of what he was supposed to be doing. "Come on," he said to me. I saw his hand twitch and start to reach for mine, and I was reminded of him doing the exact same thing as he led me into his bedroom. Focus, Vee. Focus. At the last moment, though, he froze, and the hand fell limp at his side.

I fell into step behind him as he walked into the office. I listened passively as he pointed out important areas, stopping every once in a while to say hi to someone or sign something. Clearly, he was an important figure at the company. I didn't understand why he had been saddled with me, though. This didn't seem like something that would be in his job description.

"And this," he announced, ushering me into a large room and jogging me back to the present. "This is my office."

He waved me inside, eagerly showing off the office. I could see why; it was large and extremely well-furnished. It was both bigger than my living room and better decorated. He had a full set of leather seats, a large shelf filled with a dizzying array of books, a small drinks table in one corner of the room, and in the other, a huge mahogany desk. Worse, there was a stunning view of the city out the window behind the desk.

"This is standard, right?" I asked. "I get an office like this too?"

"You're lucky you get an office," Cam said. "When I was starting out, I had to share a desk with three other interns. Three!"

"Yeah, but I'm not an intern," I said, smiling sweetly.

"So, I hear," he said. "You're the genius editor who's going to revolutionize our ancient department."

"Oh, you've heard about me?"

"Without knowing I was hearing about you. Does that make sense?"

"I think so…"

"Anyway, congratulations, Yvette. I'm sorry I didn't ask, but I'm glad you're here."He sounded earnest, and it was a little uncharacteristic.

"Thanks," I said. "Now, are you going to show me my office or what?"

"Right. Right. Before that, I'm supposed to give you this brief on what the company does, our policies and guidelines, and all that. There's a couple of style books you're supposed to read, and… let me see… oh, yeah, you're supposed to buy everyone drinks after work tonight."

"What?"

"Long story. It's kind of our hazing ritual that the newest employee has to get everyone drunk, which is the fastest way to get to know people around here."

"Okay…"

"Hey, I don't make the rules."

"Will you be there?"

"Oh, I wouldn't miss it for the world."

The rest of the tour was uneventful. It was mostly my fault, though; I was distracted all through it, even as Cam was trying to break down where each department was and how they interacted with each other. I told myself I would figure it out eventually, ideally when Cam wasn't hovering over me, or throwing suggestive looks at me in the middle of innocent sentences.

Penguin Publishing was one of the largest publishing houses in the country, and it certainly seemed like it. This was only my second ever job out of school, and already it dwarfed my last job in every aspect. It was larger, more complex, like a living organism fueled by a thousand moving parts. It was inspiring and terrifying all at once.

Cam finally pushed me into a small office in the corner of the second floor and declared proudly that it was my new home.

"It's not much," he said, "but everyone has to start somewhere, you know?"

"I love it," I said in earnest.

True, it wasn't as big as Cam's, or as luxurious, but it was a little removed from the rest of the office. It seemed like the kind of place I could disappear to or use as a hideaway. I would have no problem getting my work done here.

"You know the best thing about it, though?" Cam asked.

I shook my head.

It happened so fast. I heard rather than saw the door slam shut, then a flash of blurred motion, and then I was being pushed onto the desk and strong hands were sliding around my waist. Cam's lips crushed against mine, hungry and eager and familiar.

It was like something woke up inside me, like that touch, the feel of him, was a sensation I had been craving without knowing. A voice in the back of my head popped up, reminding me of where I was and that this was inappropriate. But Cam tasted so good, and he smelled wonderful, and I had missed the fiery exuberance of his kiss and the intoxicating feel of his hands on me. So, I closed my eyes, and I let him kiss me, and boy did he kiss me.

Everything seemed to dim; sound and sight, and all that was left was the magic of that moment. Cam's hands were on my back, and then they were on my ass, and then they had somehow found the soft skin of my thighs, and I was panting from the effort of standing up, from the agony of keeping my legs pressed together.

He lifted me in one fluid motion, and I felt my thighs settle on the cold wood of the desk. His hands were fumbling with the buttons of my blouse, so clumsily that they kept brushing past my breasts and agitating my already hardened nipples. Or maybe it wasn't so clumsy after all. Maybe he knew what to do to get me going. I couldn't argue that fact; in a few short minutes, he had rendered me wet and needy.

I didn't know how he unbuttoned the blouse, but the next moment, his hands were sneaking into my bra, and that woke me up. My eyes flew open, and I broke the kiss and pulled away from him. I was panting as I jumped off the desk and stepped away from him. I walked over to the window and threw it open, desperate for some air.

"I'm sorry," Cam was saying. "You just looked so damn sexy in that skirt; I couldn't help myself."

I loved the rush I got when he said things like that. And yet…"We can't do this," I said, still breathing heavily.

"I'm sorry?"

"It's my first day here," I explained. I needed him to understand. "I really wanted this job, and I was so excited when I got it. I know we didn't talk much over the weekend, or when we met, but I'm actually pretty passionate about books, and this field. I would like to make a difference. I know it sounds silly, but I hope to one day inspire someone to read, just like I was inspired when I was a child.

"I'm sorry. I'm rambling. The thing is, Cam. We can't do this here. I don't think it's a good idea. I like you, obviously, but I don't want this to complicate the job for me."

"What do you mean, you don't want to do this here?" Cam asked. I thought I noticed an edge creep into his voice.

"I mean us," I said. "This. Whatever it is. It was one thing when you were just my neighbor. But my boss… it changes things. It's different…"I was failing miserably at getting my point across, but somehow, I knew Cam understood exactly what I meant. I knew, because his face went from puzzled to shocked and then to casually indifferent, and it was heartbreaking.

"I get it," he said. He adjusted his tie and brushed off imaginary lint from his coat. "No mixing business and pleasure. I totally get it."

Before I could say anything else, he opened the door and walked out, and I was left standing by the window, my lips still throbbing from his kisses, but with the sinking feeling that I had just ruined everything.

Chapter 6

Cameron

My old man was waiting for me in the driveway. He always did, every time I visited. And it always made me feel guilty as if I didn't visit them nearly enough, and so he wanted to make the most of the time I was there.

Even at 70, Richard Palmer was still in excellent shape. Full head of thick grey hair. Sharp, intelligent eyes hidden behind thick glasses. Skinny—he had always been skinny—but strong and healthy. He stood tall and regal, waving a hand as I pulled in, a slight smile on his face.

"Son," he said as I got out of the car.

He reached out a hand, at the same time I was stretching out for a hug. We paused, comically frozen in our individual poses. I went to switch mine, reach for his hand instead, but he had the same idea, and he dropped it just as my hand was coming forward. It was exactly the kind of relationship I had with my dad; neither of us was comfortable with expressive affection.

In the end, he clapped me on the arm, and I nodded.

"Hey, Dad." I reached back into the car and pulled out the box I had brought with me. "I didn't have time to gift-wrap it, but here you go."

He took the bottle from me, a pained look on his face.

"What?" I asked him. "What's wrong?"

"Is this a Macallan 25?" he asked.

"Yeah. I tried to swing for the '72, but it would have bankrupted me. I'll work on it for your next birthday, yeah?"

Dad shook his head, still staring at the whiskey.

"Seriously, Dad, what's going on? I've never seen you look

33

so mournfully at whiskey."

"This is a lovely gift, son, but I can't accept it."

I scoffed.

"Or, I suppose it's more accurate to say, your mother won't let me. She's trying to get me off the bottle."

"Shit, really? Since when?"

"A couple of months."

"Has she?"

"For the most part, yes."

"Why, though?"

"Something about taking care of myself now that I'm advancing in years." He brought his hands up to do air quotes, drawing a smile from me.

"Come on, Dad. You're the healthiest person I know. Certainly the best looking 70-year-old I've ever seen."

"Hey, what can I do? You know what your mother is like."He tried to push the bottle back to me, but I shook my head.

"It's your birthday, Dad. Keep it. I'll talk to her about letting you have a glass every once in a while."

"Good luck with that," he said.

We walked to the house together. I started to ask him about his plans for the birthday, but I got my answer as soon as I stepped into the house.

The house was decorated and set up for a party. It looked nothing like the house I grew up in; the walls were covered in streamers and brightly colored decorations. Dad's photos were strewn all over the place, most of them featuring his trademark frown. The living room was filled with people, all of whom turned around when we walked in.

"You didn't tell me there was a party!" I whispered to my dad, but he only shrugged. Which meant it had not been his idea; knowing Mom, she had probably been organizing this for weeks, and Dad only learned of it today.

She came walking up to me, smiling broadly. Unlike Dad, she had no problem showing emotion or affection, and she wrapped me in a tight hug. "We weren't sure you'd come," she said, stepping back and examining me as if determined to commit my features to memory.

The one thing the Palmers all shared was that tall, proud gene; my mother was just as tall as my dad, but where he was restrained and almost shy, she was the exact opposite. Everything about her screamed 'life of the party.' She was beautiful and social, and she always knew just what to say. Dad liked to joke that they would not have gotten together if she hadn't made the first move; that's just the kind of person she was.

"I wouldn't miss Dad's 70th," I said. "Or this party. When did you do all this, Mom?"

"Oh, it was nothing. Made a few phone calls, that's all." But she beamed with pride as she said it. "Your father wanted a small dinner with just us; can you believe it? I told him it's not every day people get to celebrate 70 years."

Dad threw me an exasperated look. I knew exactly what it meant; she had overruled him.

"Well, it looks great, Mom."

"Aww, thanks, darling. Of course, if I knew this was what it would take to get you to visit…"

"Oh, stop it, Sheila," Dad interjected, coming to my defense. "You know how busy Cameron is with the company."

"Right," Mom said, but her face fell, and I felt a pang of guilt. "Of course. We're happy to have you, darling." She patted me gently on the cheek. "Come. I'll introduce you to our guests."

Their guests consisted of people from their immediate circles, Dad's oldest law school buddies along with his friends from the neighborhood, and Mom's 'gang,' her tight circle of girlfriends she had maintained since her college days. Most of them were familiar; I had met them on occasion or knew them from childhood. Still, Mom made a point of marching me through the room, her hand tucked securely in the crook of my elbow, and introducing me to every single one of them.

The pride in her voice was evident; from the way she spoke about me, I could tell she had been talking me up to them for some time, and she was finally getting to show me off in person. I smiled and made small talk as best as I could, but my attention was slowly being drawn to something else.

I had noticed it when I entered the room, but only peripherally. There were a lot of younger ladies in attendance, none of whom I knew. Mom's trip around the room with me in tow somehow skipped all the younger women, and it was only when we were done that I felt bold enough to bring it up.

"Is that everyone?" I asked her, smiling.

"Hmm?" Her eyebrows shot up in a perfect imitation of surprised confusion.

"I couldn't help noticing your introductions didn't extend to… everyone at the party."

"Well, I thought you could do the rest on your own. Do you know? Makes a better impression when you do it personally."

"Why would I need to make an impression, Mom?" I kept my eyes on her, searching her face, letting the intensity of my gaze roll over her and beat down her defenses. She had an excellent poker face, but I knew her well. She was definitely up to something.

"Mom?" I asked. She pretended to wave at someone in the far corner of the room. "Are you trying to set me up?"

She gasped, her hand going to her chest in mock horror. "I would never!" she said.

"Right."

"But now that you bring it up… is there someone you would like me to introduce you to?" She was very slick; I had to give her that. Not at all subtle, but definitely slick.

"We've already talked about this, Mom," I said. "I'm not

really looking to get into anything serious. You know what happened the last time I did."

"Just because you have one bad experience doesn't mean you should shut yourself off completely. Victoria wasn't right for you. But someone else might be."

"Someone at this party, you mean?" I smiled despite myself.

Mom shrugged, which I assumed, was meant to appear innocent. "How is Victoria anyway? And how's my granddaughter?"

I shook my head. "They're fine. I'm supposed to be spending this weekend with her. Emma that is."

I was supposed to. Up until it happened, I had no idea whether or not it would happen; that had been the unfortunate thing about planning to spend time with Emma. More often than not, something came up, or Vicki and I failed to agree on the minutiae.

"You should bring her over some time, you know," Mom said. "Spend some time with us."

I nodded. She wasn't wrong. But it wasn't a discussion I was ready for, and thankfully, she realized that. As if on cue, one of the young ladies chose that moment to walk over to us, and Mom shushed and nudged me in the ribs.

"So, you *are* trying to set me up," I whispered to her.

"I don't know what you're talking about," Mom said, but she couldn't hold back the smile.

By which time the lady had gotten too close, and I had to bite back the retort that sprang to my tongue.

"Hi," the young lady said, extending a petite, well-manicured hand.

She was actually very pretty; she had short brown hair that framed her oval face perfectly. She was tall, and she had a nice, full figure. I reached out to shake her hand and was struck by just how green her eyes were.

"I'm Melody," she said.

"Cam," I told her. I turned to introduce my mom, but she had vanished into thin air. Very slick.

Melody held my hand in place a little longer than necessary. Her smile was knowing, almost like she understood the situation and was as amused by it as I was. "I know this is weird," she said. "My mom has been trying to set me up for months too."

"Only months?" I commented. Melody threw her head back and laughed. It was a high, trilling sound that was infectious. I pictured her mother watching us from a corner in the room and nodding in approval. *That's right ... laugh at all his jokes. It helps.*

"Yours too, huh?"

"Oh, she has been on my case for years," I said. "The minute I finished college... actually no. Even before I went, she was always engineering these situations where I would bump into someone, and I was supposed to fall in love with them. She got pretty good at it, too."

"Why would she need to?" Melody asked. "I mean, you're a gorgeous guy. Surely you don't need any help with the ladies."

Someone passed by over Melody's right shoulder, throwing us a suspicious look as she went.

"I could ask you the same question," I said.

"Oh, I definitely need help," Melody said. "I don't really have time for dating. Or any social situation outside work, really."

"Funny, I'm a bit of a workaholic myself," I told her.

"Ah, then we're perfect for each other."

"You think so?"

"Totally. We would make such an efficient couple. Quick breakfasts while on the commute, check-in twice a day at work, meet back at home after eating out. It would be a partnership more than anything else, really."

I laughed, trying to imagine what that arrangement would look like. "Sounds like a business arrangement."

"Why not?" Melody asked. Her tone turned serious, and she took a confident step toward me. I gulped, jerking my head upward to stop myself from disappearing down her cleavage. "Most marriages are based on some archaic notion of love and companionship. Do you know what has a better foundation? A business partnership. Two parties coming together, each clearly stating what they want from each other. No false attachment. Just a practical arrangement that works for them both." She was uncomfortably close to me now. I could smell the fragrance on her neck, the wine on her breath.

"I'm sure what you're proposing has its merits," I said because I had no idea what else to say.

"So how about it then?"

"How about what?"

I felt the contact first. I looked down, and Melody's hand was on my chest, her fingers working their way in.

"Do you find me attractive?" she asked.

"What? I mean, of course, but..."

"I find you attractive as well. We're both adults. We might as well do it."

It took a moment for her words to sink in, for me to understand exactly what she was trying to say. Apparently, the hypothetical scenario she had been drawing up wasn't very hypothetical.

"I'm... I don't..." My mouth felt dry, and I suddenly couldn't think of a single thing to say. Her hand was still on my chest, and I felt her growing bolder with every passing second. It was actually shocking how quickly we had gone from innocent banter between strangers to a straight-up proposal. And very unnerving.

"Can I borrow you for a minute?" a voice said from very close behind me, and I turned around with relief to see my dad standing there.

"Yes, please," I said, turning and walking away with him

before Melody could say anything else.

Dad put an arm around me and led me away, and it was only when we were well away from her that I felt it was safe to talk.

"Jesus Christ, Dad, thanks," I gushed, letting out a deep sigh.

"Sure," he said, smiling. "Looks like you needed rescuing. I know your mom invited a few neighborhood ladies."

"You knew about this?"

"Not exactly, but come on. You know your mother."

"Well, women are definitely getting more confident. The woman just proposed to me, Dad."

"Really? Within minutes of meeting you?"

"Yup."

"I know her father. She's some cutthroat business manager."

"I got that impression, yeah."

"Well, it wouldn't be a party without someone being inappropriate. Come on, let's sneak away and try that whiskey. It *is* my birthday, after all."

We grabbed a couple of mugs from the kitchen and let ourselves out through the back door. Mom was lost in conversation with her gang, and she didn't notice us leave. Dad grabbed his coat, within which he had hidden the whiskey, and we walked around the house to the clearing on the side of the house.

It was the spot of many heart-to-heart conversations I'd had with my dad over the years, most of them about the trajectory of my career. He put his coat down, and we sank onto it with identical sighs.

It was almost religious, the way Dad opened whiskey bottles. Once the cap was off, he lifted it to his nose and took a deep breath. His eyes slid shut, and when he opened them, they were misty.

"This is very rich," he said, pouring a little into each of the mugs.

"Happy birthday, old man," I said, lifting my mug to his.

"To many more," he said as we clinked mugs.

I took a tentative sip, then a deeper swig. The whiskey burned straight through my chest.

"How are things with your daughter?" Dad asked me after some time.

I took a deep breath, looking up at the moon. Suddenly, I wished I was back here, a young boy with no worries in the world, no expectations, and no complicated problems to deal with.

"Okay, I guess," I said, but only because I knew what the old man was really asking, and I wasn't sure how to respond to that.

"You know what I'm most grateful for today?" Dad asked, looking intently at me.

I brought the mug to my lips and tipped it to avoid the piercing glare.

"The fact that you still have full mobility?" I joked, but Dad's lips barely twitched.

"You," he said seriously. "And your mother. I know you haven't even begun to worry about legacy and all that, but let me tell you, son. There's no greater joy than family. Money and career are all very good, but at the end of the day, you'll look around you, and the thing you'll be most content with will be the family you've surrounded yourself with. Now, I know things between you and Vicki are complicated. But that's no reason for things to be complicated with Emma as well. Children have a way of giving us perspective. Think about that, yeah?"

I nodded. A lump was forming in my throat, the old guilt I had grown accustomed to pushing down.

"I'll make more of an effort to see her," I said after a quiet pause.

"That's all you can do," Dad said.

Chapter 7

Yvette

The first days have always been difficult for me. They give me so much anxiety, and I literally overthink everything.

It started way back in elementary school when I got so upset at my mom leaving me with strangers I cried for the rest of the day. And then that memory became the lasting one in the eyes of my classmates, and it became a running joke for the rest of my time in school.

From that point, I tried to dodge the first day altogether. I would call in sick and show up the next day or hide away in my room until the buzz and excitement of the first day died down, and then I would venture out.

But none of my experiences in the past were as nerve-wracking as my first week at work.

It seemed destined to go downhill right from that initial disagreement with Cam. I never got a chance to speak with him again after he walked out of my office. I tried, but there was already a mounting pile of work needing my attention, and I think he was avoiding me. It would explain why I didn't see him the whole week, even though I was sure he was coming in to work. Several times I walked past his office in the pretext of going over to the printer, which happened to be just around the corner from his office. But he wasn't in any of the six times I checked.

I couldn't locate him anywhere else either.

It was almost comical that the way I ended up figuring out the Penguin Publishers building was because I kept trotting around hoping to bump into him.

Not that I had any idea what I was going to say to him when I did. Our last interaction had been weird, but he had come away from it with a misunderstanding. I wasn't trying to cut off all contact with him, I just wanted us to keep things professional at work. I wanted to explain that to him; I needed to make him understand that part. I didn't know why it was so important, but it was.

But that was the least of my problems.

On my second day, I got called into the boss's office. Or at least that's what she seemed to like. The office I walked into had the nameplate WYATT BANKS, but its occupant was a woman. I recognized her, though. She was the one who interviewed me; Meredith. There was something different about her. A certain tautness in her posture and expression. I knew right away this wasn't going to be the happy, banter-filled dynamic we'd had during the interview.

"Hi, Yvette," she said. "Please sit."

I sat down across from her and crossed my legs.

"How are you settling in?" she asked, although I sensed it was more a need for verbal foreplay than genuine interest.

"Very well, thank you," I told her. "Everyone has been so nice and welcoming. I'm enjoying my time here so far."

"I'm glad to hear that."

"I didn't get a chance to thank you, by the way, for hiring me…"

"Oh, you don't need to do that. You were the best candidate for the job by far. You earned it."

"Thank you."

"Sure." She cleared her throat and reached for a small heap of folders, which she pushed onto the desk in front of me. "I'm sorry I wasn't available to conduct your orientation in person. I had some personal business to attend to. Now, I know you've had a chance to speak with Mr. Palmer, our Managing Editor, about the general scope of your duties?"

"I… yes."

Meredith frowned at me, her eyes burning holes into me

from behind her bifocals. "Right," she said, and I knew she wasn't convinced. I wasn't convinced myself. "Well, primarily, we'll need you to maintain our database. I'm sure you've had some time to visit our library downstairs, so you'll know where we keep all our documents? Right. So, the first task I'm going to assign you is a rigorous review of our existing physical database. I want you to go over all our old manuscripts, come up with a different filing system, and then we can get started with the migration. By the end of the year, we should have switched completely to an online database. But I want us to start with the manuscripts. Do you think you can handle that?"

"Of course. Gladly."

"Good. I know it's a lot of work, and I don't mean to put pressure on you, but the faster you can get it done, the better."

"I'll get on it right away."

"Excellent."

I uncrossed my legs and started to get up, but Meredith held up a finger.

"One more thing. These are some new manuscripts we've been waiting for, from some of our most promising young writers. Now, as part of our policy at Penguin on encouraging young writers to get their stories out, we solicit and publish one story every year. These are the manuscripts we shortlisted. We'll be publishing one of them, which means we'll need to do a little weeding out first. I want you to take them home with you, give them a look and see which is the best. This isn't as urgent, obviously. You can take your time with them, which is why I suggest going home with them, maybe reading a couple of chapters every night. I trust you'll make a good decision on the most deserving one."

"I'll do my best, ma'am," I said, but the panic was starting to creep in.

Meredith nodded, seemingly satisfied, and she waved a hand to indicate I could leave.

I grabbed the manuscripts and dashed out of the office. I

didn't stop until I got to my own office, and then I sat down and let the enormity of the workload settle over me.

It was a lot of work. There was no doubt about it. So much so that I would have to carry it home with me every day for God-knows how long. And I wasn't even sure what I was supposed to do. There had been no 'briefing' with Cameron. I knew where the library was, but I also knew it contained rows upon rows of manuscripts, and I shuddered to think that I was required to go over every single one of them.

Already, I felt overwhelmed.

I sat there like that for a long time. My lunch break came and went, and I was still lost in thought and self-pity. Eventually, though, I remembered what Meredith had said, albeit dismissively. I was the best candidate. I had earned the job. It had to mean something that she was trusting me with this much work. Important work, too. She was basically leaving it up to me to pick the next manuscript Penguin published. It was an enormous responsibility, one I didn't think she would take so lightly. It must have meant she had faith in my ability. Either that or she was testing me. Whichever the case, this was an opportunity for me to show what I was made of, and I wasn't going to waste it.

I got started on the manuscripts right away. I figured the best approach was to make reading them the activity I carried out when my hands were free, or on the little breaks I got every now and then like on my commute to and from work.

In no time at all, I had a fairly clear picture of what I was dealing with; I was able to make an early decision with the first manuscript; the story was derivative, and it felt unoriginal, so I put it aside. But the next two were very well-written and had very compelling stories. I was hooked immediately by the third, and it quickly became my favorite. So, by the end of the week, I had narrowed it down to three, and I was tearing through them faster than I had expected.

It was the longest week of my life. Every day I got home completely drained, and I often went straight to bed after eating. I was so exhausted I was able to resist the temptation to walk over to the window and peer across to Cam's apartment.

When Friday finally rolled around, I gave a long exhalation as if I was emerging from a tunnel after a long, dark journey. I was happy with the work I'd done with the manuscripts, but less so with the database; I wasn't even close to figuring out how to go about it.

As always, I carried the manuscripts home with me, intending to finish them over the weekend. I knew Meredith had told me to focus on the database first, but I felt that it made more sense to free up my time first, pick out the best manuscript, and *then* turn to the library.

It wasn't like I had any other plans; Tyler had called to check in and apologize for not being able to come over and celebrate my first week at a new job with me. Since he wasn't going to be there, I decided there wasn't really a reason to go all out in the name of celebration. A simple glass of wine would do, and a nice, long bath to take my mind off things.

Not for the first time, I found myself wishing I lived in the apartments across from mine. And not just because they were better; the compound also had a pool, which I wasn't initially aware of. I saw it as I was returning from the grocery store. It was on the other side of the building, away from the entrance; I hadn't noticed it because the first time I walked into the building had been in the dark, and since then, I had been too swamped with work. It looked so inviting, the blue water almost winking at me in the dim lighting of the setting sun. And just like that, the idea popped into my head.

It would be a great place to relax and unwind. I could bring my manuscript, sit by the pool, and thumb through it. Once the seed was planted, I simply *had* to do it.

I waited till around midnight when I was sure everyone was asleep. It was impossible not to think back to that first night as I walked across the street to the other side. It seemed so long ago, the wind whipping my nightgown around my ankles, my mind filled with lust, and my body primed.

I made it to the pool without incident. Cam had mentioned to me that there was an elite security protocol around the apartments, but he hadn't elaborated. I kept looking out, expecting to see a burly security guard bearing down on me, but there was none to be seen. Not that I was going to complain.

I dipped a toe in the water. It was nice and warm. I threw all caution to the wind, cast aside my gown, and slipped into the pool. I could feel the tension leave my body as I floated in the middle, just lying there and letting the water carry me. It was so easy to drift off, I thought. I was weightless, carefree, and therefore stress-free. I could get used to this.

I was so in the moment I didn't hear the soft footfalls approaching the pool, or my name being called out. When I opened my eyes, though, I was suddenly aware of a dark figure crouching on the edge of the pool, staring right at me.

My heart leaped right into my mouth. My first thought was that the security guard had finally come for me, and I was about to get kicked out. But then I wiped the water from my face and eyes, and I realized I knew those chiseled, striking features. I knew them a little too well.

"Couldn't stay away, huh?" Cam asked. His grin was so warm and familiar it was almost like no time had passed since that afternoon outside that van when he looked down at me and ignited my soul.

"Honestly, no. I couldn't. This pool has literally been calling me by name." I knew he had been talking about himself, but I wasn't about to give him the satisfaction.

"Right. The pool." His grin told me he knew exactly what I was doing.

I paddled my way over to where he was at the very edge of the pool. He was in beach shorts and a very small white T-shirt that hugged his every muscle.

"Have you been avoiding me?" I asked him.

His eyebrows came together in a frown, but after a moment, he smiled. "Maybe a little," he said. I was surprised by his honesty.

"Because of what I said in my office?"

"Perhaps," he said. He straightened up and reached for the hem of the T-shirt, taking it off with one fluid motion. "Mind if I join you?" He didn't wait for me to respond. He arched his body, twisting it beautifully as he dived into the pool, sending the water splashing in every direction. Including my face and, incidentally, my mouth.

I waited for the water to settle and for his head to pop back up, and then I splashed as much water at him as I could. Naturally, it evolved into a spirited water fight, and the two of us were soon squealing and giggling like kids.

"So?" Cam asked me when I finally lifted my hands in surrender. "How was your first week at Penguin?"

"Extremely hectic," I said immediately, and Cam laughed.

"What, Meredith is riding you too hard?"

"Not at all. But she has dropped a mountain of work on my desk, and I'm still figuring out how to approach it."

"Let me guess. She wants you to review the old database?"

"Yes! And it's this enormous thing! There are rows and rows of boxes and files and papers, and I just can't."

"Oh, I know. That was my first task, too, when I joined Penguin."

"Really? What were the manuscripts made of, papyrus?"

"You know, I missed that sharp tongue of yours, Yvette Matthews."

"For real, though. Can you at least help me figure it out?"

"Sure. I'll give you a couple of pointers, don't worry."

"And will you stop being mad at me? Please?"

Cam swam over to me, closer than we had been in days. I thought for a moment he was going to kiss me, but he pulled his hand out of the water and stretched it out to me. "I'm not mad.

But let's call a truce anyway."

I shook his hand, a smile spreading out on my face. "Truce."

Chapter 8

Cameron

I couldn't shake this feeling that I was forgetting something. I stood at the door to my apartment for almost five minutes, trying to figure out why I felt so discombobulated. It had been a bad idea to spend the better part of the night with Yvette. Once we got out of the pool, she pulled out a bottle of wine and called me a pussy when I tried to say no to it. And so, we drank, and we stayed up chatting and catching up. I had missed her more than I was willing to admit at that point, more than I had realized. We had such an easy banter, such effortless chemistry I didn't even notice how late it was getting until one of my neighbors emerged from the building, fully dressed for work.

At that point, the bottle of wine had long been drained, and both Yvette and I were starting to slur our speech. I walked her back to her apartment, managing the supreme effort it took not to go in for the kiss, then I went back to mine and collapsed on the couch.

Meredith's phone call woke me hours later. It seemed like minutes as if I had barely closed my eyes before I had to open them again. Indeed, I had only slept for three hours.

Apparently, Wyatt had slipped in the shower and almost broken his leg, so Meredith was with him at the hospital and wouldn't be able to go into work. She needed me to make a quick trip to the office. Some important documents needed approval, and it had to be done before noon. I couldn't say no. Her words about recommending me to the board were still fresh in my ears, and I knew this was another test she was throwing my way, another chance to prove my mettle to the board.

So, I dragged myself to the shower, and I got some coffee into my system. It was enough to revive me, even though I knew I would be on zombie mode for the rest of the day. The only problem was the niggling feeling that there was something I ought to have been doing.

Eventually, I shrugged and gave up. It would come to me, I reasoned.

I got through Meredith's job easily enough; she had an impeccable filing system, and it wasn't difficult to find the documents she had been referring to. I wondered for a moment why she didn't just take over from Wyatt herself; she was already doing his job, and she had been for years. But then I took a look around the office, and I noticed she had not even moved in there yet. Everything was exactly as Wyatt left it. Family photos, his stationery, all undisturbed. And I realized she might never have wanted this life, that she had been content being part of his company but had no interest in running it.

I headed back to my office deep in thought. Would I ever get to that point myself? Would I ever be able to walk away from the job? Somehow, I doubted it. It was all I knew; my whole life had been studying and then starting a career I had always dreamed about. I didn't know what I would do if I didn't have this...

I stopped dead in my tracks, right in front of my office. The horror started deep in my belly and spread, like hot lava, all through my body. I hadn't forgotten something; I had forgotten someone.

I turned and ran from the office as a man possessed. I got to the parking lot and fumbled with the keys, my fingers trembling uncontrollably. Emma. I had forgotten to pick up my daughter.

I was speeding long before I got on the highway. I put my foot down on the pedal as often as I dared, taking risks I knew I shouldn't but not caring. My heart was pounding deafeningly in my ear. The horror had not left my belly; it was now a dull ache of shame, slowly morphing into the cold, hard realization that I had fucked up badly. Knowing Vicki, there would be no coming back from this.

I screeched into her driveway and bolted from the car before the engine was off. I ran, breathless, to her front door and knocked.

After a few more increasingly loud knocks, the door swung open, and Victoria Marsh was staring at me with a mixture of disgust and pity.

"I'm sorry," I said.

Vicki shook her head. "No."

"I got called into work unexpectedly," I said, pleading. "I thought I'd run to the office and be out real quick. I miscalculated.I'm really sorry."

Vicki threw a quick glance over her shoulder, then she stepped out of the house, closing the door behind her."I told her you're not coming," she said.

"What? Why?"

"Because you weren't."

"I was Vicki. I was just running a little late."

"Oh, you had to rush to work on a Saturday? Again. That's not a winning argument, Cam. And not an excuse you want to keep making to your daughter."

I dropped my face into my palms."Please, can I just speak to her, apologize to her?"

"I don't think that's a good idea," Vicki said. She crossed her hands and pursed her lips as if I didn't already understand the gravity of the situation. "I've made excuses for you too many times, Cameron. I know you think I'm a bitch because of it, but it's not fair to Emma, and I'm not going to let you keep doing this to her."

"It happened one time, Vicki," I said, a little defiance creeping into my voice.

"Really? You actually want me to bring up the instances in which you've disappointed your daughter? How about the time you forgot to pick her up from school? Huh? And she waited on those steps for an hour before you remembered you had a child?"

"That was a misunderstanding, Vicki. And I've tried to

explain this to you so many times. I got the times mixed up. I thought I was supposed to be at the school at four."

"And what was your excuse at that time? Same as the one you just used. Work. Something came up at work. You had to rush in to save the day at work. It's always that damn job, Cam. And where are you now, huh? What has all this time you've given them earned you?"

"I really don't want to fight with you, Vicki. I just want to take my daughter to Six Flags, as promised."

"And I already told you, that's not going to happen. I told Emma something came up, and you wouldn't make it. I promised her I would take her to Six Flags myself."

"I don't think that's necessary—"

"You know what else I'm going to do?" She sounded vicious now. I knew her well enough to recognize when she was ramping up to something, and it was never good. "I'm going to file for full custody. I'm going to ask a judge to revoke your parental rights, since you never wanted her anyway, and she was always the thing you had to sacrifice your job for. So, I'm going to take that burden from you. You can stay married to your job for all I care, but I'm done letting you hurt Emma."

"You can't do that," I said, but there was a note of desperation in my voice.

"I guess we'll see," Vicki said. I stared at her, looking for a trace of compassion in her eyes. There was only anger there. Deep-seated anger I doubted she would ever let go of. And it grew every time she looked at our daughter and saw my eyes.

"Please," I said. I didn't know what else to say. Somehow, I didn't think it would have made any difference. Vicki's jaw was set, as was her mind. At that moment, I was well and truly powerless.

"I won't let you," I told her. "I won't let you take her. She's my daughter too."

But my threats fell on deaf ears. Vicki threw me one last scathing look, then she turned and walked back into the house.

She made sure to slam the door, too.

"Cam. Buddy. Please stop pacing."

I looked up at Gabriel, then down at my feet. I hadn't even noticed I was pacing. I nodded absently, then walked over to the nearest chair and sat down. Gabriel got up from his chair on the other side of the desk and came over to me. He put a hand on my shoulder and gave it a gentle squeeze.

"She can't do it, can she?" I asked. "I mean, really. Can she?"

"Technically, she has the right to file for termination of your parental rights and to sue for full custody. But she would need to have very compelling arguments to make her case. Especially with parental rights. She would have to show that you have been negligent or abusive toward the child; otherwise, it's pretty much a shot in the dark."

"But she can do it?" I asked again.

"She can, yes."

I shook my head.

"Surely she has no case?" Gabriel asked me. "I've known you a long time, Cam. I don't think anyone can argue you're capable of doing anything that would warrant the revocation of your parental rights."

"You don't get it, man. It's true I haven't done anything negligent or over the top. But some things have happened that could make me look bad. I know Vicki, and she would definitely spin them to help her cause."

"What things?" Gabriel asked.

I sighed. "I forgot I was supposed to pick her up this morning. She was to spend the weekend with me."

"That's not bad!"

"Another time, I was supposed to pick her up from school, but I got the times mixed up, and she waited for me outside her school for like an hour."

"Okay, that's not great, but it's still not nuclear."

I couldn't tell whether he was trying to convince himself or me more. But I didn't like that he had gone from easy confidence to "maybe it won't be so bad."

"So? I should be worried, right?" I asked him.

Gabriel thought about that for a long time. His eyes glazed over, and I knew he was mapping out the scenario in his head, figuring out the best and worst possible outcomes. It was what a good lawyer did he liked to say. "I think we should nip this in the bud," he announced after some time. "I think the best course of action at this stage is prophylactic. You need to stop Vicki from going to court if she actually intends to go to court. She could be bluffing."

"She isn't bluffing," I said right away.

"Well, then get back in her good graces. Beg, grovel, apologize. These things always come down to a conversation between the two parties. Even if you go to court, the two of you will eventually have to come together and agree to terms. Might as well do it now and save yourselves the legal fees."

"What if I can't?"

"I'm sure you can."

"Okay. Positive thinking, I know. But lay it out for me. Worst case scenario. I try to talk her out of it, and she refuses to budge. What then?"

"Is she really that bad?"

"You have no idea, man."

I knew exactly what he was alluding to, the question he was dancing around. Weren't you two all over each other at some point? I didn't know how to respond to that question. He wouldn't be the first person to ask it either. Even *I* couldn't believe just how toxic my relationship with Vicki had gotten, especially considering how inseparable we were back then.

Vicki and I met a few years back, at a launch her public relations firm was doing for one of our books. Our connection was instant, and the sparks flew freely. Our relationship burned very bright and very fast; it was hot and heavy the first few weeks, and then we slowly started to see each other, and everything just fell apart.

We both made efforts to make things work, to no avail. And then, after finally deciding to go our separate ways, Vicki found out she was pregnant. We had our biggest fight and the most revealing one. We both knew there was no future for us after that. But there was the small matter of the pregnancy. That news hit me harder than any of the rest of it. And the realization that we would essentially be tied together for life was more than I could bear.

As soon as Vicki realized I wasn't on board with it, she changed completely. Her frustration and vitriol sharpened to a dangerous point, and she angrily declared she didn't need me. Not in her life, and certainly not in her child's.

"You don't pay child support, right?" Gabriel asked, frowning.

"She wouldn't let me. Made it a point to show me she didn't need anything from me."

"Okay," Gabriel was saying. "If she were serious, then she would sue for custody. The two of you aren't married, so that makes things a little easier for her. She will go out of her way to prove her stability as a parent and discredit yours. The fact that you aren't paying child support works in her favor here, anything to show she doesn't need you in the child's life. The court will decide on what's best for the child. You would probably get some form of visitation privilege, depending on how the case goes. Unless she denies you even that, but that's the absolute worst scenario."

"Right." I tried to swallow a growing lump in my throat.

"But it won't come to that, remember?" Gabriel said, putting on an encouraging smile. "You're going to make peace with Vicki, and that will be that."

He said it so matter-of-factly I was tempted to believe him.

Maybe I could get her to back off. I wasn't sure it was a good idea to hang the future of my child on a maybe.

Chapter 9

Yvette

The first time I heard of the annual company retreat, I pictured a large hotel with tables and tables of delicacies lined up from wall to wall. And, just outside, a large sprawling space with brightly colored obstacle courses and beaming instructors. I imagined meeting some of the people I worked with in casual clothes, maybe sweatpants and khakis instead of slacks, and polo shirts in place of buttoned-up dress shirts. I pictured a large dinner with the bosses, and afterward, stiff speeches from the senior employees talking about upward mobility and the company vision.

I did not imagine the words 'football' and 'competitive' would feature. It's why I was confused when, a few days after starting at Penguin, the talk around the office suddenly switched to the company retreat and a 'flag football tournament.'

Naturally, I sought Cam out to get a proper explanation.

"Ah, yes," He lifted his legs onto his desk, exposing bright pink socks, and his eyes got a certain look like he was reminiscing on very happy times.

"The flag football tournament is usually our opening ceremony for the company retreat. And, as you will learn if you work here long enough, the single most important event in the whole year. Bigger than our book fest. Bigger than a bonus day. The flag football game is our Superbowl, so to speak."

"Okay… and what happens at this… Superbowl?"

"We fight," he said, a tad too dramatically, slamming his fist on the desk for emphasis. "We fight to the death."

And then, when I continued to stare blankly at him, he sighed and shook his head.

"Okay, so basically, it's a competition between the various

departments. All are free to enter, of course, but it's really a battle between Editorial and the jocks over in Sales and Marketing. And I mean a battle in every sense. Since the company started, there has always been this debate about which department is more valuable; mostly just water-cooler talk. But then we realized we could actually use the tournament to see who was, in fact, better, and it evolved into this annual thing of epic proportions."

"Who usually wins?" I asked.

"I'll give you two guesses."

"Sales? I imagine they're in better shape."

Cam laughed. "That's actually a fair assessment. Sales have been whooping our asses for three years in a row, and I simply won't have it this time. This year, we exact our vengeance."

I shook my head, convinced Cam was pulling my leg. Because no one could take a game that seriously, could they?"And what does the winner get?"

"Bragging rights, for one. Exclusive use of the rec room for the next month. And, most importantly, a dinner with some of the bigwigs at the very top of the company. But you know, the key thing here is bragging rights."

"I don't have to participate, do I?" I asked.

Cam turned to me with a frown."You're part of the editorial team, are you not?"

"I mean, sure, but I'm new. Don't newbies get an exemption?"

"Absolutely not. I happen to be a team captain, and I need my best people there." He paused, thinking. "You look athletic. Did you play any sports in college? High school?"

I shrugged. "They didn't have flag football at my college."

"Very funny, Matthews. Seriously, though. Did you?"

"I ran track in high school for a minute. But that was a long time ago."

Cam's eyes lit up, and he let his legs drop, got up, and

walked over to me with excitement written all over his face. "Oh, that is excellent news. You might just be the secret weapon we need."

"I don't—"

Cam raised a finger to my lip to shut me up. The unexpected contact took me completely by surprise, and that more than anything else made me trail off.

"I suggest you start getting loose, Matthews. I'm picking you first come Wednesday."

The office pretty much went into shutdown mode over the next few days. It was nearly impossible to work; anywhere I went, people were talking about the retreat, speculating on who would win the tournament, and generally *not* being productive. I tried to keep myself out of it, focusing on my work in the library. But it was futile. By the time Tuesday rolled around, I was just as excited as everyone else.

We were driven, by two company buses, into the heart of the city. I had heard, in passing, that the retreat was taking place at the home of one of the board members of the company. If that was true, then our host was extremely well-off. The buses pulled into a luxurious compound that had the largest house I had ever seen in real life. The compound alone was jaw-dropping; enormous swathes of green as far as the eye could see, a large pond right in the middle of it all, what looked to be a small forest at the very edge of the property, and the general aura of wealth and opulence. It was actually a perfect place to host a retreat; there was plenty of open space for physical activities of all sorts.

We drove for almost ten minutes after getting into the compound before we finally pulled up in front of the mansion. There, we were greeted by a small group of people, two elderly men, and two women.

I recognized Meredith right away. And, from the photos I had seen in her office, I figured the sickly-looking man beside her must be her husband and the company CEO, Wyatt Banks.

Except he looked nothing like the man in the photos; this man was skinnier, his skin pale and ashen. I suddenly understood why I hadn't seen him at the office.

The couple next to them was far more arresting. I guessed right away that these were our hosts. The man was tall and very sharply dressed in a three-piece suit. His hair was all grey, but he had the refined posture and easy confidence of someone who owned a little island in the middle of the city. The woman next to him was just as stunning, and a little more impressive. She was in a simple frock that shimmered and danced with the slightest breeze, the little gold patterns on it appearing to wink in the light.

"Hi, everyone," the grey-haired man said, his voice booming out and silencing the chatter that had been going on since we stepped off the bus. "My name is Brian Flores. I'm one of the Board members for Penguin Publishers and a personal friend to Wyatt and Meredith here. Today, however, I also happen to be your host and a very proud one at that. This is my wife, Grace, and we would like to welcome you all to our humble abode."

"Not very humble, is it?" a voice whispered in my ear, and I whipped around to find Cam standing next to me. I hadn't heard him approach; he had this sneaky way of popping up right next to me that I was beginning to find unnerving.

"It's okay, I guess," I said, shrugging.

"Not very easy to impress, are you?"

"Oh, I am. You just have to know how to do it."

Our host was rattling off a speech about the tradition behind the company retreat, but I was finding it hard to pay attention. I was standing right in the middle of the pack, and Cam was pushed up right behind me. He was so close I could smell his aftershave. And I could feel the heat pouring from his body. It was very distracting, particularly when someone pushed him even closer to me and I felt something hard prod me in my butt.

"Are you okay back there?" I asked, turning my head slightly to the side, a big smile on my face.

"Oh, yeah, that's just my phone," Cam mumbled, taking a small step away from me.

"Right," I said, still smiling.

"You know..." Cam leaned in, so close his breath rustled my hair. "Technically, we're not at work." The way he said it, a little breathy and hushed, sent a shiver down the back of my neck.

"I'm not sure I know what you mean," I told him. But I was stalling. Just like that, Cam had sent me back to that night at his place. I realized then what had been missing in our banter; up until this point, Cam hadn't been flirting with me as blatantly as he used to.

"Oh, I just mean that—" I felt his hand rest on my lower back, and I was sure he stepped back up to me because of the heat and pressure on my butt were suddenly back.

But then I noticed that some people had turned to look in our direction.

"Cam?" Brian Flores was calling out, scanning the heads in the group.

"To be continued," Cam whispered to me, and then he stepped past me and walked over to where our hosts were standing. It was a promise, I knew. Almost a challenge. And it had me tingly all over.

What had I told him, exactly? In the office? For some reason, I couldn't remember a single thing from that day. Except him. The way he looked at me, the urgency in his touch, the reckless abandon with which he picked me up and planted me on that desk. His lips, too. I remember those; rough and soft all at the same time, urgent and demanding and intoxicating.

I shook my head, willing myself to focus on what Cam was saying upfront. My cheeks felt hot, as did the rest of my body.

"...the rest of the day, okay? So, we'll go in for a quick snack. It's actually a great opportunity for us to get acquainted with each other, introduce ourselves. We do have some new faces around, as most of you will have noticed."

A dozen pairs of eyes turned to me all at once. I smiled and gave a little wave. When Cam looked at me, he gave me a playful little wink.

"Okay. If you'll all come with me…"

The mansion was exactly as splendid as I thought it would be. High arching ceilings, with glittering diamond chandeliers hanging in the foyer. Flawless marble floors. Vintage chests and furniture, and fine drapes hanging from large, Victorian-era windows. There was a collective gasp from the group as we walked in. Several oohs and aahs were met with appreciative chuckles from the hosts. Their foyer alone was larger than my whole apartment.

Brian asked if anyone wanted a quick tour before settling down, and a loud clamor filled the room.

"Okay, then. Follow me."

He nodded to his wife and the Banks, and they walked off, disappearing through a door on the right. The procession followed Brian out of the room, their shoes making squeaking sounds as they crossed the marble floor.

I hung back a bit and joined the back of the group, my eyes still traveling up and around, marveling at the spectacle of the mansion.

It happened so quickly. Strong fingers closed around my wrist, and I felt myself being tugged away to the left of the room. I let out a little scream, and then the room shifted around me, a burst of light hit me in the face, and I think I saw a door open and close.

It must have been a secret door, hidden right at the place where those large curtains were. Or maybe I was too distracted to notice it. Either way, I found myself in a small, airy room with large windows through which the sun was streaming. And, in which Cam stood, grinning.

"Where were we?" I asked.

Cam drew me to him with another tug of my wrist, and I

was crushed against his torso. I looked up at him, too stunned to speak. He had been here before, I realized. He had to have known about this room and the side door, and he must have waited until I was right outside to intercept me and drag me in.

His fingers snuck into my hair, and then he traced a line down to my jaw and tipped it up a little more so that I was staring right into his eyes.

Cam leaned down, or I may have been the one who lifted myself up on my toes. Our lips met, soft and inquiring, and I felt his hands circle my waist and hold me fast.

I might have convinced myself that it wasn't a good idea to do this, but my body seemed to have other ideas. It came alive at Cam's touch; every nerve lit up, and shockwaves began shooting through my whole being. The kiss was a sharp reminder of just how easily Cam could turn me on; it was familiar, sweet, and passionate, but it was also different from every other kiss we'd had. He held me rather than grabbed me. His touch was impossibly soft, as was his kiss. His lips slid along with mine, slow and almost shy like he was deliberately holding back. It was infuriating.

I reached up and tried to drag him closer to me, deepening the kiss. *Pick me up, dammit. Pin me against something and take me!* Instead, he let the motion of our embrace sway him forward and then backward, and he let me go, breaking the kiss with a final peck as chaste as the first one. My eyes fluttered open, and I knew I looked furious, if only because he was grinning that devilish grin of his.

"We should head back," he said, looking out the window as if expecting to see the faces of our co-workers plastered on them, peering inside.

"Right," I said in a small voice. A voice that betrayed the frustration, the anger.

He was teasing me. Toying with me. He knew my reservations about this, about us, and he was telling me he didn't respect them. Showing me. Daring me to resist him because he knew I couldn't. He could turn me into mush with a single word, and we both knew it. It set my blood to boiling.

"Tournament's starting in a few, by the way," he said casually as we walked back out into the corridor.

I nodded absently. The tournament. Right. The faint outline of a plan was forming in my head. He thought he could toy with me like that? Well, I would toy with him right back. I didn't know the policy on switching teams, but I was going to be on the team playing against Cam. And I would be damned if I was going to let him win.

Chapter 10

Cameron

There was a reason everyone looked forward to the annual company retreat, and specifically the flag-football tournament. It was an opportunity to get everyone's aggression out in the open, to channel the frustration that came with the job, which we were normally forced to suppress while working.

On the field, however, there was no room for decorum or professional courtesy. It was the one time during the year when you were allowed to run over whoever you hated from the office. You were encouraged to, actually.

By the look of things, this year's event wasn't going to be any different.

The aggression started early. Joshua Jackson, Head of Sales, walked up to the table where I was seated and tapped me not-so-gently on the back.

"I hope you're ready for your annual beatdown, Palmer," he said, loud enough to draw the attention of everyone around us. He looked down at me with his trademark grin, and I had to actively resist the urge to punch him in the face.

Josh was the closest thing I had to a work enemy. Not that we were enemies in real life; I actually liked Josh. He had an intensity and single-mindedness that made him an excellent department head. In another lifetime, we would even have been friends. But at some point in time, one of us had thrown down the flag during a tournament, and the competitiveness that ensued pitted us solidly against each other from that moment on.

I shared that trait with Josh; both of us were fiercely competitive to the point of ridiculousness. Once, in the lead up to the annual tournament, Josh and I had stopped speaking to each other completely, even in the context of work. We would use interns or aides to send messages to each other or leave voicemails when we had to communicate. It got so absurd we refused to attend meetings where the other would be. Always, we went back to being work colleagues the moment the retreat was over. But in the lead-up to it, and on the day of the tournament, there wasn't anyone in the world I despised more.

"Oh, I wouldn't be so smug if I were you," I told him.

"Let me guess," Josh said. "This is the year you finally end the losing streak?"

"Worse. This is the year I break your spirit."

"You know, Palmer, I actually hope you do. It must be incredibly embarrassing to lose *three* years in a row. I can't imagine anyone would still have the will to live if they lost four."

"It's a good thing we won't be losing, then."

"Well, I just came over to wish you good luck. You'll definitely need it." He leaned in a bit so he could whisper to me. "I have a little surprise for you, by the way. I hope you like it."

"What are you talking about, Jackson?"

"Oh, you'll see," he said, his voice crackling with glee.

"Your mind games won't work, you know. They never have, and they never will."

Josh straightened up and grinned. "I'm almost tempted to tell you what it is, but no. It'll be way better when you walk up to that field and see it. I can't wait to see the look on your face when you do."

He gave me another hefty clap on the back, then turned and walked away.

I looked around to see several eyes on me, as expected, and as Josh had intended, several people had been watching the interaction. Our hosts, Mr. Flores, gave me a small smile from the head of the table, then he turned and went on speaking to his wife. My eyes scanned the room, looking for, and eventually finding Yvette. She was seated on the other side of the room, literally as far from me as she possibly could be.

I couldn't help smiling.

I had not meant to tease her at all. I had somehow found myself standing right behind her, far too close to her, and the contact had reminded me of our night of passion. Up until that point, I had been doing a very good job of keeping her out of my mind, primarily by keeping her out of my sight. It all came rushing back, the feel of her, the smell, the way she moaned in short gasps. It was all I could do to suppress my boner when Brian called me up to the front. I followed her as we proceeded into the house, my eyes trailing her as she found a wall and leaned against it. Shy? Or maybe she was stunned by the sheer enormity of the house; I had been too, the first time I came here.

The thought slipped into my mind unbidden. I needed to touch her, to hold her. I needed to feel that porcelain skin underneath my fingers, to fill my nostrils with her essence. Once I thought about it, there was no going back.

The kiss wasn't part of the plan, either. Not that I'd had any plan other than to get her alone. In fact, I knew the kiss had been a bad idea. She had been very clear about it; she didn't want anything romantic to happen between us. I had every intention of honoring her wishes. But as I stood in front of her, it suddenly felt like those were not her wishes at all. Her body was saying something different to me, and I made a snap decision that I was going to listen to.

All of which meant she was angry at me. She had been angry the second I broke the kiss, and she was still angry now. There was a clipped, formal quality to her words when she spoke to me. I had been with Vicki too long not to recognize the danger behind that cold, rigid smile.

I stood up and walked over to her. She watched me quietly, her lips pursed, and her eyes flashing. I didn't know what to make of it, but I felt suddenly afraid of her.

"The team's meeting out front in ten minutes for warmups," I told her.

There was no response from her. She looked away from

me as if she hadn't heard me, and after a few awkward moments, I took the cue and walked away. Yup, this year's tournament was definitely shaping up to be explosive.

Yvette didn't show up for warmups. I waited as long as I could, as long as the rest of the team would let me. After about eight minutes had elapsed with no sign of her, I was finally forced to name someone else to start in her place. I had been looking forward to seeing how Yvette performed during the warm-up; it would give me a sense of her athletic ability, and I could come up with a game plan for that. The one thing I knew for sure was that she was incredibly flexible. Not that her ability to lift her leg over the back of her head was something I could apply on the field. And it was probably a bad idea to go down that road, I reasoned.

At exactly noon, a bell sounded somewhere in the distance, signaling it was time for the tournament to begin.

She wasn't coming. Even after picking someone else, I kept looking over my shoulder, expecting her to suddenly bound up to where we were stretching.

"Come on," I said to the team. "Let's go. We're playing the first game."

Morale was low, even by our standards. Like me, the team had assumed we would have this secret weapon on our side, and when she didn't show, it was a harsh wake-up call. I could see it in their expressions, the way their shoulders slumped as they jogged wearing their identical red T-shirts with the company logo. None of them believed we could win.

"Listen," I said, stopping and signaling for them to huddle up around me. "I want you guys to remember that this is supposed to be fun. We're supposed to have fun. I know there has been a lot of pressure over the years, but this is not about the competition. I mean, would it be nice to finally silence those idiots over in Sales? Without a doubt. But you know what would be even better? If we all left here having had the time of our lives. Okay? So, let's do just that. When you get out there on that field, don't worry about anything other than making sure you're enjoying yourself. The rest will fall into place."

It wasn't the most motivational speech, but it would have to do.

Indeed, by the time we got onto the field, the team looked considerably sharper. I had recruited the fastest people in the department, three men, and a woman. One of the earliest lessons we had learned was that speed was everything in the game; Sales constantly beat us because of it. So, I had sacrificed a bit of strength and athleticism in favor of speed.

The Sales team took the field to considerable cheering. Already, the rest of the guys had gathered around the field on either side and were making their voices heard. It wasn't hard to figure out who they were cheering for. I looked through the faces, scanning the sidelines, looking for Yvette...

My mouth fell open. I saw her walking on to the field in a bright blue T-shirt, along with Josh and a smug-looking group of Sales department guys, and I was momentarily speechless.

Josh's words came ringing back to me, his taunting at lunch; this was what he had been talking about. They had found a way to snatch the slight advantage we had hoped to have.

Yvette caught my eye, and there was a savage pleasure in the way she smiled at me. It hit me then, what this was really about. This was payback for out little encounter back in the storage room. I thought I had detected a little stiffness in her gait as we left the room, and her eyes had definitely flashed with something resembling anger. I hadn't really thought of it as leaving her hanging, but I could see why she would take it like that. An unwelcome tease that violated our initial agreement not to get intimate in the office. It had been impulsive on my part; I couldn't help myself. Not that there was any way to convince her of that now.

The ref for the day, a pimply young man I recognized as one of the interns, signaled for the teams to come together, and we walked to the center of the field.

"I was right to wait," Josh said as we faced each other down. "It was worth it just for the look on your face. Priceless."

"You can't just switch teams," I said, turning to Yvette. "You work in Editorial."

"Ah, I thought you might say that," Josh cut in as if Yvette was incapable of speaking for herself. "I think the ref would agree with me that the lady can play where she wants?"

We both turned to the youthful ref, who instantly turned red at the attention.

"I'm just supposed to ref the game," he mumbled in a small voice.

"There you go," Josh declared happily.

I knew it was pointless to argue. There wasn't a rulebook or anything of the sort. He was right; the lady could play wherever she wanted, and none of the expressions of disgust and betrayal I threw at her could change that.

The ref quickly listed the rules of the game. We were to play two ten-minute halves. We each had a light paper flag attached to a belt around our waists, and the objective of the game was to score without losing the flag.

After reminding everyone to keep themselves safe and avoid endangering each other, the ref put the whistle to his lips and started the game.

I knew it was going to be difficult, but I couldn't have anticipated just how much. Yvette immediately stood out. I wasn't surprised at her athleticism, but her speed seemed to come completely out of the blue. She was skinny and tiny but incredibly elusive. On the first few plays, Josh simply handed the ball to her, and she danced and dodged her way through our entire team to score twice in quick succession.

It took her by surprise too; she was constantly looking around and gritting her teeth as if expecting someone to hit her, and then she would spin or shimmy and find herself alone, and the joy would spread through her face. She was like a little kid stepping onto a field and realizing she was better than everyone else there. It was adorable to watch and very frustrating.

On the third play, I walked over to the guy who was supposed to be guarding Yvette and tapped him on the shoulder. "Let me deal with her," I told him. "You go over to that side and guard Sheila. They're using her as a decoy, so you don't need to worry about her getting the ball."

He nodded, more than a little relieved.

Yvette's eyes locked on me as we switched places, and I stood right across from her. I smiled and gave her a little wave, and then just before they snapped the ball, I gave her a little wink. Josh, who was playing quarterback, dropped back, scanned the field, and then turned and handed the ball over to Yvette. Except Yvette was busy looking at me, distracted by the faces I was making.

I took off right at that moment. I covered the distance between us in a few short bounds.

The handoff wasn't clean, but Yvette recovered in time. She grabbed the ball and immediately looked up, searching for a running lane. But there wasn't one. I was bearing down on her fast, and I could see someone else from my team sprinting in her direction as well.

She realized there was no way she was going to getaway. She tried a little sidestep, turning her hips almost completely to the side and trying to work around me. If I had gone for her, it might have worked. But I lunged for the flag instead. It was dancing just behind her, swaying invitingly in the wind. My fingers closed around the very tip of it, and I yanked, grinning as it came away.

The ref blew the play dead.

"Nice try," I said to Yvette, giving her a playful pat on the butt. "But I'm on to you now. No more easy runs."

On the very next play, Josh tried a quick pass, but it sailed harmlessly over his receiver's head. It was the turning point in the game. Seeing me tracking Yvette so closely forced him to go elsewhere with the ball, and by halftime, we had pulled within six points of them. It helped fire up the 'troops.' We entered the second half with more energy and a real belief that we could win.

And we did rally. I had come up with a smart strategy for dealing with Yvette's speed. I shadowed her wherever she went, making sly jokes that only she could hear. Inappropriate jokes as often as possible. I reminded her of that night at my place, and then the morning in her office. The idea was to distract her as much as possible, and it worked like a charm.

If I could get her off her game even a little, it gave me an advantage. I could see where the ball was going and get there immediately. As soon as Josh handed it or passed it to her, I was right there, disrupting the play. With Yvette out of focus, the game was surprisingly more evenly matched. Josh grew increasingly frustrated as his passes went uncaught, and as Yvette got de-flagged for lost yardage.

On our side of the ball, we were finally having some success. We moved the ball well, mixing in runs and passes at random to keep them guessing, and with a minute left to play, the game was tied.

"This is it, guys," I said to the team as we huddled up for the last time. "All of you have played a great game. We've actually kept them in check pretty well. This is it, though. Final drive. Stay focused, and let's put together a winning drive. Stacy? I need you on this one. They're not expecting us to pass to you, so we're going to do just that. I'm going to buy as much time as I can. Get downfield as fast as possible. Run your ass off. Okay?"

Stacy nodded, though she looked terrified.

It was a good strategy. Josh's team had identified her as the weakest part of our team, as I had hoped they would. What they didn't know was that Stacy had great hands. If I put that ball in the air, chances were she was coming down with it.

"I bet you're regretting your decision to switch sides now!" I called over to Yvette.

She shrugged but didn't respond. Smart. Refusing to take the bait because she had been doing so all game.

As soon as I got the ball, I dropped back, looking in the direction opposite from where Stacy was supposed to be going. I held the ball, dancing on my feet, trying to draw the opponents to me, sucking them in. And then I let it fly.

It happened almost in slow-motion. The ball left my arm, spiraling through the air like a dart. Twelve pairs of eyes all went up at once, tracking the ball, watching it cut through the air, and then begin to dip.

There was one defender who had been running with Stacy, but he spotted the ball a second too late. By the time the ball dropped, Stacy was almost alone a yard shy of the endzone. She reached up and grabbed it, and from there, it was all too easy to simply walk in and score, untouched.

The sidelines erupted. A cheer rose up from our side of the field, and before I knew it, bodies were pushing toward me, and I was soon caught in a tangle of limbs and screaming people.

"We won!" somebody yelled in my ear.

It seemed so surreal, all of it. I couldn't believe it, long after I extricated myself from the throng. It was only the first win; we still had around three games to win the whole thing. But we had broken a three-year duck, and that was quite something.

I spotted Josh making his way off the field, shaking his head, and it made the win even more special.

There was only one thing that could, and did, sully the feeling of elation; the sight of Yvette walking quickly off the field, her head bowed.

Chapter 11

Yvette

I heard the knock on the door and knew it was him right away. Of course, it was him. He had probably come to gloat and rub it in my face. He had found a way to win without me, and I wasn't sure how to feel about it. Not only had he beaten us, either; he had gone on to win the flag football tournament. I felt slightly ashamed that I had gone against my department, in the spirit of exacting vengeance for something so silly and personal. As far as payback went, that had been a particularly weak attempt.

It was weird; I had been furious at Cam before, and in the course of the game, he went out of his way to rile me up even more. But now, I didn't even know why I had been so mad in the first place. It's not like I didn't enjoy the kiss. True, he wasn't supposed to be dragging me into rooms and 'taking advantage of me.' But I couldn't pretend it wasn't something I had been thinking of since that day in the office, and our interaction in the pool. There was always an undercurrent of something between the two of us, try as I did to deny it.

No, if I was mad, then I was mad at myself. Cam had a way of turning me into mush, but I wasn't the victim I had talked myself into believing I was.

The knock came again, spurring me to my feet. I was in one of the rooms at the very top. It was almost like an attic; the ceiling was low and slanting, and the windows barely let in any light. It was part of the reason I chose it. Not only was it so far from the rest of the house I could be alone with my thoughts; none of the other guys wanted it, so I didn't have to share a room with anyone.

I got up from the small four-poster bed and walked to the door. I swung it open, and as expected, Cam was standing in front of me.

I don't know what I was going to tell him, but the words died in my throat. Cam looked the best I had ever seen him look; he was in a fitted black suit with a white dress shirt and a neat little bowtie. He looked rakishly handsome. It was very unnerving.

"I think you have the wrong room, Mr. Bond," I said, finally finding my voice.

Cam smiled. "Can I come in?"

I stepped aside to let him in. He walked past me, leaving his scent washing over me. I closed the door and turned to face him.

The room looked much smaller with him in it. It suddenly occurred to me just how big he was, tall and big and looming.

"Congratulations on your win, by the way," I said.

Cam waved a dismissive hand. "Oh, it was nothing. I'm sure we'd have completely obliterated them if you were playing for us."

There was a long pause, an awkward moment that seemed to stretch on forever. His eyes were like bright embers, staring into my soul, accusatory and yet friendly.

"I'm sorry I ditched you for Sales," I finally said. "It was dumb."

"Why did you do it? Although I think I have a fairly good idea."

"Really? Why do you think I did it?"

"I got the sense you were upset at me."

Now it was my turn to stare at him silently, letting the awkward tension drag out until he couldn't bear it.

"I'm sorry about earlier," Cam said after some time. "In the storage room. I shouldn't have kissed you, especially after you made it clear you didn't want us doing anything of the sort. I just sort of got carried away."

"Right."

"It won't happen again, I promise."

There was a little twitch on the corner of his lip, and I knew he had stopped himself short of adding, "Unless you want me to." He may have said he was sorry, but if I knew one thing about Cam, it's that he was an incorrigible flirt.

"So?" I said to change the subject. "Why are you all dressed up? What's the occasion?"

"Ah." Cam straightened his bowtie, grinning. "That's actually why I came to see you."

"Okay..."

"I had mentioned to you earlier that the winner of the tournament gets to go to dinner with some head honchos at the company, right?"

"Right."

"Exactly. Now, traditionally, it's a one on one sit-down with one of the board executives or something like that. You know, a chance for a junior employee to impress, set themselves out in the eyes of management. But seeing as I was the organizing chair for this getaway and that I'm head of the department, I thought it would be a good idea to ask someone to come with me."

"You're asking me?"

"I am, yes."

I shook my head, confused. "But I played for the Sales department. And we lost the game."

"I know you did. Not that it matters, but you're Editorial, and if anyone asks, I planted you in Sales to sabotage them from the inside. But more importantly, I'm asking you to come as my plus one."

"Oh."

Cam's hands went up. "I'm not asking you out on a date, Yvette. It's just that... these types of dinners are usually snoozefests, and I could use some company. Plus, the way I see it, you should have been part of the team which won, and I would have asked you to come with me anyway."

"I don't know, Cam..."

"Please?"

"Who is it with? Dinner?"

"Wyatt and his wife. Our hosts might be there as well, I think."

"I don't have anything to wear," I said, my last resort.

Cam grinned. "Is that a yes, then?"

I narrowed my eyes at him, sensing a trap. "It's a maybe. But you're not listening. I didn't bring any cocktail attire."

Cam walked back out of the room and returned, moments later, with something dark draped over his hand. He held it up to me, a dark blue dress with shimmering studs all over, and a nice little silver belt around the waist. It looked short, but it was a beautiful dress.

"Where did you get this?" I asked, unable to resist the temptation to reach out and touch it, letting the fabric run through my fingers. It was impossibly soft, like silk.

"Mrs. Flores let me into her closet. I thought it would look great on you."

It probably would. I almost wanted to try it on just to see if he actually got my size right.

Cam checked his watch and tutted. "Come on, then. Go get ready. Dinner's starting in half an hour."

For whatever reason, I had been expecting a large, over the top dinner. Like, a huge ballroom with endless rows of candles suspended from a high ceiling, or immaculate chandeliers that twinkled and winked at you wherever you were standing. I expected a long table lined with an assortment of food and drinks, with well-dressed, incredibly polite servants buzzing around with platters and bottles of century-old wine.

Instead, the dinner turned out to be a simple set-up, a small table set with simple but elegant high-backed chairs and a candlelit ambiance. It was lovely, intimate, and classy without being over the top. I had expected to see Brian Flores, his wife, Wyatt, and Meredith Banks. But there was only Grace Flores. Regal, beautiful Grace Flores.

She stood up as we walked to the table. I thought I felt Cam's hand slide over my lower back as I went to greet her. I glanced over at him, but his expression was blank.

"I'm so sorry; my husband couldn't make it," Grace said as she hugged me. Her fragrance was flowery and heady, and it seemed to pour out of her hair. Even now, she exuded a quiet grace and poise, in a bright red frock with pearl earrings.

"Wyatt will be joining us shortly," Cam said, which explained the fourth place on the table.

"Good job today, by the way," Grace said, and my attention snapped back to her.

"What?" I said, not sure what she was talking about.

"I watched you play. In the flag football game. I thought you were wonderful, even if this one was bullying you a bit." She gave Cam a push, but her smile was good-natured.

"Thank you," I said.

"Please, sit."

Cam made a great show of pulling my chair out for me, then hovering behind me as I sat, waiting to push it in. He leaned over me and whispered something, but I was slightly distracted by the hand he had on my thigh. I was sure the contact was accidental, but still… I swallowed hard and nodded.

"You look lovely, by the way," Grace told me. "That dress on you, absolutely gorgeous."

"Thanks. You have wonderful taste."

Cam cleared his throat, and Grace looked over at him with a small smile.

"Shush, the girls are bonding," she said.

"Oh, no, no. Please. Carry on."

A serving lady drifted past us, setting a bowl of soup in front of me. Identical bowls were set out in front of Cam and Grace. My stomach gave a low rumble; I hadn't realized how hungry I was.

"How long have you been with Penguin?" Grace asked me.

"I just started," I told her. "This would be my third week."

"That's great. I've been telling my husband for months now that we need to get younger people in, at least try and modernize the company. Don't you agree?"

"Of course. I think it's important to identify the trends of the reading culture and respond to them."

"What trend would you say is taking over at the moment?"

"I'd say… we're getting less and less time to read, and our attention spans are generally shorter, so the type of content people go for tends to be bite-sized. If they can consume it on the go, then that would be great."

"But hasn't that always been the case with books?" Cam jumped in. "You can always carry it with you, read a couple of pages on the way to work, or just before bed…"

"True," I said. "But we live so much of our lives on our phones now. Younger people are likelier to read something if it's an app on their phones or an image shared on social media. I'm not saying we should get rid of books. Only that we should think about the media which works best for the current generation, and the coming ones."

"Well said," Grace said with an encouraging smile. "She's incredibly sharp, Cam. You should definitely hang on to her."

I felt my cheeks grow hot and averted my eyes, looking down at my bowl of soup instead.

"Oh, I definitely will," Cam said. I didn't even need to look up at him to know he was grinning with mischief, as he always did.

"Excuse me for a moment," he said. He pushed his chair back, and stood up, walked briskly from the room. I picked up a spoon and took a sip of the soup. It was delicious.

"He likes you," Grace said suddenly.

I swallowed too fast and almost choked. "What?"

"Oh, trust me. I know that look. And the way he touches you…"

"You saw that?

"I may have noticed it, yeah. I was young once. I remember what it was like."

I blushed again.

"I don't mean to make you uncomfortable," Grace said, waving a hand. "You're a lovely girl, and you're smart. Of course, Cam has taken a liking to you. Hell, *I've* taken a liking to you, and I only just met you."

I smiled, feeling incredibly awkward and flattered at the same time.

I was spared from answering by the return of Cam. Grace gave me a little wink and made a gesture of zipping up her lips and throwing away the key. I decided I liked her.

Cam was accompanied by someone else, a stooped, frail-looking figure I recognized as Wyatt Banks. He looked so weak I was concerned he was going to fall over any second. Cam held out a hand to help steady him and guided him over to the table.

Wyatt looked from Grace to me with watery eyes. He squinted, frown lines breaking out on his forehead like he was trying to remember if and where he had seen either of us.

"Hi, Wyatt," Grace said, taking his hand and shaking it. "Nice of you to join us."

Cam turned him to me and spread out a hand by way of introduction.

"Mr. Banks, this is Yvette Matthews," he said.

Wyatt nodded, comprehension dawning on his face. "Ah, yes. This must be your wife."

I opened my mouth to say no, but Cam gave me an almost imperceptible shake of the head, and I fell silent. "Yes," he said to

Wyatt. "Fiancée, actually."

"Wonderful," Wyatt said. He sank into his seat, and Cam took him as well.

I didn't know what was happening, but I could tell Cam expected me to play along.

"I didn't know you two were engaged!" Grace said, looking from Cam to me.

I started to speak once more, but Cam chipped in right away.

"Oh, we had hoped to keep it under wraps for as long as possible. Neither of us is a fan of the whole drawn-out process. We plan to keep it simple, spare the expenses for a good honeymoon."

"Ah," Wyatt said again. His eyes had an odd, unfocused look about them like he wasn't really sure where he was, but he was determined to push on until he figured it out. "I did that with my wife, Meredith. Except back then, it was called eloping."

"Did you really?" Cam asked, genuinely curious.

"Yeah," Wyatt said. He sank back in his chair, and a wistful look came over him. Meredith's parents were not particularly fond of me, this hotshot young journalist with no money and no ambition, at least according to them. But we were in love, and we weren't about to let that stop us, so we put together all our savings and planned a trip to Africa because we were both fascinated by the history and the literature, and when we came back, we were married."

"And how long have you two been married?" Cam asked.

Wyatt looked at him blankly. He stared at him for a long time, and then, without a word, he picked up a spoon and started to eat his soup. It was a strange moment, but then I remembered hearing about his condition, and I realized it was just his mind and memory slipping away from him. It must have had something to do with this whole act Cam was putting up.

"What about you two?" Grace asked. She was looking

pointedly at me, and I was finding it increasingly difficult to meet her gaze. "What's the story there?"

"There isn't much of a story," Cam said. He turned to me and smiled. "Why don't you take this one, honey?"

I aimed a kick at him under the table. My foot connected, but he barely flinched. "You tell it much better than me."

"Okay. Okay. If you insist."

He turned back to Grace and Wyatt, who were looking at him expectantly. I couldn't help smiling; this was a test of Cam's improvisational skills, and I had a front-row seat.

"So, a couple of months ago, I was in Chicago on business. I think we were looking to partner with a local bookstore there, stretch some of our sales in the region. And I happened to visit this cute little café in the middle of town. So, there I was, making my coffee order. And out of the blue, I hear this relentless clacking sound, which I realize is coming from the table in the corner of the room. I look over there, and I see this stunning woman, bent over a computer, typing away furiously, completely oblivious to her surroundings. Of course, I go over to say hi because I was fascinated and curious. Turns out, she is scrambling to write a review she was late to submit, and that little restaurant was the only place she could get any work done without distractions.

I stayed there longer than I had expected. We got to talking, and even after she finished her work, we just sat there, chatting. I was only in town for a couple of days, so I didn't get to see her that much afterward. But we exchanged contact information, and we stayed in contact through the next weeks. I made a point of visiting her every month, and we went out, got to know each other better, and before I knew it, I was head over heels in love with her.

So, it was a pleasant surprise when she called me one day and told me she had gotten an opportunity to come work in my city, and that she would keep me posted on how it went. It turned out she had not only gotten a job here, but she was the newest member of my department at *my* place of work.

I asked her to marry me a week after she moved here. It felt right, you know? Like everything just fell into place perfectly."

I nodded, smiling sweetly. Cam had been so convincing I had to remind myself that none of it had actually happened. But Grace and Wyatt looked like they had bought it.

"That's such a wonderful story," Grace said. "I thought I detected a little heat between you two. Turns out I was right, eh?"

The conversation flowed a little more freely after that. I was surprised by how easy it was to slip into character as Cam's fiancée, and I particularly enjoyed the thrill of filling in our backstories as we went along. No preparation, no prior communication, just the two of us improvising.

As the night wore on, and the main course was finally served, I tugged on Cam's shirt and asked him to show me to the bathroom. He nodded, gave me a kiss on the cheek, and stood up to pull my chair out. Grace was watching us with a wry smile, and I felt a bit guilty for lying to her, especially since she had been so nice to me.

As soon as we were out of sight, I turned to Cam and pushed him against the nearest wall.

"Ooh. I think I'm getting a wave of déjà vu here," he said, raising his hands in mock surrender.

"What's going on?" I asked him. "Why are we pretending to be engaged?"

"It's nothing really. I'm sure Wyatt will have forgotten about it by morning."

"You haven't answered my question," I said.

Cam sighed. "It's complicated, Yvette. Maybe I can tell you about it some other time…"

"Give me a summary, then."

"I've been to a couple of these dinners with Wyatt. In the one before this one, I brought someone I was dating at the time and introduced her to Wyatt as my wife. It was a bit of a joke, really. She had been my girlfriend, but… Like I said, long story.

85

Anyway, Meredith didn't think it would be a good idea for Wyatt to come to dinner today. As you may have noticed, his condition is getting worse, and the doctors have asked her to keep him at home as much as possible. But the old fox is stubborn. There was no way he was going to miss this company retreat, and he flat out refused to miss the dinner."

"Okay…"

"Right. Now, because of how sensitive his memory is, it's important not to throw a lot of new information at him. His short-term memory is in shambles, and it makes it harder for him to stay lucid. So, I figured there was no reason to throw new information at him. He thinks you're the person he saw me with years ago. I didn't think it was too important to correct him. As I said, he won't remember any of this tomorrow."

"But what about Grace?"

"Meredith hasn't gotten around to telling people about Wyatt's condition. There's a lot going on at work, so I think she's trying to get everything in order first. She'll tell them when she's ready. Although, knowing Grace, she's probably figured it out already."

"Well, that was quite a story you told back then. I almost believed you, even though I knew for a fact it was bullshit."

"You weren't too bad yourself, 'honey.'"

"Stop it."

"Come on; we should get back before they think we've gone to do it in the bathroom."

Chapter 12

Cameron

"Hey, Emma. Over here."

Emma whipped around, clearly surprised to see me, and then she ran up and threw herself into my arms. I hugged her tightly, noting with satisfaction that she had gotten much heavier. She pulled away, looked into my face as if to confirm that it was really me, and then she buried her head in my chest once more and reached as far around me as she could with her little arms.

"How are you doing, kiddo?" I asked her when she eventually let go.

"I thought I was in trouble!" she said. "They just said to come outside; I didn't know it was you."

"That's right. I wanted to surprise you."

"I missed you, Daddy." Her voice was small and a little wounded. I pulled her in and hugged her once more.

"I know, baby. I missed you too. I'm sorry I couldn't make it for our Six Flags date last time."

"Mommy said you were busy."

Knowing Vicki, she had probably told her much more.

"Well, I'm here now. Do you have your things?"

She nodded happily, lifting a heavy-looking bag and shaking it in my face. A dull, rattling sound came from the depths of the bag.

"What do you have in there, rocks?" I asked her.

"Pebbles," she said. "For a science project."

I smiled, but it felt a little tight. Maybe Vicki had a point. I needed to try harder to be in Emma's life. I had no idea what was going on with her, and that wasn't good.

"Come on, then." I took her by the hand and led her out of the school, opened the car door, and watched her climb in on her own. Another development I had missed; she used to insist on being carried up to the seat and buckled in. Not today. She slapped away my hands when I tried to reach for the seat belt and did it herself. I felt a surge of pride tingled with mild amusement.

"I see someone is a big girl now," I joked. Emma nodded proudly.

"Where are we going, Daddy?"

"Oooh, it's a surprise. You'll just have to wait and see."

"Won't I get in trouble for leaving school early?"

"You won't. I spoke to your teacher." I turned around from the driver's seat and looked at her.

"But let's make this our little secret, okay? No telling Mommy, promise?"

I extended my pinky finger to her, and she twisted hers against it. "Okay. Promise."

It was bittersweet, hearing about what had been going on with her. She had already set herself apart so fast in school her teachers were talking about skipping her a grade. And she was class prefect, a job she took extremely seriously, and which she said 'made all the girls hate her but not the boys.' Speaking of which, there was a boy who always brought her an apple from his own lunch box every day, and she wasn't sure why, but she had started bringing him a snack from home, too.

Her mom was pushing her to start music lessons, and she thought she might one day like to be in a band, but she wasn't too keen about it just yet. It would mean giving up sports, which she loved very much.

"You don't have to give anything up, sweetie," I told her. "Not if you love it."

"But I would have to skip soccer and basketball practice to attend music lessons."

"Is your mom getting you a music teacher?"

"She wants to. But I met her, and she's mean."

I pictured a short, stern woman with horn-rimmed glasses standing over Emma as she tried to play the piano. "Maybe the lady can come over the weekend? When you don't have practice?"

"Mommy says weekends are no good for her because she has to work."

"Hmm. I'm sure you'll figure it out, don't worry."

"Are *you* busy during the weekends, Daddy?"

I glanced at her through the rearview mirror. She was biting her lip and wringing her hands in her lap. I knew what she was asking. It was something I had thought about many times, but I hadn't figured out a way to make it work.

"Not all weekends, no."

"Can I come to visit you when you're not working? And then maybe Mommy can let me take music lessons at your place instead?" It was like a knife was being shoved into my heart. Her voice broke as she spoke, too, and I realized just how much she really cared about this.

"Tell you what, sweetie. I'll speak with your mom, and we'll work it all out, okay? I'm sure we'll find a plan that works for both of us, and of course, for you."

Emma nodded, but she was silent for the rest of the way.

It was only when we pulled up outside Coldstone Ice Cream Parlor that Emma burst out of her moody bubble.

"Ice cream?" she gushed. "Really, Daddy?"

"Of course. I said I'd make it up to you, didn't I?"

She unbuckled her seat belt and threw herself at my back, her little hands going around my neck as she hugged me from behind. I reached over and pulled her to me as she squealed in excited glee. I found her tickle-spot with ease, and pretty soon, she was laughing uncontrollably.

I loved seeing her bouncy and happy. She was like a little dynamo, bobbing up and down on her feet, pointing at ice cream flavors and then changing her mind and pointing to others. She must have sampled every single flavor before finally settling on a mix of just about everything. With a generous helping of sprinkles and a waffle to top it all off.

It was a crazy amount of sugar, I knew. But if I couldn't spoil my own daughter every once in a while, what was the point?

We sat at a table by the window, and Emma decided to regale me with her newly acquired talent for identifying cars. She would point at them as they drove by and tell me the model, sometimes by no more than the side view. It was very impressive.

"How did you get so good at this?" I asked her.

"Mommy's boyfriend works in a place that sells cars," Emma said. I froze, the spoon halfway to my lips. "He lets me walk around the shop naming the cars."

"Mommy's boyfriend?" I repeated, speaking through a lump that seemed to have lodged itself in my throat out of the blue.

"Yeah. His name is Mike, and he's really nice."

"Mike, huh. How long has he been Mommy's boyfriend?"

Emma dropped her spoon and stared away, thinking, counting in her head. "Six months," she finally said.

I paused, doing my own math. This information was… interesting, to say the least.

"Is everything okay, Daddy?" Emma asked.

"Of course, sweetie. Go on, eat your ice cream."

Emma pointed toward the play area just past the door to the back of the building. "Can I go play?" she asked.

I glanced at my watch. I was supposed to be meeting Gabriel in a couple of hours. "Okay. But finish your ice cream first."

She nodded happily. She started to take large spoonsful and shovel them into her mouth, her speed so fast I had to slow her down. But in less than ten minutes, she was scraping the

90

bottom of the cup and bouncing up and down in her seat, and I waved her away with a rueful shake of the head. She screamed her thanks and dashed from the table, her cute little ponytails dancing behind her as she ran.

She had taken after her mother, Emma. She looked a lot like her, and she had that irrepressible sense of adventure, as well as fierce confidence. It was what made her so good in school. And it made her seem older than she really was. But underneath all that, the child still lurked in all her innocence. Which was why I was furious that Vicki hadn't told me about this so-called boyfriend.

It wasn't that I had any issues with her dating. Before we split up, and just before we found out she was pregnant, there had been talking of an open relationship. No, Vicki could date whoever she wanted to. The problem was her introducing these men to my daughter without so much as telling me they existed. And, clearly, this Mike had already spent a considerable amount of time with Emma.

Against my better judgment, I pulled out my phone and dialed Vicki's number. She was probably still at work.

"No," was the first thing she said when she answered the phone.

"I'm sorry?"

"No, Cameron. Whatever it is you want, the answer is no."

"You know, Vicki, I expect at least a little civility from you. I mean, I'm only the father of your child."

"Only in the most technical sense. What do you want? I'm in a meeting."

Now that I thought about it, Emma was nothing like her mom. She was sweet and patient, and kind.

"I want to know why you're introducing my daughter to other men without my knowledge."

"What?"

"You heard me."

"What is this? Have you been spying on me?"

"Why would I spy on you?"

"Wait... Did you... Let me call you back."

The line went dead. I kept staring at the phone in my hand, waiting for that call, letting the anger build slowly. It had actually been a bad idea to call her. No doubt she was now connecting the dots, figuring out I was with Emma and building up a dose of righteous fury.

The phone rang.

"Tell me you didn't just take Emma out of school," Vicki said. Her voice always got high-pitched when she was mad. And that was a tried and tested strategy of hers; always counterattack, always pivot and dance away from the real issue.

"I believe I asked you a question, Vicki. Don't try and change the subject on me."

"My sex life is of no concern to you. I think you'd agree that our daughter's safety is more important, surely?"

"Oh, because she isn't safe when she's with me?"

Just to confirm, I stood up and peered over the glass window into the playground. Emma was sliding down a large chute.

"That's not what I..."

"It sounded like it. It's a narrative you've gone back to over and over again. Just because I was late to pick her up once. Once."

"I'm not getting into this with you. Not now. I can't believe you pulled me out of a meeting for this shit."

"Who. Is. Mike." I said through gritted teeth.

"He's my boyfriend. Not that it's any of your business."

"I think it became my business when you introduced him to my daughter."

"Mike is a great guy. He has a daughter himself, and he's a great dad."

"So that's what this is about? You're doing this to spite me?"

"Believe it or not, Cam, not everything I do in my life is about you."

"I can't believe you, Vicki," I said, finally getting to my boiling point and then shooting right past it. "You give me all this shit about being a better dad, being in Emma's life more, but then you go out of your way to frustrate my efforts to see her. And then as soon as some other guy shows the slightest interest in you, you decide to replace me with him? No. I won't have it."

"She's my daughter too!" Vicki said, and now she was getting fired up as well. "I do all that to protect her from disappointment. Because you're not here when she's crying and asking me why 'Daddy couldn't come to see her' or why you're always working or if you even love her. No, I'm the one who has to deal with that. And by the way, you're not doing yourself any favors by dragging her out of school for God-knows-what."

"I'm doing what you told me to do! I'm trying to spend more time with her! I'm sorry I don't have a car dealership to throw at her."

"You know what, Cam? Fuck you. I'll have you know I didn't introduce Mike to Emma until a year after we had started dating. I won't make any apologies for moving on with my life."

"I'm going to take her," I said, the thought jumping into my head and then pouring out of my lips before I even knew what I was saying.

"What?"

"Emma. I want my daughter to come live with me."

"That's not going to happen, Cam."

"I guess we'll see about that."

I hung up and dropped the phone onto the table, somehow resisting the urge to throw it against the nearest wall.

That had been impulsive, without a doubt. But the more I thought about it, the more the idea appealed to me. Why not? I could provide for Emma just as well as her mom could. Granted, I would have to get some help due to my busy schedule at work, but it was nothing I couldn't ultimately adjust to. I looked at my watch again. It was a good thing I was meeting Gabriel. He had advised me to play nice with Vicki, to avoid risking her going to court. But I was the one going on the offensive this time. It was the only language Vicki understood.

"So, talk to me, man. What's the plan?" Gabriel stretched out on my couch, his long limbs nearly knocking the glasses of whiskey off the table.

"I'm not sure yet," I told him. "That's kinda why you're here."

"And here I thought you wanted to hang out like old times."

"I do, obviously. But this shit just came up, so I need you to put on your lawyer hat for a minute first."

Gabriel frowned. It was never a good sign.

"It's okay," I told him. "You can be honest."

"I don't think it's a good idea, man. There's too much that could go wrong. And the outcome you want is unlikely, to put it lightly."

"What do you mean?"

"If she's going after your parental rights, that's a case we can talk about. But if you're the one suing for sole custody, then you have to prove without a shadow of a doubt that you're the better parent. The child support thing certainly doesn't help; you've essentially been out of Emma's life completely, so you have to show why you want back in now. That, and you have to prove that Vicki is a bad parent."

"Ah. So, what you're saying is I have no chance of doing that."

Gabriel shrugged in that way he did when he was trying to be polite. "Look ..." He straightened up, sat upright, and swept his hand around the living room where we were seated. "You know what I love about this place?"

"Free alcohol?"

"True. But also, the fact that this is a single man's haven. A bachelor pad, if you will. I mean, look around, man. Exercise equipment. Magazines. Take-out food. I love you, but this is no place for a child."

"Then I'll make it one. I'll redecorate."

"Okay. But do you know the first thing about taking care of a child? I imagine there's a reason you left that part to Vicki?"

"Part of the reason. I felt she could do a better job..." I trailed off, realizing I was making his point for him.

"Exactly. Vicki has her faults, but she has been a good mom up to this point. Any judge will see that. But that's not even the most pressing issue. I think this could all come down to your work."

"What do you mean?"

"You're kinda married to your job, dude. And Vicki is going to use that against you. Didn't you just tell me the old man is leaving Penguin Publishers and that they're looking to promote you? That just means more work and less time here. Realistically, I don't see how you can convince a judge that yours would be a better home for Emma."

It was all very diplomatic, the way he said it, but I knew he had a point. He was just being nice by skirting around the issue. I couldn't argue with the fact about work. Even if I could make the schedule work, I still needed to learn how to take care of Emma and prove that I could do it. It was a tall order, to say the least.

Now that I'd had time to think about it, I couldn't remember what had possessed me to make that threat in the first place. A faceless stranger going by the name Mike. Anger, definitely. And frustration. Not emotions anyone ever benefited from.

"How about you sleep on it?" Gabriel said. "Just think about it. If you still want to do it, then we'll figure out how to go about it. Okay?"

"Okay, man. I hear you."

A timid knock sounded on the door just then, and Gabriel and I exchanged looks.

"Are you expecting company?" he asked me.

"Not that I know of," I said.

I got up and walked over to the door. I peered into the keyhole and was pleasantly surprised to see Yvette, in her usual bathrobe. I opened the door, trying to keep my eyes from straying to the very short hem of the robe, and the creamy thighs below it.

"Hey, hubby," she said, pushing past me and into the house.

It was a mark of how close we had gotten that she felt this comfortable in my house.

"Hey, lover," I responded.

"I need to borrow something. Do you have…" She trailed off. She had just looked into the living room and seen Gabriel, who was now standing watching us, an amused expression on his face.

Yvette immediately turned scarlet. Of all her quirks, that was the one I found most adorable; she couldn't hide it when she was blushing. "Why didn't you tell me there was someone here?" she whispered to me, and I laughed. "I'm practically naked!"

"What I'm hearing is that you came over naked because you knew I would be alone."

"Oh, stop it," she said.

She tried to adjust her robe, pulling it down as much as possible. Then, still red in the cheeks, she went over to Gabriel to say hi.

I followed her, still grinning.

"Hi, I'm Yvette, his neighbor from the slum across the street," she said, offering her hand. "And, incidentally, his employee."

Gabriel shot me a look and said, "I'm Gabriel, his best friend."

"I don't know about best friend, buddy," I said.

Yvette turned back to me. "I wanted to borrow your cake mixer. I'm making brownies."

"It's in the top cabinet in the kitchen," I told her. "Save us some, will you?"

"We'll see," Yvette said, padding away. She grabbed the cake mixer and practically fled to the door, behind which she disappeared after a hurried 'Bye!'

"Well, that was interesting," Gabriel commented.

"What was?" I asked.

"You didn't tell me about this hot neighbor who also happens to work for you."

"There's nothing to tell, really. Can we get back to the case?"

"Hubby, huh?"

"It's considered rude to eavesdrop, you know?"

Gabriel shook his head. "Why do you even have baking equipment? It's not like you can actually cook."

I held up a hand, struck by a sudden idea. I don't know why I hadn't thought of it before.

"Brownies," I said. I'm sure my eyes were large and wide.

"What?"

"Nothing says 'happy home' like the smell of baking, right?"

"Okay...?"

"I just got the craziest idea."

"Are we still talking about hot Yvette, or is this about the case?"

A smile spread out across my face. I clapped Gabriel on

the shoulder and couldn't resist letting a little mystery creep into my voice.

"Both, my friend. Both."

Chapter 13

Yvette

"You're a terrible best friend," Tyler declared, rolling his eyes for good measure.

I re-entered the living room with a tray full of brownies and laid them out on the table. Tyler reached out to grab one, but I slapped his hand away.

"Take that back first," I said, smiling sweetly at him.

"But it's true!" Tyler protested, reaching once more for a brownie, and getting his hand slapped away again.

"How have I been a terrible best friend?" I asked him, sitting down and crossing my arms.

"How about the fact that I haven't heard from you in over a month?"

"That goes both ways, you know. You haven't called me either."

"Okay, okay. What's your excuse?"

"It's not an excuse. I've been busy. I have a new job, and I just moved to a new town."

"Sounds like an excuse."

"Seriously? I got assigned this mountain load of work on my first day there. And then it's been one situation after another since then."

"Oh, you mean the situation with the hot neighbor?"

"You remember that?" I asked. It seemed like such a long time ago when Tyler and I were ogling Cam as he carried those boxes into the apartment.

"Of course, I remember. That man was too gorgeous to forget just like that."

I bit my lip and looked down. He had no idea how right he

was.

"What's that?" Tyler asked leaning in and looking me right in the eye.

"Hmm?"

"You just blushed and looked away. There's definitely a story there."

"I have no idea what you mean," I said, but my cheeks were definitely hotter. I leaned forward, grabbed the tray, and passed it under Tyler's nose. "Brownie?"

"Oh, now I *know* there's a story there. Come on, bitch. Spill."

I grabbed a brownie and stuffed it whole into my mouth. Tyler always said I had the most open face of anyone he knew. I couldn't hide what I was thinking to save my life. It was a real problem.

"You slept with him, didn't you?" Tyler deduced, his face breaking out into a satisfied smirk.

I started to choke on the brownie, sputtering and coughing loudly until Tyler leaned forward and clapped me on the back.

"I see you still have that excellent poker face," Tyler said.

He got up and disappeared into the kitchen, returning moments later with a glass of water. I grabbed it from him and took several quick gulps, coughing to try and clear my airway.

"I don't know what you're talking about," I said when I finally regained my breath.

"Okay," Tyler said, lifting his hands to imply surrender. "I guess it's been so long I can no longer read my best friend." But his eyes were twinkling, and I knew exactly what he was doing. He was betting I would volunteer the information of my own accord eventually, that the need to share would be too much for me to remain silent. It was a smart strategy.

"How's the restaurant?" I asked him. Stalling. Desperate to change the subject.

Tyler sighed, and for the first time since he arrived, a dark shadow flitted across his face. It was fleeting, but I caught it.

"What?" I asked, suddenly worried.

"Eh. I don't want to worry you with my shit. It's nothing."

"I demand that you worry me with your shit, Tyler."

He laughed, then his face turned serious once more. "The restaurant's not doing too good, to be honest," he said. "In fact, Gale is thinking of selling."

"What?"

Gale was Tyler's aunt. She had been running the restaurant with him for as long as I had known him. It was practically a family business.

"Yeah. Been a tough couple of weeks. There's a new fast food joint right across from us... opened soon after you left... they've been running us ragged. Taking customers right out of the restaurant."

"I thought the biggest pull was regulars?"

"It is, but that's no longer enough. Not with the flashier place right across from us. We've tried everything: promos, social media marketing, daily events, live bands... none of it has worked. The fact is, people seem to prefer the new restaurant."

"Have you thought of upgrading?"

"How do you mean?"

"You know... renovating the place, sprucing it up a bit. I know the family room aesthetic is a staple of the restaurant, but maybe you could do a little makeover, modernize the place some. Aren't you always talking about these grand plans you have for running the place if you were in charge?"

Tyler shrugged noncommittally. "Those were just ideas, Vee. Dreams, more like. I wouldn't know the first thing about that. And I don't think Gale would go for that right now. She seems set on selling."

"Come on, Tyler. I know how you feel about that

restaurant. You don't like to admit it, but I know you care about it too much to let it go like that."

Tyler shrugged again. "I don't see anything that can be done about this particular situation, though, to be honest."

I fell silent if only to let him figure it out on his own. Tyler was incredibly smart, but he could be very tentative, never taking any risks unless he had no choice. I wasn't about to let him off that easy on this one.

"I mean, I get what you're saying," he said after a while. "And there's obviously merit to the idea of starting fresh. But…"

"But what?"

"It's a lot of work, Vee. And it would cost more than Gale and I have between us."

"Excuses," I told him. He grinned at the callback.

"Don't think I don't know what you're doing," he said.

"Besides talking some sense into my best friend?"

"You're trying to distract me from the elephant in the room."

I looked around theatrically, then back at him with a puzzled expression. "No elephants here."

"Right."

"So? What are you going to do about the restaurant?"

"I'm not sure. I don't want to think about it just yet, which is why I came all the way over here; to get my mind off things. You're not doing me any favors with your relentless questioning."

"Well, we'll figure it out. I'll help you."

"I know you will."

"Great!" I reached over and grabbed another brownie. I was just about to pop it into my mouth when Tyler reached over and put a hand on my forearm.

"Might want to slow down on those," he said with a wry smile.

"Why? Because they go right to my hips?"

Tyler laughed. "Please. We both know you couldn't put on weight if you tried. Just... maybe one is enough?"

I turned to him with narrowed eyes. Tyler had an expression of guilt and mischief, and it only took me a second to figure out what was happening.

"What? You did not!"

I lifted the brownie up to my nose and took a deep sniff. I didn't know why I hadn't smelled it before, but it was right there.

"Dude! You laced my brownies!"

"I'm sorry!" Tyler said. "I meant to mention it, and then it slipped my mind."

"When did you even...?"

"While you were out getting the thing from your neighbor."

"Not cool. How much did you put in?"

"Not much. I told you, I just want to chill and have fun with my best friend. Like old times."

I stood up, walked to the window, and back to the couch. I brought my hand to my face and flexed my fingers. I didn't feel any different.

"It hasn't hit yet," Tyler said with a smile. "Give it a couple more minutes."

I suddenly felt naked and very self-conscious. It had been a while since I did weed with Tyler. If my previous reactions were anything to go by, I was about to get very animated and very paranoid.

"How come you haven't had any?" I said, sitting back down. I grabbed a brownie and pushed it into Tyler's face. He took it from me and wolfed it down, his eyes lighting up.

"That's more like it," he said. "Now, come on and tell me about the hot neighbor."

I shook my head, still not believing what Tyler had done. It was typical if I was being honest, I should have seen it coming. A month apart and no hijinks? Of course, he would want to blow things up. In the back of my mind, I realized my self-control was slipping. I suddenly wanted very much to tell him all about Cam.

Oh my God, Cam. That beautiful, frustrating man. Why was I suddenly visualizing his tall, athletic frame? The way his skin glistened after he broke a sweat. The sharp V of his torso as that soft tuft of hair disappeared down his pants. The cords of muscle in his thighs, powerful and thick, just like his arms, and every inch of him. I drew my legs together and squeezed my thighs against each other. It felt like my pants were soaked through, just like that.

My skin felt tingly and incredibly sensitive. I was definitely high.

Right on cue, I heard a knock on the front door, which seemed overly loud and intrusive. I glanced over at Tyler, who shrugged and went back to his brownie.

I had a feeling it was him. Who else would it be? I hadn't made any other friends in the building. Holy shit, I hadn't made any friends at all. I needed to do something about that. I was fully unpacked, and I was starting to really think of this place as home. It would be a good idea to familiarize myself with the people. Put down roots, as it were.

The knock came again. It may have been louder, more urgent, or I could have been imagining it. I got up, so very slowly, and marched to the door.

Cam beamed down at me as I swung it open. Ever so beautiful. Always grinning like he found everything funny. Or perhaps it was me he found funny. I reached for the nearest wall to keep myself steady; the combination of Cam in that tiny white tee and the world suddenly decided to spin was playing games with my balance.

"Smells good in there," Cam commented brightly.

"No!" I said without thinking. And then I realized that the conversation I was responding to had only happened in my head.

The one where he asked if he could have a brownie.

"What?" Cam said, frowning.

"Nothing. How can I help you?" It came out cold and curt, which wasn't at all what I was going for.

"Uh, I need to speak to you. I have a huge favor to ask."

"Now?" I asked, looking back at Tyler on the couch. Cam followed my gaze, looking over my shoulder.

"Oh, I didn't realize you had company. I could come back another time…"

Yes, please do.

I thought I said it out loud. I was sure I did. But I realized when Cam turned to walk away, that it had only happened in my head again.

"No, no," I said out loud. I reached out and grabbed his arm, turning him around and pulling him back.

"Give me a minute," I said.

I ducked back into the apartment and mumbled something to Tyler about being back in a bit. Then I skipped back out, closed the door behind me, and signaled for Cam to follow me.

I don't know when the idea popped into my head, but I knew right away it was a great one. I wasn't sure what he wanted to ask me, but there was only one place I felt was private enough, and that's where I led him to.

We took the stairs all the way to the top floor. I felt Cam's hand hover over my lower back as we went like he was thinking about sliding it around my waist. He seemed to decide against it. We were mostly silent as we walked, and my mind kept churning out increasingly bad ideas for small-talk topics. Eventually, we got to the very top of the building, where a small, rectangular trap door was hidden away in the ceiling, almost indistinguishable. I reached down and felt around for the nook I knew was there. My fingers closed around it, and as the door opened, a tiny step ladder came down all the way to where we were standing.

Cam paused at the foot of the step ladder, a curious expression on his face.

"The roof?" he asked.

"Yeah. It's really cozy, actually. I discovered it a few days ago."

He nodded, apparently impressed. He stepped aside, indicating that I should go first, and I obliged. It was quite similar to the first time we met; me in front, feeling increasingly conscious of my ass and his eyes behind me. Not unlike the first time, I didn't mind it too much.

I stepped out into the brightly lit rooftop, squinting as my eyes got used to the abrupt change. Cam followed me out, his face scrunched up too.

"Wow," he said, looking around us.

"I know, right?"

The rooftop was easily the coolest thing about my apartment building. It seemed like a part that was never meant to exist; an extension of the building the owner probably had no idea was even there. It was a large, open space, stretching all the way around to the low walls overlooking the city. The brick finishing on the walls was different from any other part of the building, which sort of confirmed my theory about the rooftop being from a different era.

You could tell, though, that people had been there before. There were signs of life all over; cigarette stubs, empty cans of beer, a lone shoe here and there… The first time I was up there, there had even been a few items of clothing, enough to suggest someone had held a party.

Most notably, though, there was a small, two-seater couch pushed away to one side of the rooftop.

I had examined it thoroughly last time. It was a faded shade of grey-black, and its cushions were thin enough to imply long use. Its legs were all gone, so it was resting somewhat unevenly on the concrete surface. But it was, for all intents and purposes, perfectly sound. Whoever left it here had done everyone in the building a huge favor.

"This view is ridiculous," Cam said, walking up to the edge and peering over it. I drifted over to him and followed his gaze. The city was laid out in front of us in all its glory, miles and miles of buildings and roads and tiny people milling about.

"It is," I agreed.

The wind was whipping around us fiercely, and I had to grab Cam's arm to stop myself from being blown away.

"Careful," he said unnecessarily.

"What did you want to ask me?" I turned my face up to him. It felt wonderful, the warm sun forcing my eyes shut, the wind swirling over and around us, the heat from his fingers burning through my skin.

"Right. Well, I don't... Are you okay?"

"What?"

"You seem... different," Cam said, staring at me intently as if hoping to figure out just what was different.

"Different how?" I asked.

"I don't know if I can explain it. Just different, I guess."

"Because you know me so well, huh?"

"I know you well enough, Yvette."

I expected to hear the drop in tone and volume of his voice, the telltale sign that he was making a subtle pass at me. But he looked serious, anxious, even.

"What's going on, Cam?" I asked.

Cam looked once more over the city skyline, then he turned and nodded to the couch in the corner. We walked over to it and sat down.

"Look," Cam said. "I *do* know you fairly well. At least I think I do. It's only been a couple of weeks, but I feel like we've gotten close, have we not?"

I nodded nervously. Why did this feel like a break-up speech?

"In that spirit, I have a little confession to make. I haven't shared with you the biggest part of my life. And that's on me. I should have, and I'm sorry I haven't. But I'm going to rectify that right now."

I suddenly wished he wouldn't. I wasn't in the right frame of mind. It felt like he was about to confide something serious to me, and I didn't think I was ready for it.

"I have a daughter," he said after a pregnant pause.

"Oh," I said. I had not seen that coming.

"I know. I know. It's a long story, most of it incredibly complicated. I'll tell you all about it, I promise. But I need a favor from you. It's a huge favor, so I'd understand if your answer is no. I really hope it's not, though."

"Okay…" My mind was reeling as I tried to imagine what he could possibly want with me that also involved his daughter. I had been right; this wasn't a conversation I was ready for.

"You remember the dinner with Wyatt and Mrs. Flores? During the company retreat?"

"Yeah?"

"Remember our little act, when we pretended to be engaged?"

"Lovebirds who met in a coffee shop? I remember."

"Well, I need you to come to play house for a couple of days."

"What do you mean?"

"Exactly what it sounds like, Yvette. I want you to pretend to be my wife for a couple of days."

Chapter 14

Cameron

It occurred to me, after I had been speaking for a fairly long time, that Yvette wasn't paying attention to me. Her eyes were on me, large and wide and lovely, but she seemed to be very far away.

I trailed off and gradually stopped speaking. Yvette barely noticed. Her eyes were glassy, I noticed. Her hand was moving between us, toward me, snaking its way to my torso.

There was something about her that seemed out of place, odd. She wasn't herself. Or the version of herself I was familiar with. There was a near-permanent smile on her face, and everything she did seemed to fill her with unbridled joy. Her movements were slow and measured; her hand seemed to float between us for a very long time before finally resting on my chest.

She mumbled something, her voice pitching up at the end. A question.

"What was that?" I asked, frozen in place as she began to caress me.

"Why did you stop?" she asked, raising her voice so I could hear her.

It was that slow, slurred speech that made me catch on. Unless I was mistaken, Yvette was high. How had it taken me so long to notice? Well, I suppose it hadn't. Not really. I knew something was up; I just didn't figure out what it was soon enough.

My first reaction was amusement. And then curiosity. I had seen Yvette buzzed on wine, but that was about it. This was clearly something different, and I couldn't wait to see what she did.

She gave me a gentle push with her hand, calling my

attention back to her.

"Huh?"

"You were telling me something," she said. "Why did you stop?"

"Oh. I got distracted, sorry."

"Distracted by what?" Her mouth spread into a wide grin. She slipped her hand inside my shirt.

I started to speak then stopped, having completely forgotten what the question was. My silence clearly infused her with confidence because the next moment, Yvette was shifting on the couch, closing the distance between us until she was practically inches from my face.

She brought her other hand to my shirt and started to fidget with the buttons. Her fingers were clumsy and impatient, but at that moment, I couldn't care less. Slowly they worked, gradually undoing the buttons, disrobing me. Eventually, she parted the shirt and ran her nimble fingers over my chest and abs. Her touch was light, her hands strangely warm.

It wasn't the best place for any of this. We were out in the open, the wind swirling furiously around us. Anyone could walk up through the trapdoor at any moment. Then there was the questionable state of the couch. All valid reasons to push her away and put out the fire she was lighting.

Instead, I brought my finger to her chin and tipped it upward. Her eyes were still slightly unfocused, but they were now glowing with an excitement I hadn't seen since our first night together. They were half-lidded too, almost sleepy, and it was unbelievably sexy.

She licked her lips, her tongue darting furtively from her mouth and running over her lips, which she then pushed out in an adorable little pout. It was invitation enough. I brought my lips to hers, pulling her into me as I did so.

A faint moan escaped her mouth as I kissed her. She slid her arm around my back and wrapped herself around me. I shifted, letting her weight push me back on the couch. With her arms still around me, she lifted herself, and then her legs were snaking around me too, and she was completely wrapped around me.

The kiss was just as slow and languid as everything else she had done. Clearly, she wasn't in any rush. She matched my motions with hers, but I let her take the lead after some time. Her lips were soft and full and slick, and they danced in beautiful poetry against mine. Her body writhed in tune, following the rhythm of her lips, rocking back and forth as we kissed.

It was by far the most sensual kiss we had shared. I let my eyes slide shut and fell into a beautiful trance. Smell, touch, taste. It was easy to forget that we were outside. Or that at any second, we could be interrupted. None of it seemed important, only Yvette, and her body twisting against mine.

As she rocked back and forth, I let my hands creep down her back, making lazy caresses down her spine, all the way to her butt. I grabbed her ass with both hands, squeezed and rubbed, the motion pushing her right into my groin and drawing another sharp intake of breath from her. Her mouth slipped from mine. She tilted her head back, the biggest smile on her face. Her hips started rocking against me, grinding, humping.

There were too many layers between us. Way too many. I slipped my arm inside the back of her sweatpants and was pleasantly surprised to find her not wearing any underwear. Wild. Exciting. And now I knew there was no turning back.

I lifted her without warning. She gasped as my arms went under her butt and lifted. Instinctively, the legs locked around my lower back tightened, and I was able to get all the way up.

"Your place?" I mumbled right into her ear.

She shook her head, sending a cloud of her perfume and scent into my nostrils. "Tyler," she said simply.

Ah, yes. The best friend from home.

"My place?" I asked.

Yvette shook her head again. "Too far."

I looked skeptically back at the couch. Yvette's lips went to my neck, prompting, urging, willing me to stop stalling.

She sighed, letting her legs drop from around me. She straightened up as she stood in front of me. Then she grabbed my hand and dragged it to the front of her pants. Her eyes were glued on me as she pushed the hand in. Feel that, they seemed to say. She was so wet it was a surprise the front of her pants wasn't drenched.

I nodded, my dick throbbing painfully, straining against my jeans. The couch would have to do.

My fingers found the edges of her sweatpants and yanked them down. Yvette grinned and reached for my own pants. There was no hesitation this time. Her whole demeanor had changed; she was more urgent and desperate.

The pants came free, and I let them drop to my ankles. It was incredibly exhilarating being in that situation, knowing where we were and that we were not supposed to be doing this. It added to the excitement in a way I had not anticipated.

I grabbed Yvette and crushed my mouth to hers. It was a fierce kiss, a possessive statement of intent. Just as she was getting into it, I pushed her away, catching a fleeting glance of her puzzled expression just before I whipped her around to face the couch.

She took the cue right away. She leaned down and climbed the couch with her knees, letting her ass trail seductively in the air. I couldn't help smacking her once across the right cheek, and then once more across the other.

I grabbed her by the hips, stepped forward so I was right behind her, and then let the heat and moistness of her womanhood guide me into her. I was engulfed by a sensation of such pleasure I felt my whole body tremble. I pushed in all the way, burying myself to the hilt, feeling with satisfaction her lips grip my shaft and squeeze.

The rooftop of Yvette's building had a wonderful view. But it was nothing compared to the view I had been presented with. Yvette was subtly thick; she had a narrow waist, but it ballooned outward into these rounded hips and thick, bouncy ass. The sight of her ass jiggling as I thrust in and out of her was incredibly enticing.

I knew almost immediately that the pace was going to be problematic. I tried going slow, driving my hips forward slowly and pulling out just as slowly. Each time, Yvette moaned, and her body trembled, and she pushed herself back into my groin.

Resigned, I placed both hands on her hips. I switched up the pace without so much as a warning, and Yvette groaned. Her knees almost gave way under her as I started to pound. The wind was still fierce, but not fierce enough to drown out the sound of our thighs smacking against each other.

I was in control, and I loved it. I played with the speed and intensity of my thrusts, feeling Yvette out, letting her show me how deep I could go, what speed was just right. And then, just when she thought I had established a steady rhythm, I abandoned all restraint and ravished her. Our joint motion was almost a blur; my knuckles were white against her hips, sweat was trickling down my thighs… and my mind was a jumble of incoherent words. She was thrusting backward, and I was pounding too, and after a while, I couldn't tell who was fucking who, and it was glorious.

Yvette was well past moaning now. She was screaming and calling out my name, her words just about reaching my ears before being snatched away by the wind. And then her body tensed, and I opened my eyes to see her fingers grip the edge of the couch as she started to orgasm. I rode her harder, faster, slamming into her now, hearing my own groans mingle with hers. Then, with a final grunt, I drove into her as deep as I could. It sent me right over the edge. My toes curled inside my shoes. My eyes rolled into the back of my head. My whole body went rigid and then limp.

When my eyes finally opened, and my breathing returned to normal, I gently slid out of her. There were faint lines on her cheeks and hips where I had been grabbing her. I didn't remember holding on so tightly. It had all happened so fast, and both of us had been completely lost in the moment.

Yvette straightened up. She reached down and pulled her pants up, then collapsed on the couch next to me.

She was silent for a long time. I wondered if she was regretting what had just happened. She had said so many times that she didn't want us to pursue this dynamic, but we kept falling into each other's arms. We kept finding each other alone together, and it was no longer possible for me to deny the chemistry we had. I wasn't sure why she insisted on doing it.

"So, tell me about this plan of yours," she said after some time. She was still looking away from me, but her hand sought mine and her fingers locked into mine.

"Oh. Right. Well, like I was saying..." *Before I was rudely interrupted by your body.* "My ex and I have a very complicated relationship. Toxic, really. For reasons best known to her, she won't let me see my daughter. She's been getting increasingly unreasonable about visitation, and recently I learned that she started seeing someone, who she introduced to my daughter, Emma.

"Anyway, there has been talking of a custody fight on both sides. I came up with this idea to show her that I would have a good chance of beating her in a custody battle if it came to it, and that's where you come in. I've invited Vicki over for dinner in a week. Nothing too complicated. Just a simple sit down. She hasn't gotten back to me, so there's a possibility she won't even come. But in the event she does, I want us to be ready."

Yvette nodded slowly. "So, you basically want me to pretend to be your wife to give her the impression you have a happy home?"

"Well, when you put it like that, it sounds a little sad." *And it was.* "It's not untrue, but I was thinking of it more in terms of 'creating a viable domestic setting.' My buddy Gabriel, who you will recall from when you flashed him your thighs..."

"Hey!"

"That wasn't a complaint. We both appreciated it greatly."

"Uh-huh."

"Gabriel thinks my home is too much of a bachelor pad. And I agree. It needs a feminine touch, at least. I want to make it at least habitable for a child. You know?"

"This is just for a day, right?"

"It should be, yes."

"I don't know, Cam…"

"I'll make it worth your while, I promise." I was beginning to sound a little desperate. "I'll pay you, how about that?" The words were out before I'd really thought about them. I realized, as soon as I said it, that offering to pay wasn't a particularly noble approach. There was a very real possibility that Yvette would feel commodified and get offended. I gritted my teeth and waited for the explosion, the angry rebuke.

The harsh words never came. Instead, Yvette smiled, and she turned to me with laughter in her eyes. "I mean, it's not exactly the proposal I dreamed of as a girl but go on. Ask me."

"What?" I stared at her blankly.

"You said you want me to be your fake wife, but you haven't exactly asked me yet."

"Oh. Right."

I got to my feet and then stood facing her. I patted my pockets, realizing I needed a ring. Or something like it. There was nothing but scraps of paper and my keys and wallet. From my back pocket, I pulled out a small wad of cash, unraveled the neatly wrapped notes, and pulled out the small rubber band. I sank to my knees, reaching for and lifting Yvette's hand to my lips.

"Yvette Matthews. Ever since I met you, I have thought of nothing else. You have lit up my life in ways I didn't think possible. In the month or so I have known you, you have challenged me, made me laugh, and inspired me. I have known, for at least three hours, that I would like nothing more than to fake-spend the rest of my life with you. Would you do me the honor of being my fake wife?"

Chapter 15

Yvette

The period leading up to the dinner with Vicki was more fun than I had thought it would be. For one, I had expected the whole thing with playing house to be awkward and weird, but it was far from it. Awkward because despite my best efforts, I couldn't seem to keep my hands off Cam. Even while I battled with my obvious attraction to him, still trying to wrap my head around it, the moment he showed up, my whole body started to tingle.

It was escalated tenfold by the weed. Thanks to Tyler's sneakiness, I was more open and vulnerable when Cam showed up than I had ever been with him. No inhibition. No shame. No tiny voice in my head telling me to rein it in. Just my body screaming for him, demanding his touch, wallowing in the bliss of his lovemaking. I could still feel Cam's hands all over me as I walked back to my apartment. I could still taste him, and my body was still tingly. It was a good thing Tyler was asleep when I got back because I wasn't sure I would have been able to keep my 'situation' from him. I hadn't even figured out how to tell him about Cam yet.

It should have been awkward with Cam afterward. There should have been some post-coital hang-ups. Neither of us brought it up, though, for whatever reason. I purposefully avoided it, choosing instead to quiz Cam about the details of our pretend marriage, and he seemed happy to go along with it. We slipped easily and immediately into the banter we had always shared, and that was that.

It wasn't weird, either. The fact was, I barely knew Cam, even though it felt like I had seen him every day since I moved to the city. I knew a lot about him, and him me, but the fact that I was just now learning about his daughter showed just how little I actually knew about him. I figured it would be at least a little weird to 'live' with him. But Cam was the Cam I had always known. Playful, funny, and very accommodating.

On the first night, he sat me down to discuss the essentials of the arrangement, after I turned down his offer of a tour. I didn't need one. I had been in his apartment too many times. It helped that he had picked that week to work from home, so I didn't have to worry about seeing him at the office as well.

"So, this is an agreement between friends, yes?" he asked me.

"What do you mean? As opposed to what?"

"Uh, I could have Gabriel draw up an official contract, something you can sign?"

"What would this contract say?"

"I… I don't know now that I think about it."

"I imagine it would include stipulations on our conduct? You know, what we can and cannot do around each other?"

"Ah, yes. That would be helpful. I have a million things I would add to that list just off the top of my head."

I scoffed. "Like what?"

"Like that thing you do when you blush, and your face turns this delightful shade of red. None of that, please."

"I can't control what my face does!" I sputtered. And, as if eager to make my point for me, my cheeks began to heat up.

"See, there you go. Now, if we had a contract, you would have voided it right there and then."

"Fine. Then you don't get to take your shirt off."

Cam laughed. "What?"

"You know what. No more walking around in these flimsy T-shirts, which you then rip off at will."

Cam reached down and started to pull the T-shirt he was wearing off. "Oh, you mean like this?"

I was treated to a stunning view of rock-hard abs, and I loudly protested and pretended to cover my eyes. It was probably for the best. My cheeks were almost certainly bright red.

"Voided!" I said.

"Okay. Okay. I get it. No contract. As long as you're comfortable with our arrangement…?"

"I am. We're adults, Cam. I'm sure we can figure out something as simple as a fake marriage."

"Are you sure about that?"

I shrugged.

"When did we meet?"

"Uh, a year ago, in Chicago."

"When's my birthday?"

"Uh…"

"Do we have pet names?"

"Sure, we have a bunch of them."

"How do I like my coffee?"

"Umm… Okay. Fine. Maybe we do need to talk it out, get our stories straight. I thought we could just wing it as we did at the company retreat dinner, but I guess that won't work."

"Oh, it definitely won't. You'll be up against someone way more formidable than sickly old Wyatt Banks. Vicki is vicious. She'll sniff out even the smallest lie within a second."

"She sounds charming," I commented dryly.

"Let's just say she's quite the character. We'll need to be on our A-game, coz it won't be so easy."

"I hear you."

Suddenly, the task seemed herculean and definitely more complicated than I had initially thought. It wasn't going to be a simple 'hi' and 'would you pass the gravy please' and then a quick exit. I would have to fully commit to this. Not unlike an actual marriage, ironically.

The tiny voice in my head popped up, reminding me that I was doing this for Tyler, my best friend. He needed the money for his restaurant, and this was a simple arrangement that would ensure he got it fast. Just a friend helping out another friend by pretending to be married to yet another friend.

There was another voice, much smaller, though. One that wondered aloud if that was really my only motivation, and wasn't it easier to just ask Cam to loan me the money? But he hadn't asked any questions when I brought it up. He seemed okay with paying me; he insisted on it, actually. It was a lot to ask, he said, and he was happy to reimburse me for my troubles.

Then there was the whole moral debate I'd been having with myself. I had been high when I agreed to all this, so I was more susceptible than usual to Cam's charms. Now, though, I wasn't so sure what to make of all this. I didn't know anything about Cam's ex beyond the largely unflattering picture he'd painted. Even so, I wasn't sure it was a good idea to get involved in something so personal.

Still, I found myself going over there, and once I sat across from him talking about our 'marriage', it was easy to forget about all the other stuff.

We spent the remainder of the day creating and going over our backstory. That was easily the most enjoyable part for me. We basically had these templates, these two characters who existed in the real world, and whose lives we then had to fabricate to reach a scenario where they would reasonably be married.

It was a rare opportunity for me to flex my storytelling and editorial skills. It was almost like being a kid again, imagining the perfect love story, and planning out the rest of my life with some handsome stranger. Except, in this case, the handsome stranger was seated right across from me, and he would occasionally chip in with a correction like, "I think it's better if we say we had one of those courtroom weddings. Nothing complicated, because then we'd have to show pictures and stuff."

"Wait, won't we still need a certificate?" I chipped in. "In case she demands to see one?"

"We will don't worry. I can download one from the internet easily enough."

Once we had the backstory nailed down, we moved on to the more practical aspects of our marriage. Cam and I had a little photoshoot; we went around the house in different outfits, staging and taking as many different photos as we could and creating the 'visual evidence of our love.' Some he sent to Gabriel, who he claimed was better at photoshop than he was. Most of the others we printed and framed, then dotted strategically around the house. By the time we were finishing, it was evening. The whole day had gone by so fast I had barely noticed it.

"I'm going to order us a pizza," Cam said, glancing at his watch and yawning loudly.

"I think I have some leftover beef casserole in the fridge," I said.

"Sounds delicious," Cam said in a falsely cheery voice that meant he was being sarcastic. "But how about I order a pizza just in case one of us doesn't want to eat leftovers, huh?"

"That's no way to speak to your wife," I said. "Especially after she slaved and slaved to get that meal ready for you."

Cam grinned. "I'm sorry, pet." He leaned in and planted a big kiss on my cheek. "You know I love your cooking."

We ended up eating the pizza because we were both too tired to make the trip over to the other apartment, and Cam was convinced the casserole would have gone bad by now.

We were so tired we went to bed almost immediately. I watched Cam undress, and his eyes were similarly sharp as I took a shower and came out in my nightgown. But neither of us said anything. When we got in bed, I felt him slide up to me and put his arms around me, and the warmth and comfort sent me to sleep almost immediately.

The planning process was much longer and more detailed than I had anticipated. There was so much that needed to be done to make Cam's house 'more domesticated' to infuse it with the feminine energy it so desperately needed, which meant a lot of pinks, randomly through the house. Pink slippers in the bathroom. Switching out the bedroom curtains from boring, predictable black to a friendlier maroon with gold stars scattered across the fabric. It also meant doing a complete overhaul of the kitchen because the man had only a basic understanding of space and utility. I could tell he rarely cooked; his drawers were full of takeout menus, and several of the things in his pantry were unopened.

For dinner, I decided to keep it as simple as possible. Chicken parmesan. The chicken was as safe a choice as you could make, and it was easy enough to make.

A few hours before Vicki was supposed to arrive, Cam snuck up behind me and snaked his arms around me.

"What are you doing?" I asked, even as I let my body fall back into his. I hated how my body just seemed to fit along with his; we had been cuddling every night, and I had gotten so used to the feel of him behind me I almost forgot we weren't actually married.

"I just wanted to say thanks for this," Cam said.

"It's the least I could do," I said, smiling. I thought I felt something long and hard prod the back of my thigh lightly.

"One thing is missing, though..."

Cam let his hands drop from around me, and I turned around to face him.

"What?" I asked.

"We're newlyweds. We're supposed to be all over each other."

Somehow, I didn't think that was going to be a problem.

"What are you trying to say?"

Cam reached for me so fast I had no time to react. Or think. Or blink. Or do anything but gasp softly as his head came down, and part my lips as he met them in a searing kiss.

It was quick and dirty. Cam pushed me both with his lips and his body. The counter was digging into the small of my back, but the pressure of his body was unrelenting. He kissed me hard, with passion and abandon as if he was trying to make a point like he had been starved of that contact for so long, and he was coming up out of the water for a breath of fresh air.

He pulled away just as suddenly. I had never felt so confused, so discombobulated. I blinked several times to remind myself of where I was. I laid a hand on my chest in a futile attempt to still my beating heart and let out a deep sigh as I looked up at Cam. My lips felt swollen and tingly. Both sets.

"That," Cam said. "That's what I was trying to say. We need to be like that in front of Vicki."

"Right," I said, although I still wasn't sure what he was talking about. It all came back to me slowly. "Oh," I said. "What does that accomplish, exactly?" Besides, make her jealous? Was he trying to make her jealous? Was that what this was really about?

"It shows her we have great chemistry, that we're good together."

"Okay," I said. But there was a little hurt in my voice, and Cam noticed it right away.

"Hey," he said. He lifted my chin to his face, as he so often did, and made me look into his eyes, those unreal pools of stunning blue. It was nearly impossible to keep looking into them.

"This isn't about her," he said. Everything about his demeanor was earnest, desperately pleading for me to believe him. "I couldn't care less about her. This is about Emma. I'm doing this for Emma. If Vicki sees that there is a home here, then at the very least she backs off, drops the idea of a custody battle, and then I can work out how to see my daughter more. That's all I'm trying to do, okay?"

I nodded and tried to force a smile onto my face.

"That kiss was unfair," I pointed out, and Cam grinned.

"Yeah?"

"Totally. Should have been included in the list of outlawed things."

"Hmm. And how about this?"Cam's fingers, which had been hovering over the hem of my apron, suddenly brushed the fabric aside and drove lower, seeking out and finding my dress and sneaking past it.

They found my thighs hot and eager. I tried to clamp my legs shut, but they practically fell open on their own. Cam brushed his hand over the soft flesh on the inside of my thighs, and I gritted my teeth and shook my head.

"Yeah," I mumbled incoherently. "That too."

The softest touch right at the front of my panties. Featherlight, causing the hairs on my whole body to prick up.

"Okay. What about this?"

The fingers brushed once more against the panties, and then I felt them lock around the sides of the panties and brush them aside.

My heart was pounding once more, loud drumming that sounded deafening in my ears. I gripped Cam, burying my head in his shoulder and biting my lower lip to keep myself from screaming.

Cam found my wetness with practiced precision. He played with the folds of my lips for a short time, then finally ventured past them, curling upward to touch the hood of my clitoris.

I was trembling now. My legs were like jelly; I suspected they would give way any time now. Now he was on my clitoris, his touch still gentle, his fingers quick as they rubbed and teased around it.

I threw out a hand, desperate to do to him what he was doing to me. My hand slapped something warm and hard, and I followed the outline of the sweatpants he was wearing, yanking at the strings, and then finding my way inside. I wrapped my fingers around his length, and the sharp intake of breath from him was almost as erotic as the feel of him. I wanted him inside me so badly… I needed it. Nothing else mattered. I couldn't remember how we got to this point, but I was glad we had. Why had we wasted so much time not doing this? How had I spent so many nights curled up with him instead of him being inside me?

He seemed to read my mind. As I stroked and squeezed his cock, he tugged hard at my panties, and I heard them tear. He reached down and grabbed me by the hips, lifting me onto the counter. He leaned in and reached between us with his hand, placing himself at my apex, teasing me with the thick head of his cock. And, as I stared into his piercing blue eyes, burying himself inside me with a quick stroke.

Bliss.

Just then, though, the shrill sound of a doorbell cut through the air, breaking into our little bubble and causing Cam to pause mid-thrust.

"No!" I said, my voice low and hoarse. I shimmied, shaking my hips, trying to get him to keep fucking me.

"She's here," he said, looking in the direction of the door.

Let her wait I wanted to say. *Fuck me, dammit!*

But I knew he wouldn't. The moment, magical as it had been, was gone.

He pulled out and backed away from me. He reached down and pulled his pants back up. His cock stuck out of the front, almost comically large and distended. He smiled at me, leaned in for another quick peck on the cheek, and then he turned and walked out of the kitchen in the direction of the bathroom. When he returned, the boner was gone.

I dropped myself from the counter with a disappointed sigh. I heard the door open and made my way over there. Cam was standing across from two people. Not one, as we had expected. The woman was clearly Vicki. Next to her, a short, balding man was pumping Cam's hand with false cheeriness.

"Hi," he was saying. "I'm Mike, Vicki's boyfriend."

Chapter 16

Cameron

Mike was short. And old. And he had a shiny bald pate he actually seemed to be proud of.

Of all the people I had assumed Vicki would be dating, this guy would never have crossed my mind. He was as far removed from her type as a person could be; Vicki liked tall, well-built, athletic men. Mike had a dad bod. It was baffling, to say the least.

But the thing that irritated me the most about Mike, seconds after meeting him, was his forced pleasantness. He beamed when he saw me. He greeted me with the enthusiasm of a fan meeting their idol. His handshake was firm if a little too aggressive. I suddenly wished I hadn't just washed my hands. He had the demeanor of a mild-mannered middle-aged teacher, and I wasn't sure why, but it made me want to throttle him. Maybe it was because I knew Vicki, and she ate men like Mike for breakfast. Vicki didn't do nice men. She dated assholes and slept with worse assholes. This was... curious.

"You can let his hand go now, Cam," Vicki said, jarring me back to the present. She looked smug.

"Right."

Mike drifted over to Yvette, who I hadn't noticed walk up. Something bright red caught my eye close to her foot, and I looked down to see the torn shreds of the panties I had just ripped from her. A reluctant smile crept up on my face.

"You must be Yvette," Mike said, bringing Yvette's hand to his lips and kissing it. Pretentious too. What a shocker.

Vicki walked over to me and leaned over to whisper in my ear. "Not bad," she commented, nodding in the direction of Yvette. "Which street corner did you drag her from?"

"The one next to the retirement home where you clearly met your boyfriend."

Vicki bristled.

"Just so you know, I don't believe this façade for a second."

"I don't need you to believe it. I need you to see it."

I started to step away from her, but she grabbed my hand and pulled me back. "Mike gives me orgasms every time we have sex," she whispered. She must have envisioned it as a surefire way to make me jealous, which could only mean she was jealous of herself. This was going to be an interesting dinner.

"Good for you," I whispered back. "I was literally inside Yvette when you rang the doorbell." It was petty and childish, but I couldn't help it. That's what Vicki did; she brought out the absolute worst version of me.

I shrugged off her hand and went over to Mike and Yvette. She must have told him about work because he was waxing lyrical about his brief experience with publishing companies.

I leaned down and picked up the panties, making sure Vicki was watching, and then I stuffed them into my pocket. I slid a hand around Yvette's waist and pulled her in close. Without missing a beat, Vicki dashed forward and grabbed Mike's hand.

"So, Vicki," I said, smiling through gritted teeth. "We weren't expecting both you and Mike." I didn't have the patience for subtlety. But I had no doubt as to why she had brought him. It was the exact same reason she was now caressing his arm slowly. Showing off her new man. Wanting me to see that she had moved on.

"I know!" Vicki said. "I'm terrible at these social things, to be honest. And Mike is the total opposite. He thrives in any social setting, isn't that right, babe? So, I figured I'd bring him along for moral support. You know?"

"And Emma?"

"She's at her music classes. We're picking her up on the

way home."

I stared at her as her words sank in. That had been deliberate. She wanted me to know that she knew what Emma and I had talked about. That I had asked Emma about music classes. And that I had suggested she shouldn't have to give up anything just because her mother said so. It was yet another subtle dig, a reminder that *she* was the active parent, and the best I could do was look on.

"Well, I'm just happy she's doing something she loves."

"Oh, she is."

We continued to stare at each other for a long time, the naked animosity radiating between us until Yvette nudged me slightly in the arm, and I snapped out of it.

"Please, join us."

We ushered them into the living room, and Yvette went to fetch them drinks. Vicki didn't sit down immediately. She walked first to the spot where my exercise bike had been before Yvette moved it, and then to the old drink cabinet where most of my photos were mounted. She stood there for some time, looking from one photo to another, her posture rigid and skeptical.

"You two make a lovely couple," she said when she finally joined Mike on the couch.

"Oh, yes," Mike agreed. He turned to Yvette, who was returning with drinks. She looked so homey and domestic, it was almost amusing, with her apron and her hair secured in a tight bun.

"If you don't mind me saying, you smell wonderful."

Yvette and I exchanged glances, and it took everything in me not to burst into laughter.

"Thank you," Yvette said.

"So, and I know this is a cliché question," Mike asked. "But how did you two meet?"

From the way he asked it, I knew Vicki had put him up to

it. And I suddenly understood why she had brought him. It was partly to flaunt her new man in my face, true, but mostly, Mike was going to play good cop. She had probably drilled him on what to ask, when to ask it, and who to direct his questions to. That way she could sit back and watch, wait for someone to make a mistake. The strategy clearly hinged on their perception of Yvette as the weak link. They must have thought they could get her to crack.

"Oh, it's such a long and tedious story," Yvette said. "How about you tell them, hun?"

"No, no. You're the storyteller. You take this one."

We had been over that story a hundred times. Back at the dinner with Wyatt and Grace Flores, the story had been created on the spot. A bit of improvisation on my part. But we had revised and perfected it over the last few days. It was watertight in addition to being charming and romantic, and Yvette recited it perfectly.

"How about you two?" I asked when Yvette was done. "I spoke with Vicki a few weeks ago, and she didn't mention you. This must be recent?"

Mike didn't respond immediately. He looked over at Vicki, who opened her mouth then seemed to think better of it and closed it.

"Uh, I'm sure she was going to tell you in her own time."

"Right."

"How did we meet? Well, I should give you a little context. I have a car dealership over on 5th and Lincoln. And one day, this little girl sprints into the store and makes a beeline for one of the cars in our window display. The problem was the display was hidden behind this very fine but very strong glass case. It's very hard to see, especially if you're running at full speed. So, this little girl didn't see it, and she ran right into it, wiped out on the floor, and started crying.

"I go over to her quickly, check to see if she's okay, but I can't get her to stop crying. Then I hear footsteps, and I look up, and the only thing I see is this blurry motion, and I don't know how, but the next moment, I'm sprawled on my ass on the floor.

"Turns out, the lady was this little girl's mother, and she thought I had done something to her daughter, so she hit me. It was quite the scene. I would have been embarrassed, but she was the most beautiful woman I had ever seen, and once we cleared up the misunderstanding, I gathered up the nerve and asked her out."

He beamed happily at Vicki, who gave him a stiff smile in return.

"I suppose that little girl was Emma?" I asked.

"Yes. And she's still obsessed with cars, that rascal. I don't know where she gets it from."

Of course. It all made sense. Emma had taken a liking to the car, and she would have pestered her mom about passing by the dealership every chance they got, just to look at it. The repeated visits must have warmed her to Mike, the flustered salesman who was always nice to her when she came by. And who seemed to like Emma.

"Can I use your bathroom?" Vicki asked suddenly.

"Uh, sure," I told her. "You can use the one down the hall."

She stared at me with her signature scowl, but she got up quietly and left.

"Emma is really amazing," Mike told me. I felt my jaw clench. "She's such a delightful child. Smart, energetic, willful… I think she has big things in her future, that one."

"You have a daughter, too, is that right?" I asked him.

"Elaine," Mike said. "She's a few years older than your Emma, but they get along very well. Hopefully, you can meet them soon."

"Definitely," I said.

I could see what Vicki meant about Mike. No doubt he could turn even the blandest topic into small talk fodder.

"We should move to the dining area," Yvette said after a

brief silence. "I think we're ready to serve dinner."

"Wonderful," Mike said. "Maybe we should wait for Vicki?"

I got up, shaking my head. "No, you two go ahead and set up. I'll go check on Vicki."

I walked over to Yvette and kissed her full on the mouth. Display of affection, just like we discussed. Mike looked away, pointedly.

Vicki wasn't in the bathroom of the hall. Which did not surprise me in the least. I went from room to room, looking for her, knowing she had gone snooping. I eventually found her in my bedroom. I should have guessed that was where she would go. The woman was calculating beyond belief.

"Bathroom's over that way," I said, pointing back the way I had come.

Vicki was standing over my dresser, rummaging through my clothes, her face pinched and unpleasant. "Who is she, Cam?" she asked me.

"Who? Yvette? My wife, of course."

"You're sticking with that?"

"What, the truth?"

"That woman doesn't live here, Cam. Please don't insult my intelligence."

"And what makes you think that?"

"No sanitary products," Vicki said, holding up a handful of my underwear. "I've turned this room over, and there's no single sanitary item here. If she lived here, there would be something."

"Wow, Sherlock. What an incredible deduction. And, incidentally, an invasion of privacy. I'm going to need you to get out of my bedroom."

"Don't you mean 'our' bedroom? Yours and your wife's?"

"Out, Vicki."

She threw the boxers back into the drawer and came storming over to me by the door.

"Like I said, Cam. I know exactly what you're trying to do. And it won't work. I'm going to have private investigators crawling so far up your ass you won't remember the meaning of privacy. Good luck keeping up this charade with your 'wife.'"

Chapter 17

Yvette

I had never been the best at reading people, but I had no problem decoding Vicki. I had never met the woman; this was our first interaction, yet I was confident I had her completely figured out within minutes of meeting her.

The thing about Vicki was, she was gorgeous. Not just beautiful, which she was, but stunningly gorgeous from head to toe. She was tall and skinny, with the kind of body you could expect to see in a magazine. Her breasts were a bit of an anomaly, though. They were large and heavy, pushed out to full glory by whatever bra she was wearing, and accentuated further by the low-cut blouse she had on. I could tell she often got her way just by bending over and giving men an eyeful of cleavage. She had long, brown hair that fell past her shoulders, and her face was thoroughly made up, the highlight being a bright red lipstick that seemed to glow in the light.

So, stunning. Without a doubt. And that was key to who she was. I doubted Vicki had ever worked for anything in her life. She probably smiled and things just fell into her lap. She had the air of someone who always expected to get their way, which obviously meant she turned ugly when she didn't. She had perfected the art of charming her way out of situations and into places. Which meant she was incredibly entitled. And when that was threatened, she became downright nasty. It explained the way she was with Cam.

From the minute she saw me, she had been assessing me. Sizing me up, and when the smile tugged at the corner of her lips, I got the sense she was satisfied she had nothing to worry about. I wondered what it was she whispered to Cam when she dragged him aside. I was dying to know what Cam told her in response because she didn't look too happy about it. I did notice, however, the subtle way he glared at her when he picked up my panties from the floor and stuffed them in his pocket. And when he slid an arm protectively around my waist. Possessively. Showing me off. Letting them know I was his.

I knew I wasn't, but it was a great feeling.

Mike was a little different. He was nice, but the kind of nice that often nagged at you and made you weary in the long run. He was friendly and conversational and clearly comfortable with pretty much any social setting. The problem with that was that I would have to be the one to deal with him. I would have to smile and nod and pay attention to his ramblings, responding often enough to encourage him to keep talking. It was the absolute worst part of being a host.

I loved everything else about it, though. Playing house. Being the dutiful, domesticated wife, which I would never have thought of myself as being. Running around, serving drinks, then sitting around to make pleasant chit-chat. It was all very 70s housewife, and I was having a blast with it.

But there was more to it. I felt it in the way Vicki pranced about the house, eager to show me that she knew her way around, that she had been here before. I heard it in her voice when she spoke, in the way she directed her questions solely to Cam and not to me. Then there was the subtle interrogation Mike was subjecting me to. I didn't need Cam's wink to figure out what was happening. We were being observed, studied, tested. Whatever it was Cam wanted her to think, she was already wise to the notion that she was being deceived and was determined to snuff out the lie. As confident as I was in our preparation, I didn't think we could survive the intensity of these two.

Cam seemed confident. There was something he wasn't telling me, a reason behind his confident smile. It took me some time to figure out what it was about them that bothered me so much. And, to my surprise, it was Mike who voiced it.

Cam had just gone off to 'check on Vicki,' which I found completely unnecessary and highly suspicious. Mike was helping me set the table, and I think he noticed me throwing looks in the direction Cam and Vicki had gone.

"Drives you crazy, right?" he said, and he flashed me a knowing smile.

"Huh?"

"Those two," Mike said. "There's so much tension between them, except it doesn't always seem like hatred. You know?"

"I'm not sure I do," I said.

"You know what they say. There's a very fine line between love and hate. A lot of negative emotion isn't that different from positive emotion. And it's all just that: emotion."

"I'm still not sure what you're saying."

Mike sighed. "What do you think of Vicki?"

"I... I don't know enough about her to have an opinion." It was the politically correct thing to say, and we both knew it.

Mike smiled. "Right. Well, what do you think of her with Cam?"

"I think there's a lot of history there," I said, but I was beginning to see where Mike was going.

"You don't have to be afraid. You can speak plainly to me. They hate each other, right? They're always yelling at each other and calling each other names, and they go out of their way to make each other miserable... But do you have any idea how much effort that actually takes? It's exhausting, carrying around that much resentment. It's enough to make you wonder, why do they do it?"

"What do you think?" I asked him.

Mike smiled. "I think it would be very easy to assume there is still some lingering affection there. I mean, they made a baby together. It's not completely unreasonable to assume they still have feelings for each other, no matter how complicated. My point was that, as the third party, I understand that worry, that nagging feeling of doubt, and I'll bet you understand too."

He was making way more sense than I was comfortable

with. I recognized all the beats he was hitting on. And I realized it was the same thought that had run through my mind, more than once, often subconsciously. Why was Cam so hung up on his ex? Why did it matter so much to him that he showed her how good his life was now? Was he only using me to make her jealous?

The problem with that theory was what it said about me. What it demanded I admit to myself. What we were doing, Cam and I; this was a business transaction and nothing more.

"I guess I hadn't thought about that," I told Mike.

He smiled again, with that frustrating knowing look in his eye, but thankfully he dropped the topic. We carried on setting places on the table, and I doubled my attempts to keep my eyes from the hallway.

Cam and Vicki reappeared moments later. From their expressions, it was clear something had happened between them. The thought popped into my mind, horrid and disturbing that maybe they had been intimate in some way. I looked over at Mike, and his face was back to pleasant and good-natured. If he was as troubled by the dynamic between Cam and Vicki, he hid it well.

Cam walked right up to me and pecked me on the cheek. His hand slid down my back and onto my ass. He cupped my right buttock and gave it a playful squeeze, surreptitious but not completely out of sight of the guests. I remembered his words; we need to be all over each other. Well, he was certainly doing a great job of that.

"This all looks wonderful," he commented, nodding at the dinner setup.

"Thank you," I said. I turned to Mike and Vicki. "Please, sit."

The chicken recipe I'd followed was my mother's, and it was one I was particularly proud of. It had turned out great, too; the chicken was tender and flavorful, and the puttanesca sauce was thick and delicious. It was a bright moment for me, watching Vicki take a bite and try to conceal the fact that she was impressed. Mike wasn't as shy with his reaction.

"This is delightful!" he gushed, taking another forkful of chicken and chewing slowly. His whole face lit up, and he nodded appreciatively. "Wonderful!"

"Thank you, Mike," I told him.

"She's a hell of a cook, this one," Cam said, looking over at me with a fiercely proud glint in his eye.

"That she is," Mike agreed. "You have to give me this recipe, Yvette. I'm not much of a cook, but if I can get anywhere close to this, I think I would take it."

"Oh, I don't know. It's an old family recipe, and I haven't written it down anywhere…"

"Well, then you must inform me next time you're making it, and I'll hurry over with pen and paper, yeah?"

"Sure."

"So," Vicki spoke over Mike, dropping her fork loudly in a bid for attention. Everyone turned to look at her.

"I hear old man Wyatt is retiring," she said, directing her comment at Cam.

Cam fidgeted uncomfortably in his seat. It wasn't hard to figure out why. No one knew about Wyatt outside the company. Or at least, no one was supposed to. "Uh, I don't know anything about that," he said, slightly defensively.

"Oh, come on, Cam. It's an open secret. Everyone knows the old man is going down fast."

"And who exactly is 'everyone'?"

"People talk, Cam. And I know a lot of people in the publishing industry. Let's just say the word on the street is that Wyatt won't survive the year and that Penguin Publishers is working on a replacement."

"Even if I knew anything about that, Vicki, I wouldn't be talking about it with you. That's company business."

"I hear it's you," Vicki went on, undeterred.

"What?"

"The replacement. I hear it's going to be you."

Cam opened and closed his mouth. I could almost hear his brain working furiously, trying to come up with a believable lie. But his hesitation was enough confirmation for Vicki, who gave her an arrogant smile.

"Of course," she said. "It makes sense, from their perspective. You've worked there the longest. You have the most experience. And the board actually likes you. I imagine it seemed the only logical choice for them. You know what, Cam. Good for you. I'm actually thrilled for you."She grabbed the nearest glass to her and raised it. She probably meant it as a congratulatory toast, but the impression I got was that she was mocking him.

"I'm sure you'll do a great job," Vicki said, her glass in the air.

Mike raised his as well, hesitated, then, noticing that neither Cam nor I was raising ours, let his hand drop slowly.

"Like I said, Vicki. I don't know about any of that," Cam said, resolute.

"I understand if you're not able to talk about it, Cam," Vicki said. "I also understand that a promotion would be problematic for your bid to get custody of Emma. You already spend half your time at that damn office already. I don't imagine your schedule is going to clear up when you have more on your plate."

"How about you let me worry about that?" Cam said, and now his voice was a little frosty.

"Right. Just thought I'd mention it, seeing as you've suddenly decided to be a good father."

"Can we not do this now, please?" Mike cut in, his voice sharper than I'd heard all night. "Darling," he turned to Vicki, "our hosts have made us this wonderful meal. We're having a nice, quiet dinner. How about we keep it that way, hmm? Maybe save the unpleasantness for later?"

Vicki dropped her fork for the second time in a row. She

looked at Mike like she was hoping to burn holes into him. But Mike didn't falter. And suddenly, their dynamic made a whole lot of sense. Mike was nice and friendly, but he was no pushover. Clearly, he had no problem putting Vicki in her place. I glanced at Cam, and we exchanged smiles.

Vicki put her hands on the table, and she moved as if to push herself out of her seat. But she seemed to be having difficulty. I glanced down at her perfectly manicured fingernails, and that was when I saw it. There was a nasty red rash spread out across the backs of her hands, and it looked to be spreading further up her hands by the second.

I pointed, horrified, unsure what to say. Vicki looked down at them, and then her hand shot to her throat, and she was choking for breath.

Mike was out of his chair in seconds. He rushed to Vicki's side and helped her up, whispering urgently in her ear. "What the...? Darling?"

Vicki was waving her hands, gesticulating in the direction of her plate.

Cam stood up too, but his confusion froze him in place.

"Wait," Mike said suddenly. He leaned down to Vicki's plate and gave it a good sniff. Then he turned to us, comprehension mingling with mild horror. "Are there pine nuts in this?"

"Uh, I... yes... I think... I'm not... No, wait. I did use pine nuts in my sauce, yes."

"She's allergic," Mike said simply. He gave Vicki a reassuring pat on the shoulder, whispered something to her, and then turned and dashed away.

I should have asked Cam to confirm any allergies once we knew Vicki was coming over. But then again, he should have known about her allergies. It was almost ironic that I had gone for this particular dish because of how simple it was, and here we were, with the guest choking. Maybe to death.

I looked over at Vicki, and I felt my heart drop into my stomach. Her skin was red and splotchy. The rash had spread all the way up her arms and onto her face. Her eyes were swelling fast, and tears were streaming freely down her cheeks. And from the way she was gripping her throat, she was having trouble breathing.

I had no idea what to do... should she sit? Stand? Lie down?

Mike returned moments later with an EpiPen. He helped Vicki back to her seat and then parted her dress slightly and administered the injection.

We watched in stunned silence as he did, and afterward, he slid into his seat beside her and watched her with concerned eyes.

It took some time, but the redness eventually started to fade. Vicki's expression softened, but only just. She still looked like a bad Halloween monster, and when she finally got her voice back, I wasn't surprised to hear the vitriol coming out of her mouth. "You tried to kill me," Vicki said, her eyes locating and staying on me.

"Don't be ridiculous, Vicki," Cam said. He had been silent so long I'd almost forgotten he was there. "Yvette would never do that."

"Come on, darling," Mike said to her. "We need to get you to the hospital. You could have a second reaction."

Vicki looked like she wanted to argue some more, but she appeared to think better of it. Mike came around and kissed me lightly on the cheek, telling me it had been an excellent meal. He shook Cam's hand and said thank you, and then he gathered their things and guided Vicki out the door.

It was such a weird, unceremonious ending to the night, neither of us knew what to say. We just sat there, silently, looking anywhere but at each other, until the awkward tension got to be too much.

"Well, I think you made quite the impression," Cam finally said.

I stared at him, my heart still pounding from the horror of what had just happened, and the mirth in his voice made me smile a little.

"I can't believe I almost killed your ex," I said.

Cam shrugged. "She'll be fine; don't worry."

Chapter 18

Cameron

The biggest thing to come out of my week of fake marriage was the adjustment I had to make at work. It wasn't as simple as I had imagined it was going to be, inviting Yvette to my home. Obviously. But the challenge I had completely overlooked was just how complicated things would get at work.

I realized, as soon as I had to go back to the office, that I had no idea how to act around her. I had never really known how to act around her, to be honest, but this was a different ball game entirely. Now that I had been that intimate with her, it was nearly impossible to go back to treating her like just another employee. But then Yvette had never been just an employee.

The awkwardness started right outside the building. Yvette had insisted on going home to change and get ready for work, but I knew she didn't want us to be seen walking in to work together. Already, the secretaries were whispering about us, and I understood her not wanting the prevailing story about her to revolve around an affair with me.

I was rummaging in my briefcase for my keycard when she showed up. When I became aware of her, rather, because her scent hit me before I looked up, and I knew right away, it was her.

I couldn't help the smile that spread across my face. I couldn't do anything about the quickening of my pulse, and the general feeling of weightlessness that stole over me.

She looked stunning. Weeks of watching her at work, and never had she looked more delectable. She was in a sharp suit;

cream blouse and high-waisted black pants, along with an expensive-looking pair of high-heels.

I had no idea what to say to her. My mind was awash with images from our married week, and all I wanted to do was remind her of some of my favorite moments. Like the time we set out to clean the house and ended up getting drenched with cleaning water and creating a game to test who could skid across the living room without falling down. Or that very memorable night when neither of us could sleep, so we stayed up all night talking. And of course, the time she almost killed my ex-girlfriend.

I was trying my best not to remember any of the sexual stuff, because I didn't think I would make it through the day if I did. Like the first day after she moved in, and because she forgot to bring her favorite sleeping gown, she spent the evening in an oversized T-shirt of mine, and the following morning naked. I was definitely not thinking about that. Or the time I was teaching her to use my shower, and I ended up eating her out right there in the bathroom.

I shook my head hard and readjusted my pants, the bulge already beginning to grow. This was going to be a difficult day, I realized.

It helped slightly that she seemed just as awkward as I was. That her cheeks flushed every time we were in each other's presence. And that she seemed as incapable of stringing together two words to form a sentence as I was.

And so we stood there, two passing ships, staring at each other, each in a world of our own until it got openly uncomfortable for us both, and we both reached for the door.

We bumped into each other again at the coffee machine. The kitchen was the most communal of all the office spaces and where the presence of other people meant we couldn't dedicate long minutes to openly lusting after each other.

"Coffee?" I asked conversationally, lifting the pot over to her.

I noticed she had unbuttoned the first two buttons of her

blouse. You could just make out a bright white bra underneath. And the creamy skin around her throat and chest area.

"Sure, thank you," she said, offering up her cup.

"I hope you like black coffee," I said. "I think we're out of milk."

"Yeah, that's okay."

I poured the coffee out. From the corner of my eye, I watched as the two ladies who were with us in the kitchen finished their tea and walked out together, chatting in low voices.

Alone. Just the two of us.

"You look gorgeous," I said to Yvette, my voice barely a whisper.

"Thank you," she said.

"It's taking everything in my power not to plant you on this counter and kiss you until you get dizzy."

Yvette blushed, as she always did, but her gaze was steady. Her eyes were locked on mine, challenging me, daring me.

"Shame," she said. "I was just thinking the same thing."

"Were you now?"

"Oh, I was. I've mapped it all out. I'd walk in here, and you'd see me and lose all sense. You'd clear the contents of this counter with a sweep of your hand like they do in the movies. And then you'd pick me up and drop me here, and I would spread my legs and pull you in, and You would kiss me. All we would have would be the stolen moments until the next person walks in, so the thrill would make it exciting and hurried and frenzied. And just before someone walks in, you'd pull me off the counter and wink at me, and we would go back to talking about something innocuous like the weather."

I nodded, impressed, and aroused and tempted beyond belief. "There's just one problem with that plan," I said.

"What?"

"You're assuming I would have the presence of mind to

stop just because someone walks in. I don't know that I would, to be honest."

The sound of footsteps came, sudden and close, and Yvette and I took hurried steps away from each other. Our eyes remained locked, however.

"Lovely work with the digitized books, by the way," I said, reaching for the first topic that sprang to mind.

"Oh, thank you. It was quite the task, but I'm happy with how it all came together."

"Which reminds me. Design sent over a few mock-up covers for some of the books. You should pass by my office after lunch, so I can show them to you."

"Sure. I will."

She nodded stiffly, then turned and walked away. Without adding sugar to her coffee. I doubted she would even realize she was carrying a cup until she got to her desk.

I watched her walk away, unable to resist the urge to follow her with my eyes. Naturally, they landed on her buttocks, firm and round, with a pronounced jiggle to them as she sashayed away.

I heard a low whistle from close by, and I whipped my head around to find a young man with a thick beard staring right where my own eyes had been.

"That's a tasty morsel right there," he said, shaking his head to illustrate his point. I didn't recognize him, but the easy confidence attitude screamed sales.

"Right," I said. My voice was way calmer than I felt.

"She's new, right?" he asked me, still staring at the spot where Yvette's ass had been.

"Not so new. Been here over a month."

"Oh, she can get all of it and then some. I would *not* mindbending her over an HR manual and showing her the fraternization policy." He chuckled at his own joke, going so far as to lift his hand, demanding a high five.

I stared at the outstretched palm, the blood pounding in my ears, wondering what would happen if I responded by punching him right in his stupid face.

But I simply smiled and nodded. "She is something, that's for sure," I said, picking up my own cup and walking away. It took a minute, but the surge of adrenaline gradually wore down, leaving the lingering question of why I had felt so protective of her in the first place.

Our next meeting was mandated. After updating Meredith on the sales figures for the previous month and projections for the next, she wondered aloud when the digital copies would be available in time for the next editorial meeting.

"I'll need a timeline for them," she said. "Everything is moving so fast; we need to be ready in the next few weeks."

"I'll find out," I said.

"Have you had a chance to look at her work?" Meredith asked me.

"Yvette's?"

"Of course, Cam. Who else were we talking about?"

"I've seen one book, I think. She did an excellent job, although I feel like she would thrive with a little more artistic help."

"How do you mean?"

"It's something I've heard her talk about. There's no point in digitizing out classic publications if we have no intention of illustrating it as well."

"Ah. Different mediums and everything."

"Exactly."

"I'll see what I can do. I might need to sit down with her again. I've just had so much on my plate lately…"

"Oh," I said, suddenly guilty. "How's Wyatt doing?"

"Worse, to be honest."

"Well, I can handle Yvette. I'll go speak with her, see where she's at, maybe pick her brain about working with a designer."

"Would you? That would be immensely helpful."

"Of course, Meredith."

"You're doing a great job, by the way. As it is, you're a shoo-in for the appointment."

Her words reminded me of Vicki and what she had said to me at dinner a few nights ago. The promotion meant more responsibility. More time here, and potentially less with Emma. But I couldn't worry about that; I would cross that bridge when I got to it.

I left her office and made a beeline for Yvette's. I quickened my step, remembering her cleavage, and the way she leaned in as she described her fantasy of me taking her on the kitchen counter.

I gave a little knock, waited a few seconds then walked in. Yvette was on the phone. She looked up when I walked in, and she smiled with such joy I couldn't help grinning myself. She held up a finger, then pointed to the seat in front of her desk. I shook my head.

I walked around to her side of the desk and stood behind her, my hands going to her shoulders. She felt stiff, knotted. I started to massage her shoulders, being met with an initial shake of her head but proceeding regardless. Slowly, gradually, I felt the stiffness leave her body, and her shoulders slumped.

"That's right," she said into the phone. "I think we can make Monday work, Mr. Cavill."

I watched as her hand tightened around the pen she was holding. And as her head lolled backward, falling onto my torso. If she wasn't on the phone, I knew she would have let out a sigh.

I took that as an invitation and sent my hands further south. I worked my way from her shoulders down to her back, then all the way up and over into the opening in front of her blouse. I reached in and squeezed my hands into her bra, cupping both breasts.

"No, no. It's not a problem at all, Mr. Cavill. We want to bring your book to a modern audience, that's all. Share your brilliance with a younger generation. It will be good for your new book, too."

I pulled my hands out and set about undoing the rest of the buttons on her blouse. Then I reached back and found the taut clasp of her bra and flicked it open, causing her breasts to spill out. I reached forward once more and cupped them, this time letting them rest in my palms, my fingers brushing past her nipples and drawing a reluctant gasp from her.

"Great. I look forward to the meeting. Right. Of course, sir. Monday it is."

She dropped the phone back onto its cradle so hard it made a clanging sound. She stood up suddenly, whipping around so fast she almost sent me falling backward.

"You can't do that!" she said, her expression wild. "Not while I'm working!"

But I wasn't fooled. I knew how Yvette looked when she was aroused, and she was checking off all the boxes right now.

"I'm sorry," I said. "I was just thinking about that plan you mentioned, back in the kitchen, and I was wondering if this desk would be a good substitute for that counter."

We reached for each other simultaneously. I lunged, and she fell into my arms. My hands found the seat of her pants and lifted. Her legs went around me, and I carried her back, planting her firmly on the desk behind her. I reached around and gave her desk a sweep, just like she had said, sending files and folders and a phone flying to the floor. Then I reached down and found her lips.

She was definitely angry. I could tell from the way she kissed me. Angry and horny, and impatient. We kissed like long-lost lovers because that's what it felt like we were. Like it had been ages since she was in my arms since my lips were dancing on hers and my tongue prying her lips open to taste the sweetness beyond.

There was an abandoned, and a passion there that I knew was dangerous, but I couldn't pull away if I wanted to. This felt right, felt like home. I was crazy about the woman, I realized. I wanted nothing more than to do this to her, with her, and that would be enough for me.

She mumbled something into my mouth, the words drowning in the urgent rhythm of our lips.

"Hmm?" I mumbled, my eyes flickering open.

"Door. Did you close it?"

"Who cares?" I asked, and I swooped back down and kissed her once more.

I didn't; I knew that much. They could all watch, for all I cared. And after a few moments, Yvette threw away her caution, too. She fumbled around with the front of my shirt, gave up, and went to undo the buttons on my pants instead. They came away shockingly fast, considering she had to work against the rigid protrusion that was my throbbing cock.

"Fuck me," she whispered. "Please."

Those words were like fuel to an already wild inferno. I pulled away from her, stepping back slightly. My fingers were trembling as I worked her pants free, and then as I yanked her panties down. I didn't have the patience to pull them all the way off, so I let them fall to her ankles and pool around them. And then I was back between her legs, finding her warm moistness with ease and plunging in with a sure stroke.

Her fingers dug into my back as I buried myself in her. Her mouth was open at my ear, and she muttered incoherent nonsense that I thought included my name.

I grabbed her back, pulling her right to the edge of the desk to gain purchase, then I started to pound. I had no intention of slowing down. We were not making love, not today. My hips rocked back and forth, slamming repeatedly into her, our bodies slick with sweat and our voices coming together in muted gasps and groans.

My thrusting was brutal, frenzied, manic. I plunged repeatedly into her, plundering her very depths, then pulling out and doing it over again. It was unrelenting and raw, and the single most intense sex I had ever had.

Her body started to quake. From her legs, I felt the jerking, involuntary twitching and bobbing. Then her torso stiffened, and she gripped me harder than before, her nails now biting into the skin on my back.

"Oh my God, I'm coming," she whispered through gritted teeth.

I was, too. I wanted to say it back, but the effort would have been too much for me. I pulled her all the way off the desk and carried her to the nearest wall. The pants around her leg almost tripped us both, but we made it there.

I lifted her legs even higher so that they rested on the insides of my elbows. Then, staring deep into her eyes, I thrust into her, once, twice, and by the third stroke, I was well over the edge. I kept thrusting still, feeling her body fall apart and enjoying every second of it. Her cries were no longer so muffled, and the slapping sounds from our bodies were fairly audible.

Slowly, I came to a stop, sliding in and out of her with less urgency and power until my own toes uncurled, and the orgasm drained my legs of all their strength.

I let go, then, setting her gently on her feet and collapsing almost immediately onto a chair.

It happened so fast. Too fast for either of us to react. Yvette was reaching down to pull her pants up. I was catching my breath, my chest heaving uncontrollably.

A sharp knock, and then the door swung open. Meredith poked her head into the room, and her mouth fell open at the scene in front of her.

Chapter 19

Yvette

It was the single most embarrassing moment of my whole entire life.

The worst part was how long it seemed to take. From the moment the door opened, everything seemed to happen in slow motion. Meredith's head, peeking in from the slot in the door; her eyes, sweeping the room, taking in Cam first, collapsed half-naked on my chair, and then swinging around to me, fumbling with the bunched-up mess that was my pants.

I had never been so mortified, and so completely paralyzed. I just stood there, the realization that we had been caught washing over me, rooting me to the spot and robbing me of my ability to think or speak.

Cam didn't seem to be doing any better. He just stared at Meredith, too stunned to even attempt to get dressed.

I don't know what I expected Meredith to do. I could think up a million scenarios, but the one that actually played out wouldn't have been one of them.

She walked quickly into the room and closed the door behind her. "Cam," she said, looking at him. "There was something else I needed from you; I forgot to tell you during our briefing back in my office. Please come see me as soon as you get a chance?"

Cam nodded, clearly unable to speak too.

"Miss Matthews? I would like to speak to you as well, ideally as soon as possible. Would you please join me in my office in, say, ten minutes? That should be enough time for you to get cleaned up?"

She spoke so casually; it was almost as if she was discussing the weather. And not like there were two naked employees in front of her. She didn't seem mad, either, or offended. Or any of the things I expected her to be. Just calm and rational and slightly terrifying because of it.

"Would that be okay?" she prompted once more, and I nodded.

"Excellent."

She turned to leave. "We really should put some locks on these," she commented dryly as she opened the door. Then she was gone.

Cam and I stared at each other silently for a long time. I was mortified beyond belief, and he seemed to be lost for words, which wasn't something I associated with him. The sight of him made it much worse; he was still slouched back in the chair, his pants halfway up his legs, his dick hanging out obscenely, limp, and ashamed.

I heard the sound of footsteps, and that spurred me into action, snapped me out of the stupor. I quickly pulled my pants all the way up, snapped my bra back on, and buttoned my blouse up. I was sure I looked disheveled, but there wasn't time to worry about that just yet.

Cam took the hint as well. He finished getting dressed just as the knock sounded on the door, and by that time, I had already gotten down and gathered the scattered items on the floor.

"Just a moment!" I yelled. My voice cracked; it felt like I hadn't spoken in a very long time. I did my best and quickest arrangement, stacking the documents in one semi-neat pile and everything else in a reasonable pile across the desk.

I glanced over at Cam, and he nodded stiffly. I reached up and patted my hair, making sure it was all in place and that I didn't look like I had just been pushed up against a wall.

"Come in!" I said.

A tall, pretty woman pushed the door open and walked in. I knew her from around the office, but I had never spoken to her.

She was, unless I was mistaken, a secretary to one of the senior managers.

"Sorry to interrupt, Miss Matthews, but a call came in for you. Mr. Cavill. Says there's a problem with your line."

The problem was that someone had swept it to the floor in a fit of passion and probably broken it.

"Okay," I said. "Thank you. I'll call Mr. Cavill back right away."

She nodded, turned, and hurried away.

I picked up my phone and dialed Mr. Cavill's number. As it rang, I stared in the direction of Meredith's office. Ten minutes, she had said. I wasn't about to waste her time when I was already on thin ice with her.

Mr. Cavill wanted to reschedule. It turned out his Monday wasn't as free as he had assumed, and he wanted to know if I could make Tuesday morning work. I quickly agreed and hung up the phone. I was far too wired for casual conversation. Or anything else, really.

My heart was pounding, and my mind kept trying to work out the variety of ways this meeting with Meredith could go. It was bad enough that I was probably going to get fired. I couldn't even wrap my mind around the scene Meredith had just walked into. How bad we must have looked. How unprofessional. And we had developed such a nice relationship, one I had been hoping would blossom into a mentorship. And now this.

It was all my fault. Right at the beginning, on my very first day here, I had gone out of my way to stop this very thing from happening. I had told Cam off, refusing to engage in any funny business at work. Yet here we were. I had been so adamant about maintaining a professional demeanor, keeping the personal stuff out of work, and I had failed miserably. Not only had I allowed Cam to charm his way past my admittedly feeble defenses, but I had also let him break the one rule I had promised myself I wouldn't compromise on. Now, this was going to be the whole story; people were going to talk, as they did, and I was going to be that woman who slept her way to the top, who only got the job because she was fucking the Head of Department. And I had worked so hard to get here.

Maybe it wouldn't be so bad if I got fired. At least I wouldn't have to walk past an office full of smirking people who looked down when I met their gaze. At least I wouldn't have to pretend not to hear their snide comments as I passed.

I knocked on Meredith's door. I waited until she invited me in, and that drew a smile from her.

"I should probably have done the same, eh?" she said, her tone surprisingly light.

"What?" I stuttered, confused by her tone.

"Come on in, Yvette. Sit." She pointed out a chair in front of her desk, and I walked to it and sat down. She watched me quietly for a while, then she got up, came around the desk, and sat down in the chair across from mine. "You don't need to be so tense, Yvette. I didn't call you here to berate you."

"I'm not fired?" I asked in a small voice.

Meredith reached over and touched me gently on the arm. It was a kind gesture, and its purpose was clearly to reassure me. "Not at all. For several reasons, primarily the fact that I like to think of myself as a feminist, I'm not going to judge you for expressing your sexuality. I mean, obviously, I'd prefer it if you didn't do it at work, but I understand the thrill. I was young once."

I looked at her, my mouth hanging open.

"Plus," she went on. "Cam is an extremely attractive man. I cannot say with any conviction that I wouldn't do the exact same thing if I were twenty years younger, and he looked at me the way he looks at you."

It was the second time I'd heard that statement. How exactly did Cam look at me? Why was I the only one who never seemed to notice it? I wasn't brave enough to ask Meredith to elaborate. Not while I was still getting my breathing back down to normal.

"I'm sorry you had to see that," I said. "It was unprofessional, and it won't happen again."

Meredith nodded. "From what I've seen of your work, Yvette, you're an excellent editor. You have that rare ability to shape a writer's work while removing yourself from it entirely. I think you're a hard worker, you deliver your work in time, and you get along well with just about everybody— some, clearly, better than others."She gave me a little wink, no doubt her way of letting me know it was safe to laugh about it all now.

"I don't think your relationship with Cam has affected your work, so I have no reason to be unduly concerned. I'm not so sure about him, though. But that's a conversation I'll need to have with him."

"What do you mean?" I asked, unable to help myself this time.

"About Cam? Let's just say he's been a bit distracted. At least now I understand why. Anyway, Yvette. I called you in here to talk to you about the next step of your work. I had asked Cam to find you a graphic designer to work with for the books you've already completed, so we can get them out as soon as possible. Is that okay?"

"Yeah, that would be great."

"Excellent. Beyond that, I wanted to talk to you about something else, something more… personal, if you don't mind."

She glanced over at the door as if checking that we were indeed alone. It was a subtle shift, but her demeanor changed almost completely. All at once, she was open and vulnerable in a way that made me feel slightly uncomfortable.

"Cam told you he invited you to the dinner with my husband at the company retreat?"

I nodded.

"I'm sure he mentioned, and you would have noticed this too… my husband is a shell of the man he used to be. The disease has advanced faster than we anticipated, and every visit to the doctor now comes with more and more bad news. I fear he may not have much longer..."Meredith trailed off, and her voice cracked ever so slightly. I was afraid she would start to cry, and I wouldn't know what to do. I couldn't imagine the kind of strength and fortitude she had, going through something this heartbreaking and still being as unbowed as she was.

"I'm so sorry, Mrs. Banks."

She snorted, and it sounded like a laugh."I've seen you naked, Yvette. I think you can call me Meredith.

"Right. Meredith."

"Anyway. I've been finalizing Wyatt's projects and clearing his backlog. I'm close to finishing, actually. Now, I'm not supposed to be telling you this, but the board is very interested in Cam taking over in the capacity of COO. I've been pushing him quite hard, to be honest; I feel like he would be the perfect fit, and he knew Wyatt well enough to carry on his legacy."

So Vicki had been on to something.

"What I'm getting at is this: As soon as Cam is appointed to the new position, which will be in the coming weeks, I think, I'm going to need someone to step in as Head of Editorial, on an interim basis while we find a replacement. I've been so busy with the transition I haven't really had time to start the search..."

"I don't understand. Do you mean you want me to do it?"

"Precisely."

"But Mrs ... Uh, Meredith. I'm new... There must be someone more qualified..."

"You're a smart woman, Yvette. Tell me, what is the median age of our staff in the Editorial department?"

I thought about it for a moment. "Around 40?"

"Try 50," she said. "I love what you've done with the library. I loved your idea about digital copies and new covers. I need that innovative spirit. Someone who can shake up the department, inject new life into it. I'm sorry, but I'm not going to take no for an answer."

I looked at her, lost for words. A few minutes ago, I was sure I was going to be fired. Instead, I was getting a promotion.

"Tell you what," Meredith went on. "I'll let you sleep on it. But I'm very impressed by you, young lady. And I hope you accept."

Chapter 20

Yvette

I was distracted during my entire commute home.

It had been one of the weirdest days since I started working at Penguin Publishers. There was a lot to think about, and once I clocked out, my feet went on autopilot, and I let myself drift off.

I bumped into someone at the door, which was how I knew my mind wasn't in the present. I barely noticed him; there was only a brief flash of a black and white suit, and then a gruff voice mumbling an apology, and then he stepped aside to let me pass.

I was flattered that Meredith was impressed enough to consider me, even though it hadn't even been two months since I started. It spoke to just how well I had settled in, and how much my work was speaking for me. That was the good news. The flipside was that I was now being thrust into a position of leadership, and I wasn't too sure how I was going to handle that.

I would essentially be taking over from Cam.

Cam.

My phone buzzed urgently in my purse, sparing me the inevitable trip down the rabbit hole of thinking about Cam. I needed to figure that bit out. I really did.

I thought it might have been Cavill again, but it turned out to be Tyler. My heart leaped. If ever there was a time I needed my best friend, now would be it.

"Just the person I wanted to hear from," I said.

"Oh, look. You remembered you have a best friend."

"Don't even start, Tyler. I've had the craziest day."

I had stopped by the side of the road, right outside a small café. I thought I saw someone staring at me from inside the café, but I dismissed it.

"Sounds unbearably exciting," Tyler said, with just a hint of sarcasm. "But before you get into that… there seems to be a huge amount of money deposited into my bank account, and apparently, it was in your name. I thought someone must have made a mistake, but they insist that there was no mistake."

"Oh, yeah. I forgot to tell you about that. It's not a mistake. I did send you that money."

"Vee? What's going on?"

"It's for the restaurant. Obviously. Do you remember? We talked about it when you were here. You said you were thinking about renovating, but you were short of money?"

"And you just happened to have five thousand dollars lying around?"

"It's a long story, Tyler. But you should definitely get started with the renovation plans."

"I told you, Vee. We're selling."

"No, you're not. That was you being afraid to take the risk. Now stop being a pussy and tell your aunt you're going to make it work."

Tyler fell silent, and I knew he was searching for another excuse.

"Where did you even get that kind of money?" he asked. The classic side-step.

"I got an advance. I'm being promoted."

It was the first thing that popped into my mind. Well, it wasn't completely false.

"No way! Really?"

"Yup. Head of Department. But only on a trial basis, to begin with."

"That's incredible, Vee. I told you you'd kill it!"

"Yeah yeah. So, you have no excuse not to follow through on the restaurant. Let me call you when I get home, okay? I'm outside this restaurant, and the people are starting to stare."

"Okay. Proud of you!"

Normally, I would take the bus or get a cab if it was too late. But today I felt like walking. I thought it would help clear my mind, but all it did was give me more time to obsess over everything that had happened.

My thoughts were a jumbled mess. I kept jumping from work to Cam to Meredith and then back in a vicious cycle, without making any real headway. I felt like I had the weight of the world on my shoulders. A mild headache was starting out at my temple, threatening to morph into a full-blown migraine.

And still, no solutions presented themselves to me.

It should have been simple, really. The promotion was a dream come true. I would be ascending the ladder faster than even my most optimistic projections. It would be a highlight of my career, young as I was, to be given such responsibility. And it was a welcome indicator that I was on the right track after all.

The simple fact was that Cam complicated everything. It wasn't just a promotion if he was involved. I couldn't work with him; I didn't know how to. I had tried so hard to do just that for the last month and a half, and it had ended with him pinning me against a wall in my office. If I were honest with myself, we were always going to end up on that desk, against that wall. There was too much heat between us, too much sexual tension. I wanted him so badly, and it clouded my judgment, especially in the most crucial moments. I barely knew who I was anymore. The Yvette Matthews who had moved here not so long ago was shy and career-focused and introverted. This woman who looked back at me through shop windows as I strode through the streets; this wild and carefree panther was almost a stranger.

I was walking past a boutique when I saw him. I almost missed him, as my eyes went from my own reflection to a brightly dressed woman on the other side of the street. But then I noticed the suit, and it hit me as oddly familiar. And then I remembered where I had seen him. He was the dark shape I had bumped into on my way out of the office.

Except that had been nearly ten blocks back, and there was no logical reason for him to be walking in the same direction as I was. It was too much of a coincidence.

I continued to walk, but I was watching him now. I took a roundabout route, walking across streets I normally wouldn't, and taking random turns every other block. Always, when I checked back across the street, he was there, walking a little distance away, trying to blend into the crowd as much as possible.

He was definitely following me.

A wave of panic shot straight through my body. I quickened my steps, no longer concerned with disguising where I was going. I just wanted to get home and lock myself in my bedroom. It was getting late, and I had never felt so scared.

I walked even faster, the temptation to break into a run growing with each passing second. Then, seized by a sudden idea, I looked around me and shouldered my way into the nearest open building I could see.

Once inside, I pulled out my phone and dialed Cam's number.

I hadn't spoken to him since the incident in the office. Part of me was angry at him, perhaps a bit unfairly. But the second I heard his voice, a feeling of calm settled over me.

"Someone is following me."

"What?"

"A man. In a dark suit. He's been trailing me since I left the office."

"Where are you now?"

"I'm not sure... uh... the Macy's downtown, I think."

Cam was silent for so long I thought we had been

disconnected.

"Hello?" I said.

"Vicki," he said simply.

"Huh? What does she have to do with anything?"

"This is her," Cam said, and there was so much conviction in his voice. "She threatened me back when she came over for dinner. She said she would hire private investigators to watch me. This must be it."

"Why would she do that?" But I already knew why. It was obvious, really. Simple.

"She doesn't believe it. The marriage. Or even if she does, she wants to make me... us... miserable, in the hope we slip up."

"This was supposed to be a quick, simple thing, Cam," I said.

"I know. I know. I'm sorry. I may have underestimated her a bit. But if she's going to the extent of hiring a private investigator, then it means she's been rattled."

"Do we know for certain, though, that it's a private investigator?" It could be a kidnapper or an opportunistic thug who had seen me use my phone repeatedly and was waiting for the right moment to pinch it.

"I'm positive it is," Cam said.

"Wouldn't a private investigator be more subtle? I don't know... blend into the surroundings? This one is in a suit, and he must be terrible at tailing if I managed to spot him."

"That's exactly why I'm sure it's Vicki's doing. She wants us to know she has people following us. She wants us to be aware of them because that makes us look over our shoulders, and we are more likely to make a mistake. I know how she thinks. This is definitely her."

"So, I'm not in any danger?"

"I don't think you are, no. But let's not take any risks. Take a cab straight home and wait for me there."

Home? As in my place? Or his?

"You mean…"

"My place, Yvette. If she has people watching us, then we're going to have to maintain the façade a little longer, at least until I figure out how to work this to our advantage. I have a quick meeting in the next fifteen minutes, but I'll be home as soon as possible, and we can talk this out properly."

The more I thought about it, the more I realized what a bad idea it had been, agreeing to Cam's little plan. Not only had it gotten way off the rails, but it was also now actively affecting my life. I hadn't been to my own apartment in so long I'd almost forgotten what it looked like. It was all very well when we spent long weekends at his place; working days were a different matter. I couldn't spend the whole day avoiding him at work only to go back to his house when it was over. It was suffocating; I felt like I was in a trap whose jaws kept drawing closer, and I had no way of getting out.

And for what? I hadn't even met the daughter this was all supposed to be for.

The only positive was the money, which Tyler was hopefully putting to good use. But beyond that, the teensy plus I had imagined would make it all worth it, that time spent with Cam, no longer seemed worth the hassle.

I requested an Uber and waited for it at the store window. I looked around, but my stalker seemed to have vanished. I wasn't convinced, though. I knew he was somewhere, waiting for me to emerge. No doubt, he would get in a cab himself and follow me.

I kept looking through the back window, trying to figure out which car he could be in. I knew I wasn't in danger, but I still felt on edge, and I finally understood what Cam had meant. Just the feeling of being under a microscope, that knowledge that I was being followed and monitored… it was incredibly unsettling.

When we arrived, I got out of the car, still distracted, still looking over my shoulder. I was so distracted I didn't immediately realize I was headed in the wrong direction. I walked all the way to the entrance to my own apartment before it hit me. Damn it.

I pretended to pull out my phone, look keenly at it, and then swivel, ever so slowly, away from the building and set off in the opposite direction. I doubted anyone watching me would be fooled. That was all the evidence they would need if they were; she doesn't even know where she's supposed to be living.

I made my way to Cam's building and got into the elevator. Only then could I breathe freely. I let out a sigh of relief, and I realized I had been balling up my fists. The nails on my fingers had dug into my palms, leaving red groves in the skin. A thin sheen of sweat dotted my forehead.

Breathe, Yvette.

I rushed to Cam's apartment, retrieving the spare key from the flowerpot, where I knew it would be, and letting myself in. The smell of his house hit me right in the face. I looked around, and it took me a second to understand why I felt so calm, why the fright that had been with me the whole ride here was suddenly ebbing away. I felt safe. In the space of only a week, this place had somehow started to feel like home.

Chapter 21

Yvette

One of my favorite things about Cam's house was the kitchen, which was wonderful to cook in, but especially the refrigerator. It was always stocked with an assortment of things. Prime cuts, vegetables, simple do-it-yourself meals. It was perfect for a bachelor who didn't have time for complicated recipes. And, factoring in the fifty or so take-out menus Cam had lying around, it meant there were always several options whenever one got hungry.

Or when they walked into the house unexpectedly after being chased by a stranger in a suit and decided they might as well make dinner.

I stood in front of that freezer for almost ten minutes, going back and forth over the alternatives. Chicken again? Steak? Something vegan? Or I could bake. It had been a while since I did, and it would be the perfect activity to take my mind off things. But I dropped the idea as soon as I thought of it. The baking equipment I had borrowed from Cam was still at my house. So, I settled for a simple dish I could make in minutes: spaghetti and meatballs.

I was setting up the counter, readying myself to cook, when I heard a soft knock on the door. Not the doorbell, as one would expect, but a dull, almost timid little rap, which I only heard because the house was eerily quiet.

My heart stopped for a second. My first thought was that it was the man in the dark suit, that he wasn't a private investigator after all, but a serial killer who had tracked me all the way to the house and was now going to kill me. It sounded ridiculous, even in my own head, but it didn't stop the brief hitch in my breathing, and when I went to answer the door, I paused, grabbed one of the knives from the rack, and held it behind my back.

I peered cautiously through the peephole. I saw nothing at first, which only heightened my concern. But just as I was about to dismiss it and turn back, I saw a flash of movement just below my field of vision, and I looked further down to see a mop of straw-colored hair. Intrigued, I swung the door open. My eyes traveled downward, and I was looking at a small, cute girl.

"Hello," she said beaming. She had a couple of teeth missing, and it made her twice as adorable. She had an air of grace about her, a certain poise that was definitely beyond her years, and a sharp intelligence behind her hazel eyes.

"Hi," I said, smiling back at her. I almost reached out to shake her hand, then remembered I was clutching a knife behind my back.

"I'm looking for my dad," she said. Her voice was high-pitched but strangely melodious.

"Oh!" I said, the shoe finally dropping. I should have picked it up right away. The hair and eyes were totally her mother's, but the easy charm and friendliness were all Cam. She had his confidence, too, in the way she spoke and carried herself.

"You must be Emma," I said. "Come on in!"

I stepped aside, and she skipped past me into the house. I closed the door, then dropped the knife surreptitiously into the nearest flower pot.

Emma waltzed in, dropped her bag on the couch, and threw herself on it.

I grinned and went up to her. "Don't you wanna know who I am?" I asked her, sitting across from her.

"You're daddy's girlfriend," Emma said, matter-of-factly.

"Who told you that?" I asked her.

"No one told me," Emma said. There was a hint of pride in her voice. "I heard Mom talk about it with Mike."

That could not have been a good conversation. I was tempted for a moment to ask Emma what her mom had said about me. But knowing Vicki, it was probably best to leave it to the imagination.

"I'm Yvette," I said. "But my friends call me Vee."

"Can *I* call you Vee?" Emma asked, all sweet and adorable.

"Of course you can," I told her. "And you know why? We're going to be best friends."

She smiled, a brief flash of pearly white teeth.

"Did you just come from school?" I asked her.

Emma nodded, but I noticed she averted her eyes. Her eyes went past me and into the kitchen, and I realized she must be hungry.

"Oh, I'm so sorry," I said. "I was just about to start cooking. I can make you a sandwich while we wait?"

"Ooh, can I watch?"

"Of course you can."

She hopped off the couch and skipped after me into the kitchen. I walked over to the refrigerator and pulled out an avocado, onions, tomatoes, and a pack of ham. I grabbed the bread from the counter and pooled all the ingredients there as well.

Emma pulled out a stool and mounted it. She was watching me so intently, her eyes wide as I buttered single slices of bread. She offered to dice the onions and tomatoes for me, but I shook my head. I worked fast; the first layer was avocado and onions, the second mayonnaise and ham and tomatoes on the third. It was a simple sandwich, but I was suddenly feeling immense pressure not to disappoint her. As a child in middle school, I was suddenly desperate for her to like me.

I pushed the plate over to her and smiled.

She grabbed the sandwich and took a bite. Her eyes lit up, and she took another big bite. A rare flush of pleasure washed over me. She didn't say anything else until she was done eating. And she ate quickly; within moments, she was brushing crumbs off her face and beaming up at me.

"Another one?" I asked her, but she shook her head.

"Do you know when Daddy will be back?" she asked instead. There was something about the way she looked over her shoulder that put me on alert. I didn't know what, but something wasn't right.

"Emma? Is there something you want to tell me?"

She shook her head a little too hard, and her eyes popped. I had not been around kids much, but I knew guilt when I saw it. "Are you sure?" I asked her. I leaned in so I could look into her eyes. She looked back for only a second, and then what little resolve she had crumbled, and she blinked and buried her head in her hands.

"I want to speak to Daddy," she said through her fingers. Her voice was heavy, and she suddenly sounded distressed.

"I'll be right back," I said, patting her gently on the shoulder.

I grabbed my phone from my pocket and dialed Cam as I walked out of the room. The phone rang a few times before I remembered that Cam had told me he was heading into a meeting. Maybe he wouldn't be able to answer the call. But just before I hung up, Cam's voice filtered through, urgent and slightly panicked.

"Yvette? Are you okay? Did you get home?"

"Yeah, yeah. I'm fine, Cam, thanks." I glanced once over my shoulder, then decided to walk further down the hallway. "Emma is here," I said simply.

"What?"

"She just showed up at the door, asking for you."

"My daughter Emma?"

"Yeah."

"Is she okay? Did something happen?"

"That's just it. She looks fine, but something seems off about her. I mean, as best I can tell, having just met her."

166

"She's supposed to be at music practice right now," Cam said, and now the concern in his voice was audible.

"I think you should speak to her."

"Okay."

I turned and speed-walked back to the kitchen. Emma's eyes looked slightly moist when I handed the phone over to her. I thought about it for a moment, then I backed up and went to stand in the living room. It felt like I would have been intruding on a private moment.

"Daddy?" I heard her say, all sweet and innocent, and I felt a stab of affection for her. I wanted to just go up to her and wrap her in a hug.

I couldn't hear the rest of the conversation, but random words floated over to me, and I could tell from the increasing pitch in Emma's voice that Cam wasn't very happy with her. And he was letting her know it.

A little over a minute later, I felt a gentle tug on my leg, and Emma was looking up to me, handing me back the phone.

"Hello? Cam?"

I gave her another little smile, then peeled away and back down the hallway.

"So, it looks like she ran away from home," Cam said.

"What?"

"Yup. She is supposed to be going for her music lessons. Her mother usually has her picked up from school and dropped off at her teacher's home, but today, she talked the driver into taking her to my place instead."

"But why?" I asked, impressed at her resourcefulness despite her age. "Why would she do that?"

"It's a long story," Cam said. "But I know she didn't want to go to music classes at all. Vicki made her, and she's been resisting it ever since. I guess this is her being rebellious, ten years too soon. Anyway. I hate to ask, but do you think you could take her home? I'll text you the address. I don't want Vicki coming back home and thinking I took her from class again."

"Uh, are you sure about that?"

"There's not much of a choice, Yvette. I'm kind of in the middle of something, and even if I leave right now, I won't make it home in time to get her and still drive her home. Not before Vicki gets home from work."

"Okay. Okay. I'll see what I can do."

"Thank you. You're a lifesaver. I'll text you the address just now."

The line went dead.

I walked back to the kitchen slowly, my mind a jumble of conflicting thoughts. On the one hand, I understood Cam's concern about Vicki finding out Emma wasn't where she was supposed to be. I could just imagine the kind of fuss she would kick up, and what it would mean for their battle for custody of Emma. A battle that was so far happening under the surface, but the tensions were definitely rising, and I had no doubt they would spill over pretty soon. This was just the kind of thing that could push them over the edge.

But on the other hand, there was Emma. As little time as I had spent with her, I could already tell she was willful and vibrant. Smart, self-reliant, and naturally happy. I hated to think she was being forced to do something she didn't want. I wasn't a parent, obviously, but it seemed kinda cruel to pack her up and send her right back to Vicki when she clearly felt the way she did.

There was a hidden dimension to all this, too. One I wasn't sure Cam had even considered. Emma having run away was actually a good thing. It could help his case if the custody battle ever came to be. I was sure it wouldn't look good to a judge that Emma had run away from her mom.

All of which meant I was torn when I walked back into the kitchen and looked into the beautiful little face of Emma.

"What did Daddy say?" she asked, her expression wary.

My phone vibrated. I glanced at it and saw the text from Cam. And then I met Emma's eyes once more, and I couldn't bear to disappoint her. "Do you know how to make a pie?" I asked her.

She didn't get it at first. There was a brief hesitation, and then her features went from confused, to cautiously optimistic, and finally settled into reluctant glee. "I can stay?" she asked her smile wide.

"We'll let your dad take you home when he gets back, okay?"

She nodded.

"But don't do that to him again. He was really worried about you, and he already has a lot on his plate at work."

"I won't." She elbowed herself off the chair and came running up to me. The hug took me a bit by surprise.

Cooking with her turned out to be a lot of fun. She had this bubbly energy, and a genuine curiosity to learn. I decided the best way to teach her was to let her do it along with me. So, I created two sets of everything. Two sets of ingredients, two mixing bowls, two baking pans. She would watch me do something and then repeat it. We had a lot of fun, throwing things around, starting and escalating a mini food fight (which she won because she was surprisingly athletic), and, finally, sliding our pies into the oven.

I got to know her a bit better, too.

While stirring her bowl, she suddenly turned to me, all serious, and asked how I had gotten her father.

"What?" I sputtered, wondering if I had misheard her.

"You and Daddy," she repeated. "How did you two become boyfriend and girlfriend?"

I couldn't help smiling. "Why? Is there someone who wants you to be their girlfriend?"

"Yes. There's a boy in my class, Harry. He always wants to sit with me at lunch. He brings me little gifts every day, and yesterday, he held my hand while we waited for his mom to come to pick him up."

"Do you want him to do these things?"

"I guess…"

"Do you like him?"

Emma blushed. "A lot of the girls in my class say he's cute, and one of them stopped speaking to me because Harry and I are always together."

"Sounds pretty serious. Listen, Emma. You don't have to do or be anything right now. You're young; you have the rest of your life to find a boyfriend, okay? But you and Harry can be friends. That way, you don't have to stop hanging out with him, and you don't do anything you don't want to."

She nodded sagely. After that, she turned into an open book. She spilled all her secrets, from the teacher she hated in school, her mom's persistence with vegan meals, and the stray cat she had befriended outside Mike's car shop.

We were having so much fun I completely lost track of time. Suddenly, it was almost ten, and as we pulled the pies out of the oven, I heard the sound of the door opening and Cam calling out from the living room. I meant to ask Emma to wait in the kitchen while I went and spoke with her dad. But she was too fast for me. At the sound of his voice, she squealed and ran from the kitchen. I followed behind her, slightly anxious.

I heard Cam's surprised exclamation. I saw him lift Emma and twirl her a bit as he hugged her. And I saw his eyes scan the room, find me, and narrow in confusion. And something close to anger.

Chapter 22

Cameron

The most annoying and simultaneously adorable thing about Emma was just how hard it was to be mad at her. She did this thing where she nuzzled into the crook of your neck, and the warmth was too much for you to stay mad. Or she turned on the charm, widened her eyes, and dropped her voice by an octave, so that you were smiling despite yourself, and returning her hug, and you couldn't remember why you had been made in the first place.

It was much easier, however, to be mad at Yvette. Especially when she looked guilty herself and made no efforts to hide it. But I would deal with her later.

"Aren't you supposed to be asleep?" I asked Emma, putting her down.

"Vee and I were making pies!" Emma said excitedly. "Come on; I'll show you."

She grabbed my hand and tugged as hard as she could, turning and walking in the direction of the kitchen. I gave Yvette a withering look as I walked past her, but the comment that rose to the tip of my tongue died when I saw what had become of my kitchen. Either a tornado had blown through, or it had recently been the scene of a shootout. Everything was everywhere. Food on the floor and counters. Dishes everywhere. But there was also a pleasant scent hanging in the air, of baking and chocolate.

"Come on!" Emma prompted again. She pulled me to the counter and patted the nearest chair. I smiled reluctantly, then settled in. Emma called Yvette over and pointed at the pies.

"Mine first!" she declared, and the pride in her voice was unmistakable.

Yvette grabbed a fork and dug into the smaller of the two pies on the counter. She carved out a piece and served it on a saucer, then pushed it over to me. It was almost comical, the way they were both staring at me expectantly like they were contestants in a competitive cooking show, and I was just about to send one of them home.

I took a forkful of the pie and chewed slowly, tentatively. I wasn't sure what I had expected, but it was much better than that. Sweet and tasty and fluffy, it almost melted in my mouth.

"Did you make this?" I asked Emma, and she nodded with a broad grin. "I guess we just discovered another of your many talents. This is wonderful."

"Vee helped me," Emma said. "She showed me how, and I followed what she was doing exactly, and she even let me work the oven."

"This is all wonderful, sweetie. But we need to talk about what happened today, okay?"

And now I was going to have to be the bad cop. I hated having to. The beauty of co-parenting with someone like Vicki was that she always ended up being the bad cop, and all I had to do when I got time alone with Emma was be a little bit nicer, a little more attentive, and a lot more indulgent.

I had rarely had cause to scoldEmma. It was something I tried very hard not to do. But here we were. Reluctance aside, I needed her to understand that she had done something wrong. I didn't even want to think about what Vicki was going to say. It was frankly shocking that she hadn't called me yet. But I had no doubt she was going to. All because of Yvette.

"Actually, Cam," Yvette said, and she gave me a significant look. "Can I speak to you real quick in the bedroom before you do that?"She didn't give me a chance to respond; she turned and walked away, expecting me to follow her. I shook my head in disbelief.

"You sit here and eat your pie, okay?" I said to Emma. "It's way past your bedtime, and tomorrow is a school day. Eat, and we'll talk when I get back."I leaned down and gave her a light peck on the forehead. She was pouting, clearly a bit disappointed that the lecture had been postponed, not canceled.

Yvette was seated on the bed when I walked into the bedroom. It was almost sexy, and it came pretty close to stirring up a different emotion in me than the one I was going for. "What the hell, Yvette?" I asked her.

She held her hands up as if begging me to be calm. "Hear me out, Cam. Please."

I pursed my lips and crossed my hands, leaning against the wall farthest from her.

"First of all, that girl is adorable as hell. You know this."

True. I couldn't argue that.

"She got me with the eyes. I swear. I was just about to tell her I was taking her home, and then she hit me with those gorgeous orbs, and I found myself nodding and changing the subject. It's very sneaky, actually."

I couldn't argue with that either. I had been on the receiving end of Emma's charm far too often not to know how potent it was.

"But. I know it's not my place, and I'm really not trying to meddle in your personal affairs. But she was miserable. She clearly didn't want to go back. I felt like there was something she wasn't telling me, something that had happened to make her run away, and I didn't want to just send her off without finding out what it was. So, I thought, you know, that *you* would have a better chance of getting it out of her than me. And that it would be better for everyone involved if we waited for you, and then, once we got to the bottom of things, you could take her home yourself."

She stopped just short of saying it, but I heard it in her voice. She didn't want to deal with Vicki again. Considering what had happened the last time they were in the same room, it really wasn't surprising. And I should have thought of that before asking her to drop Emma home.

Her argument wasn't unreasonable, either. There was just one slight problem. "Vicki," I said. "She's going to freak out." I pulled my phone out, still surprised that she hadn't called me.

"Speaking of which," Yvette said, and now her tone was almost conspiratorial. "I had a thought. I probably shouldn't be thinking about this kind of thing, but doesn't this help your case against Vicki? The fact that Emma ran away? It can't look good for her."

I stared at her for a long time. It hadn't even occurred to me. I had been too busy, too worried about Emma. She wasn't wrong. Damn it; she hadn't been wrong yet. Vicki was always ragging on me about forgetting to pick Emma up that one time. This would even things up quite nicely.

"So, as you can see, my decision to let Emma stay wasn't just a whim."

I nodded slowly. "And you decided to destroy my kitchen to validate your decision?"

"Oh, that's your daughter's work. We had a little food fight, and she was a bit too fast for me. Kept making me miss. She's quite something, Emma. I have to admit."

That brought a smile to my face. Reluctantly. "You two got along pretty well it seems," I said.

"We're best friends for life."

"Thanks for looking after her," I said after a while. "Really. I know she can be a handful..."

"Nonsense. Emma is nothing short of delightful."

I smiled again, and the anger seemed to have all dissipated. "And I get why you let her stay. You're right. Maybe there's more to it than meets the eye. I'll go talk to her, see if she'll confide in me."

"Okay."

I got to the door and turned back. "I feel like she would want her best friend there. You know, for moral support."

"Right," Yvette said. And she sprang up and walked out of the room with me.

Vicki called some time later as expected. What I didn't expect was how calm she sounded. There was none of the swearing or insult-throwing I had been bracing for. She simply wanted to know if Emma was okay, and when I told her she would be spending the night and going straight to school in the morning, she didn't even put up a fight. It was as uncharacteristic as it was unexpected. Vicki told me she would bring a change of clothes for Emma in the morning, and then she hung up.

It was her attitude, more than anything else she said, that set the alarm bells off in my head. For as long as I had known Vicki, I had never seen her let anything go just like that. If she was letting me have Emma without so much as a word of protest, then it meant something was up.

It took some coaxing, but I eventually managed to get it out of Emma.

She wasn't very sure about it, and she was clearly reluctant to be 'snitching.' But according to Emma, Mike and Vicki had had a huge fight the previous day. Huge as in epic, and loud enough that they woke Emma, who had been asleep. She couldn't make out the words, of course. But she heard the anger in their voices and the biting tones. And, when her mom dropped her off to school in the morning, Emma thought her eyes were slightly bloodshot.

She had dreaded going back home all day. She didn't know what was happening, what would happen. She didn't want to listen to the low rumble of them arguing through the walls. And a tiny part of her was scared for her mom. So, as soon as she was done with school, she instructed her mom's driver to take her to my place instead of the music teacher's. And she told him to deliver a message to Vicki that she had gone to her dad's and that she was fine.

It broke my heart because it brought home the fact that despite my intentions, and Vicki's best efforts, Emma was still experiencing the effects of a broken home. The only thing that made our arrangement worth it was the knowledge that Emma was better off growing up away from toxic parents, which Vicki and I would undoubtedly be together. It was a shame that she was dealing with that anyway.

I imagined Emma had idealized Mike as a bit of a father figure. Clearly, they had been pretty close, and that fight had brought home to her the possibility that he would be leaving and had probably been too much for her.

I understood how she was feeling, even if she didn't know it herself. And I was deeply grateful to Yvette for letting Emma stay until we figured things out.

Emma fell asleep while we were talking. She must have been very tired, and she had gone well past her bedtime. I lifted her from the couch slowly and carried her to the guest bedroom, which Yvette and I had thankfully cleaned when we were preparing to live as husband and wife. I lay her down and tucked her in. This was it, I thought. This was the moment I was missing every night; this and many more. And just like that, my resolve to get her back strengthened. No matter what it took, I was going to get my daughter back.

Yvette was on the bed once more. But this time, she was in her nightgown, and when she held out her hands, it was an invitation. I grinned at the contrast. I stepped out of my pants and pulled my shirt off, then I walked over to her and fell into her arms.

Her body felt warm and soft. Her arms felt so natural around me, and her torso lined up perfectly against mine. I could get used to this, I thought.

"That was... interesting," she whispered, her lips inches from my ear.

"I thought so too," I said. "You parented the shit out of her if I say so myself."

"You weren't too bad yourself," Yvette said. I felt her smile, heard it in her voice. I was too comfortable to even lift my head.

"This has been quite the day," I commented.

"It really has," she agreed. "It was only a few hours ago I was sure I was getting fired."

"What?" I exclaimed. "Why?"

"Um, I was only caught sleeping with my boss. By *his* boss. Or did you forget?"

"Meredith wouldn't have fired you for that. Sending out a manuscript with grammatical errors? Instant dismissal. But she wouldn't bat her eyes over a little office romance."

"That must be why you were so calm when she walked in."

"I was caught off-guard; I won't lie. But I didn't think you were in trouble, or at least not your job."

"Funny story. She actually offered me a promotion."

"No way, really?" I lifted my head from the halo of her hair so I could look at her face.

"Yeah. She offered me your job."

I laughed. "Very slick, woman. Charming your way into my pants and then stealing my job."

"I did no such thing. It's not my fault you can't keep your hands off me."

"I could say the same thing about you," I said.

We stared at each other, then burst out laughing at the same time.

"Congratulations, though," I told her. "I knew Meredith would be looking for someone to fill my position once I moved up, but I didn't think she'd be so bold."

Yvette started to protest, but I silenced her with a finger to the lips. I felt a gentle stirring in my pants.

"Don't get me wrong," I continued. "I'm not saying you're not qualified for the job. Or that you don't deserve it. I think you'd kill it, just like you've been doing. I meant that there are a lot of old vultures who would have expected the job to drop into their laps, and I'm glad Meredith skipped right past all of them."

"I don't even know if I want the job, to be honest," Yvette said. "I'm supposed to be sleeping on it."

"I can help you decide," I commented. I freed my hand from beneath her and reached for the hem of her nightgown, slipping past the soft fabric and caressing the impossibly soft flesh of her thighs. Yvette closed her eyes and moaned lightly.

"Okay," she whispered. "I'm listening…"

Chapter 23

Cameron

My old man once told me that you never really know you're married until you can read each other's minds; when the two of you are so in sync that you don't need to speak to each other. It made no sense then because I knew my mom well enough to know she couldn't go more than a few minutes without speaking.

This morning, though, his words came ringing back in my ears, and it was quite jarring.

I don't remember falling asleep the night before. I woke up to a sharp sensation in my left arm, and when I blinked my eyes open, I realized I had fallen asleep holding Yvette, and she had slept on my arm the whole night. The pins and needles sensation crawled all over my left arm when I finally extricated it from beneath her, and it wouldn't function properly for at least an hour after.

It took me a minute to get my bearings, and then I remembered we had to get Emma ready for school, and I swung into action. I shook Yvette awake, and we staggered into the shower. I was still groggy, and I ended up turning the wrong shower knob so that instead of hot water, the jets that hit us were ice cold.

It was the perfect wake-up call. And, it turned out, the most effective way to keep our shower short. We got dressed fast and rushed to the kitchen. Yvette made pancakes while I prepared the coffee and set the table. Just as I was preparing to go wake Emma up, the doorbell rang, and I knew it was Vicki.

Her eyes did look redder than usual, and her whole demeanor was different, albeit in a subtle way. Her posture wasn't as rigid and upright, and her voice was ever-so-slightly shaky.

I moved to step aside and let her in, but she shook her head. She held out a small bag, and I took it. I watched her eyes travel past me, over my shoulder, and rest on Yvette, who was scurrying around looking for something. Her lip curled, and for a second, she looked like her old self.

I was so tempted to ask about her and Mike, but I held my tongue. No need to get Emma in trouble.

"We just made breakfast," I said. It was a half invitation, an act. I wasn't really asking, and I knew she would never say yes anyway. Indeed, she shook her head and turned to leave.

"Emma needs to be in school in the next hour," she said as she walked away.

Yvette and I worked perfectly together, like a team of synchronized swimmers. Or seasoned parents. Shower, breakfast, dressing; we did it all without saying a word to each other. Emma was still groggy, so she wasn't as conversational as usual. Yvette and I kept looking at each other over the table, and then at Emma.

I knew exactly what she was thinking because I was thinking about it too. We were crushing this parenting thing. We were excellent together; we always had been. And then I remembered my dad's words, and I shook my head to dislodge the fantasy.

Surely, there wasn't a reason for this charade anymore? The breakup with Mike meant that Vicki would be too busy to deal with us. And even if she wanted to keep up the investigation, I now had a rock I could throw at her glasshouse: Emma running away. I would have to ask Gabriel, but I was fairly sure we were in the clear.

Which only left one thing: Yvette. My fake wife, Yvette.

She had performed admirably in the job. She had actually done more than I expected of her, more than I would have asked. Granted, it was ultimately a business transaction. But I had pulled her completely from her life, asked her to go along with a plan that was objectively mad and, I admit, legally questionable, and she hadn't so much as groaned in protest. I had no idea how to even begin to thank her.No doubt she would be happy to learn she could go back to her own place, and that we wouldn't have to keep playing husband and wife.

I had no problem admitting that it had been a lot of fun. Somewhere along the line, I had gotten lost in the performance, and things had started to feel a bit too real. Like walking into the house to the smell of pie and the sight of my daughter running up to me. Or waking up tangled in her legs, wrapped completely in her scent, the faint memory of our lovemaking playing in my mind.

It had been better than I could have hoped. But I knew I needed to pull the plug soon.

We dropped Emma off and promised her she could come over whenever she wanted, but she would have to speak to her mum first. Then, with the panicked realization that we were running late ourselves, we got back in the car and headed to work.

"Do you think this will look weird?" Yvette asked me after some time.

"What's that?"

"This. Us. Driving in together."I could tell she had been thinking the same thing I was. And she clearly wanted us to start severing the ties we had created to each other.

"I'm sorry," I said. "I could drop you off a few blocks away, and you can walk in on your own."

"Where do you usually park?"

"Basement."

"There won't be many people in the basement?"

"Only one way to find out, I guess."

I wondered why she was suddenly so reluctant to be seen with me, something that had never happened before. Before, we had even been flirting openly. And then it hit me; she was thinking about our little incident in my office from the day before. She was worried that word had gotten around, and knowing how quickly gossip traveled, she would be right in the middle of the banter. Possibly, she was worried about how it would look if she was seen walking in with me, and then a week later being promoted to my old job. Or maybe she just didn't want people talking, as the sight of us together was bound to get them doing. There was so much to it, and I was suddenly sorry for how complicated I had made her life.

"I'm sorry," I said as I pulled into the basement.

"Huh?"

"I realize now what you meant when you told me you didn't want to complicate things at work. I disregarded it, and now everything is complicated. I'm sorry about that."

"It's not a problem," Yvette said. "Besides, I'm not an innocent victim. As you said, I've had some difficulty keeping my hands off you myself."

I grinned as I pulled the handbrake up and switched the engine off. I turned around in my seat so I was facing Yvette directly. We looked at each other, the heat and tension growing between us, and I wanted to kiss her so badly it was almost physically painful.

"I think I should head up first," she said, breaking the tension. "And then you can come in later."

"Sounds good," I said.

Married, I thought as I watched her swing her long shapely legs out of the car and walk away.

My first thought when I walked into the office was that I was in the wrong place. It seemed deserted. Granted, it was only eight, and most people wouldn't be arriving for the next half-hour or so. But even with that, the office was still strangely empty. I scanned the first few offices as I made my way to mine, rapping on doors and peeking inside. There was no one in the offices I checked.

I started to get concerned when I got to the break room. There was always someone in the breakroom. Except for this morning, apparently.

I dropped my things in my office and made my way to Yvette's. I knocked, waited, then swung it open and stuck my head inside. Yvette wasn't in her office either. I frowned and pulled out my phone. Whatever was going on, it was very unusual.

But before I could dial Yvette's number, I heard the clacking of heels on the concrete floor, and I whipped around to see her walking up to me.

"Hey, what's going on?" I asked her. "Where is everybody?"

It wasn't until she got to me that I registered her expression. Horror, mixed with dread, and the puzzled look of someone who doesn't know what to do or say. I grabbed her by the shoulders, almost instinctively, because it looked like she was going to fall down.

"Meredith is looking for you," she said.

"What's going on?" I asked her again. I could feel my pulse quickening, the slow spread of tension through my body.

"Most of the staff are gathered in Boardroom A3. I'm not sure I've heard it right, but someone was talking about Wyatt Banks… something about…"She trailed off, unable to finish. But she didn't need to. I put two and two together easily enough, and the blob of horror that had been building up in my chest sank with a thud into my stomach.

I sidestepped Yvette and walked to Meredith's office, eventually breaking into a run. I turned the corner, pushing the door and bursting in a bit more forcefully than I would have liked.

Meredith was seated on her desk. On her desk, not a chair; she was perched precariously on its edge, her hands white as they clasped a phone she was speaking quickly into. Her eyes shot up when I barged in, and she lifted her eyebrows to acknowledge me, then she went back to her phone call.

I stood there, listening to her speak, and I knew from her voice that the worst had indeed happened. I couldn't standstill. My legs wouldn't let me standstill. I walked to one end of the office, turned, and paced to the other. I thrust my hands in my pockets, then pulled them out and started to crack my knuckles.

Meredith's phone call seemed to take forever. She did eventually hang up, and she turned a gaunt, pale face toward me.

"Why didn't you call me?" I asked, walking up to her. I reached out and hugged her. I thought she felt lighter than usual, a little weaker, maybe.

"I meant to," she said. "I've been on the phone the whole morning."

"What happened?" I asked.

"Brain aneurysm. This morning. Completely out of the blue, although according to the doctor, his brain was deteriorating really fast."

"I'm so sorry, Meredith."

Meredith nodded. Her head dropped. When she spoke again, her voice broke, but she powered through. "This is the worst thing about Wyatt's condition. You know it's coming. It's like this giant cloud, looming in the distance. And you don't know when it will swoop down and engulf you in darkness. But you know it will, one day, maybe today, maybe six years from now. You allow yourself to hope, to dream. One morning, he's completely lucid, and he remembers everything, and you think, maybe we'll have more days like these. But the next day is bad, and the one after that even worse, and you have to realize all over again that he isn't going to get better."

It was gut-wrenching hearing her talk. Particularly because I had always known Meredith to be a very strong woman, and this had clearly undone her.

"Does it make me a bad person," she went on, "that I'm relieved? I'm devastated, of course. Wyatt was the love of my life. But I've been preparing for this moment for months now. Dreading it. Waiting for it. Running from it. And now that it's finally happened, there's a part of me that just feels relief. At least he isn't in pain anymore."

I put my hand on her shoulder and gave it a little squeeze.

"You shouldn't be here, Meredith," I said.

"What?" she frowned, her misty eyes searching mine.

"You should be at home. I know you have a lot to do, people to speak to…"

"Are you kicking me out of my own office, Cameron Palmer?"

"I'm saying you shouldn't be working, Meredith. Let me handle all this, and you go home and get some rest, okay? There's nothing urgent enough for you to be here."

"But… I have to…"

"No, Meredith. You don't have to do anything but take care of yourself."

"The staff?"

"I'll deal with them, don't worry."

She looked down again, this time for so long I almost thought she had fallen asleep. Then she nodded slowly, and after a brief hesitation, she held out a hand, and I helped her off the desk.

"I'll call you a cab to take you straight home. I'll come to see you as soon as I'm done here, okay?"

"Thanks, Cam. Really."

The meeting with the staff was easily the hardest thing I had ever had to do. I dreaded walking into that boardroom. I felt like it would be inauthentic to do so without first processing my own feelings about what had happened. I just didn't know if I could do that in the thirty minutes I was expected to.

In many ways, Wyatt was the role model I had always needed at work. From the moment I joined Penguin Publishers, he took me under his wing and showed me the ropes. He had a perfect understanding of who everyone was and their unique abilities, and he spotted my own strengths right away. It was because of him that I rose through the ranks so fast. It was his vision that had inspired the Penguin to get to where it was now.

Meredith had been one hundred percent right about his death. We were always aware of it looming around the corner. Almost expecting it and yet never ready for it. I had never really thought about it happening, even though Meredith kept telling me the prognosis was getting progressively worse. This was sudden and shocking, even though it shouldn't have been.

I felt someone slide up to me. Felt, rather than heard, because my mind was too far away. There was that familiar scent I knew and loved. There she was, showing up just when I needed a little push.

"I know he meant a lot to you," Yvette said. "I'm so sorry."

"I don't know what to say to them," I said. "I thought I did. But I don't think I'm ready."

"Yes, you are. Meredith trusted you to lead because she knows you can. I trust you, too."

I glanced over at her. Somehow, her assurance seemed bigger, broader in context. "You do?"

She nodded. "They need to know what's happening. They've been getting snippets from random people, from obscure contacts in the publishing world, and that uncertainty is only making them more anxious."

I took a deep breath, let it sit, and then blew it out in a long, slow exhale. Yvette snuck her hand into mine and gave me a reassuring squeeze. It was weird to think that an hour ago, we had been so worried about being seen together. Now, we walked into the room together. It was the only way I was going to get through this. With her by my side.

Chapter 24

Yvette

Wyatt Banks was an incredibly popular man. He was well-loved too if the attendance of his funeral was anything to go by.

The ceremony was held in his home, a large, sprawling estate with lush vegetation and a haunting feeling of emptiness. It was ideal for so many reasons, primarily the size being perfect for the sheer number of people who came to say their last goodbyes.

I arrived early to help Cam, and for the better part of two hours, we were walking around saying hi to the guests. I had never been more in awe of Cam than when I was watching him walking around, clearly in his element, aware of every single person and intimately familiar with them. When he introduced me to the former COO, for example, he remembered that the man's daughter had been doing some work with underprivileged children in Africa, and he wanted to know how she was doing.

With another board member, he was quick to bring up a long-standing bet as to which department would contribute the most to the annual profit margins, and the two had a lighthearted exchange about it.

Cam was completely at ease as he waltzed around, meeting and greeting, sharing in the collective grief of those who came to celebrate Wyatt.

In the course of one week, everything had changed between us. I could point to the exact moment when it did, too, outside the boardroom at Penguin, just before he officially informed the company employees that Wyatt had died. There was a moment when he was as vulnerable as I had ever seen him. I had reached out to comfort him, to let him know I was right there with him. It was a simple gesture, me holding his hand. But it had endured to this day. Since then, Cam had no problem showing me affection, even in public. He didn't care anymore if people saw us together, or if they whispered to each other when they did.

Today, it felt like I was on his arm. He introduced me by name, or in some instances as the person who would be stepping into head Editorial. But his arm was never far from mine, or from my waist, and I got the sense he was being possessive without saying it outright. I felt like he needed me, and he was refusing to let me go.

And I was totally fine with that.

"Okay, okay." Cam put a hand on the small of my back and steered me slowly around. "This is a big one. You see that lovely couple over there?"

I followed the direction he was pointing. A tall, handsome man with thick gray hair was lost in conversation with a woman just as tall and regal.

"Yeah?"

"Those are my parents. Wanna meet them?"

"What?"

"You're right. I shouldn't have to ask."

He gave me a little push while I protested, and he kept up the pressure, leading me slowly toward the couple, my weak protests falling on deaf ears.

His parents were stylish and beautiful; there was no other way to put it. His mother was beautiful in a simple but elegant black dress and a hat with a large white bow tipped to the side. She had an easy smile that reminded me of Emma, and she seemed to radiate kindness. Her husband was a greyer, gruffer version of Cam. He was pleasant and conversational, even while being somewhat aloof.

"It's a shame Cam hasn't brought you home to meet us sooner," his mother said. Sheila, she insisted I call her. "And that we're meeting under such circumstances. But Richard and I are thrilled to meet you. Aren't we, darling?"

"Oh, absolutely. I'm afraid my son hasn't told us all that

much about you, my dear."

"Come on, Dad. You know how busy I've been at work."

"So you've said. But surely, even a phone call would suffice?"

Sheila grabbed my hand and led me away from the two men. She had a broad, friendly smile on her face as she led me to one of the food stands.

"Once those two get started, there's no telling how long they'll be at it," she said.

"They're a lot alike, aren't they?" I said. "Like two bad copies of each other."

"Very astute, dear. And yes. Quite right. They're both stubborn and frustrating and set in their ways. But they're also soft little puppies, even if they don't like to show it."

I let out a reluctant snort. "Not Cam," I said when Sheila raised her eyebrows at me. "I don't think I would ever use the word puppy to describe Cam."

"Are you sure about that?" she asked me. "Because I've watched for over an hour while my son worked the room, and I saw the way he waltzed with you, leading but never allowing you to fall behind... how he presented you every time he introduced you to someone. I saw the stolen glances, the way his gaze lingered on you long after you looked away. That, my dear, is what I'm talking about. They're subtle men, these Palmers, but they don't hide their emotions very well."

I wondered what *I* looked like when I was with Cam. I felt like I was the one who was always stealing glances at him, staring longer than I should, like I was constantly conscious of touching him. My God, I hoped I didn't look that lovestruck.

The ceremony started shortly afterward. I lost the Palmers as I went to look for my seat. Cam had wanted us to sit together, but he was right at the front row with Meredith and Wyatt's friends and family, and I insisted I would feel out of place there, so he reluctantly agreed to let me sit in the back with the some of the people from work.

It was probably for the best. I got emotional as soon as the service started. Every person who spoke about Wyatt did so in glowing fashion. The tributes poured in, each more heartfelt than the last, and every one devastating. My eyes kept misting up, and when it was Cam's turn to speak, I felt the lump in my throat finally morph into an actual sob.

"A lot has been said about Wyatt Banks," Cam said. His delivery was slow and measured, his voice low. I knew it was his way of keeping himself under control.

"And rightly so. He was a giant among giants. Every single person in this room has experienced Wyatt's kindness, brilliance, and generosity of spirit, directly or indirectly. So, I know you all understand me when I say that he was the best man I knew. I wouldn't be where I am today if it wasn't for him. Nothing I can say will ever be enough to convey my gratitude to him. I can only hope to one day inspire someone as he did me."

I was completely gone by the end of the speech. The tears came freely, thick and fast, and try as I might, I couldn't get them to stop. My poorly stifled sobs were starting to draw attention, so I got up and walked from the place as fast as I could.

I quickened my steps as soon as I turned the corner. I didn't stop until the sound of the microphone was too far in the distance for me to hear. I found a wall and leaned on it. Only then did I allow me to let go.

It took some time for me to get myself under control. Slowly, gradually, the tears slowed and stopped, and by then my handkerchief was drenched. I was sure I looked like a total mess.

"Here," a voice said from frighteningly close by.

I jumped, startled, having been sure I was alone. Someone was handing me a handkerchief… someone who I realized a moment later was Vicki Marsh, the person I least wanted to see at that moment.

"No thanks," I said.

She gave the handkerchief a little shake as if to ask, 'Are you sure?' I shook my head once again.

"It's heartbreaking, isn't it?" Vicki said.

I wondered how long she had been standing there, watching me. I felt violated like a private moment had just been stolen from me.

"He was a visionary; there is no doubt about it," Vicki went on, seemingly unaware of just how much I didn't want to hear from her. "But a lot of this bloviating is pretentious and selfish. As most funeral speeches are. Anyone who actually knew Wyatt would tell you he was actually—"

"You need to shut the fuck up," I said. My voice was low, and I didn't say it with any real conviction, but it still cut right across what she was saying, and effectively shut her up.

"I beg your pardon?" Vicki said, and her eyes flashed.

I turned to her, all restraint I had been holding on to disappearing. "I said that you need to shut the fuck up. What are you even doing here? I'm sure you met Wyatt once, at best, and I doubt you were memorable enough to warrant your presence at his funeral. And yet you feel entitled enough to badmouth him? At his own funeral? You're unbelievable."

Vicki bristled. "You know nothing about me," she said through gritted teeth.

"You know what? You're right. I don't. Because I don't care. You're nothing to me."

She shook her head. "You think you're so smart, don't you? You think you have everything figured out, huh? So, you'll know, then, the story of how Cam and I met? Has he told you that yet? How he helped me steal clients from Penguin for years, right under his beloved Wyatt's nose. Did he tell you we fucked in every room in that office? Or maybe you're laboring under the impression that you're the first office romance he's ever had?" She laughed, a loud, cracking sound that was unnerving and irritating. I felt the air begin to grow thin.

"That's just what Cam does, sweetie. He finds the most gullible little women, and he charms them into thinking he's in love with them. He used me to climb that ladder, leveraged our relationship and my contacts to convince Wyatt to promote him. Then as soon as I was no longer of any use to him, he dumped me. With his baby. You didn't know that, did you?"

I shook my head, refusing to believe any of the things she was saying. I knew Cam. I had lived with him, worked with him. I had been intimate with him. There was no way he was the person Vicki was describing.

"You think you're different, huh? You think he isn't doing that with you. You're probably telling yourself that he loves you, and the two of you are going to get married and build a life together... I saw through your pathetic married act in a second. I knew what Cam was doing, and I thought you were smart enough to realize it on your own. But I see you'd rather fool yourself that he's in love with you even though the truth is right in your face. You know he's using you. Deep down, you know it. And you know what's going to happen when he gets done with you."

I didn't realize the tears were rolling down my cheeks again until Vicki got blurry, and I felt the wetness on my face. I blinked them away furiously, determined not to let her see me cry, but it was too late. I brought the handkerchief up and tried to dab my eyes.

Vickismirked, sensing victory.

I was convinced she had said all that to mess with me. I knew it. But there was a sliver of doubt, a fragment of truth in her allegations, and it stuck, even as I actively rejected it. It had been Cam who came up to me with the plan to play married. On my first day at work, he had tried to sleep with me in my office, and even after I asked him not to, he went on seducing me at work. All of which culminated in me almost getting fired because of him.

I wanted so badly to focus on the time we had spent together, and the man I had come to know at that time. But there was a niggling question mark, and Vicki had pushed it out and made it impossible to ignore.

"What do you want?" I heard myself say. I hated that my voice had dropped back to a tame, almost mewling quality. "Why are you telling me all this?"

"I just thought you should know," she said, her voice calm now. "You've been carrying on like you have all the answers like you're special just because Cam fucked you a couple of times. I simply wanted to correct that idea. You're one of many. I hope you've been using protection because he makes a really shitty dad." She gave me one last smile, then, with a final sweep of her hair, she turned and walked away.

Chapter 25

Cameron

"I like her."

Mom nodded in thoughtful appreciation. It took a moment for me to figure out what she was referring to.

"Of course, you do. She's delightful."

"When I heard you two were married..."

"What?" I had been watching Meredith in the far corner of the room, only partially listening to my mother. I snapped my attention back to her. She had a smug smile on her face, the kind that said she knew enough, but she was fishing for more gossip.

"I'm assuming it's a joke of some sort," she went on. "Because I just know my son wouldn't take such a big step without telling me."

"Maybe I wanted to keep it a surprise," I said, playing along. "Or maybe I've been too busy with everything at work."I made a sweeping gesture to indicate the wake, with people milling about in dark clothes and even darker expressions.

"Too busy for a phone call?"

"Okay, fine! There was no marriage, okay? You can stop looking at me like that."

Mother simply smiled. "Of course, there was no marriage. I knew it was a lie the second I heard it. But you know what? I almost believed it."Her eyes were bright with an intensity I had not seen in a long time.

"What do you mean?" I asked her.

"I saw you two together," Mom said simply. I waited, but she seemed to have concluded the thought.

"Uh-huh?" I prompted, slightly impatiently.

"Well, it's a bit obvious, isn't it?" she said, and now there was a note of exasperation in her voice like she couldn't believe she had to explain it to me.

"I'm pretty sure I have no idea what you're talking about, Mother."

Mom sighed again. "Why do you keep scanning the room?"

"Huh?"

"Your eyes, your body. You've been looking across the room since we started speaking. Scanning. Searching. I also noticed, and I'm sure this is no coincidence that the lovely Yvette hasn't been in since the ceremony. Plus, I saw you two together earlier. The way you were with her, the way you two looked at each other... It wasn't so unbelievable that you two could be married."

I frowned; my lips dry as I tried to think of what to say.

I had never really thought about how Yvette and I were perceived. I mean, I had considered it once, when she had wanted us to go into the building separately to stop the gossip mill from coming for us. And maybe before, in the office, once or twice, I had avoided openly flirting with her. But it had all receded to the very back of my mind after Wyatt's death. Suddenly, it seemed like a lot of work for no good reason. Why would anyone care what Yvette and I did? Why would anyone even think about that at a time like this?

It was subconscious, I suppose, how I acted around her after I decided to stop holding back. I barely noticed it, but she was right beside me, or she had been before the ceremony. When she stepped away, I reached an arm out and pulled her back in. I went everywhere with her; I kept her in my sights. She was an anchor in a difficult moment. I needed her with me. I couldn't do this without her.

"Like I said," Mom whispered, snapping me back to the room. "I like her."

I smiled. "That's not much of an endorsement, Mother, to

be honest. Remember the crazy woman you threw at me during Dad's 70th birthday party? You liked her too."

Mother waved a hand dismissively. "Oh, never mind her. This is different. Yvette is different."

"Is she now?"

I found my eyes traveling across the room again. Not for the first time, I wondered where Yvette had disappeared to. And then I realized my mom was watching me, her smile widening, and I cleared my throat and reached for my phone. My fingers started to dial her number, more out of habit than anything else. I stuffed the phone back into my pocket and thrust my hand in along with it.

Mother reached up and touched me lightly on the cheek. It was at once unnerving and incredibly tender. It was almost like being a child again, standing in front of her, knowing she could see right through my lies and feeble attempts at secrecy.

"Have I ever told you the story of how your father and I met?"

"More times than I can count, Mom. You courted him. Love at third sight."

"Your father watched me from across a room, not unlike this one, for the whole night. I could feel his eyes on me the entire evening. Hot, intense, unbelievably arousing."

"Jesus, Mom."

"But he never made the move. I could tell he wanted to. I wanted him to. I did all I could to encourage him. Still, we shot darts at each other with our eyes for the entire night, and finally, my friends told me it was time to go, and that was that. I agonized over it for the whole week. I stayed up at night, regretting my cowardice, wishing I had taken the initiative. So, the next time we met, I wasn't going to repeat my mistake. I walked up to him, and I told him how I felt, and it was the bravest thing I've ever done, and the most satisfying, and the proudest."

"This is wonderful, Mom. Really. But what does it have to

do with anything?"

"You should tell her how you feel, Cam. It's so obvious to me, and your father, and anyone with eyes, really. Why isn't it to you?"

"I..."

"I don't know about this fake marriage. I'm sure there is an innocent story behind all of it, which I hope I'll get to hear someday... What I do know is that it has brought you and Yvette together, and that was clearly a good thing. Don't be like your father. Don't let her get away just because you can't figure out how to say what you feel."

Yvette was nowhere to be found. I looked all around the house, going from room to room. I stopped everyone from work I saw and asked them if they had seen her, but no one seemed to have seen her since the ceremony.

It was a large house. One of Wyatt's quieter accomplishments, but it was gorgeous. He had planned to have a large family, but work always seemed to get in the way. I went from room to room, growing increasingly uncomfortable. It was strange, and it felt like an intrusion.

Suddenly, I had so much to say to Yvette; stuff I had been holding on to, things I had been thinking but had been too afraid to admit, at least out loud. I had always known this moment would come. The death of Wyatt had come at a terrible time, and it was a tragedy in every sense. But it had also forced everyone, I included, to push everything else into the background. I would have liked to think that I would have reached my epiphany without my mother's intervention, but who knew? It didn't matter, at the end of the day. I had gotten where I needed to be.

I was just about to give up when I heard voices coming from one of the rooms down the hall. Or rather, a voice, just loud enough to carry over to me, and, as I got closer, it started to sound familiar. And then I got to the very end of the hall, and I heard the angry, clipped tones that could only belong to one person.

I backed away, slowly, hoping I could get away before she heard me. Just as I was turning around, though, I felt my hip connect with something hard. I whipped around, stretching my hands out in anticipation. But I grasped only thin air. I saw the vase fly, inches from my fingertips, and finally crashing to the hard marble floor. It was loud and raucous, the noise reverberating and bouncing from the walls and echoing down the hall.

In the room at the end of the hall, the voice went silent. I froze, hoping she hadn't heard me. But moments later, the sound of footsteps came, and with them, the curious, twisted face of Vicki Marsh poking out from the door.

"Cam?"

I should have left. I should have walked away and not engaged, because that was always how I got in trouble with Vicki. And I would have. But something about her face drew me in. It made me curious. I remembered the way she had sounded when we spoke on the phone, back when Emma had run away. Defeated, resigned. The Vicki I knew was many things, but resigned was not one of them. And so, I took a step forward instead of away.

She stepped aside to let me into the room. As I walked past her, I noticed the redness in her eyes was still there. Her face was pale, strained. There was almost nothing of the vibrant, aggressively confident woman I knew.

"Is everything okay?" I asked her.

She closed the door behind her, her hand lingering on the lock as if she was trying to decide whether to turn it or not. Her phone was in her other hand, the screen still lit. Her expression was strange; pensive and open.

Her phone buzzed as she continued to stare at me. My eyes darted to the screen, and even from a distance, I could make out the name Mike. That would explain why she had been yelling. They were in the middle of a fight.

I wished I had followed my initial instinct and left. I had no intention of getting in the middle of whatever this was. Even though a part of me flushed with pleasure at the thought that they were not as perfect as they had initially seemed. Maybe I could sneak away while she answered the call?

But she didn't answer the call. She hung up, and when he called again a moment later, she let out an angry huff and flung the phone away. I heard it thud into a corner somewhere.

"That fucking asshole," she cursed under her breath.

Don't engage, Cam. Walk away.

"What did he do?" I heard myself ask. I was genuinely curious. My initial reaction to Mike had been colored somewhat by the anger at his closeness with Emma, but even then, I thought he was a nice guy. Too nice to be with Vicki, for one. I couldn't imagine him doing anything that would make Vicki call him an asshole.

"It's complicated," Vicki said with a shrug. Dismissive. She didn't want to talk about it. And in doing so, she was giving me an out. If I was going to leave, then this was the perfect moment.

"I didn't mean to eavesdrop," I said. "But you seem agitated. More than usual, obviously."

Vicki smiled. "You always did see me so clearly, Cam. You know, I think you understand me better than anyone ever has. It's why we were so good together."

"We were not good together, Vicki," I said, shaking my head.

"Maybe not at the end," Vicki said. "But when we first got together? We were like an inferno. Do you remember?" She lumbered toward me. It was the first time I noticed how unsteady she looked on her feet. And that was when it hit me that she was drunk. Or at least slightly buzzed. Her speech was starting to slur, too.

"Do you remember?" she asked again. She swayed this way and that, trying to compensate for her lack of balance by taking longer strides. The result was that she sort of fell toward me, her feet not being quick enough to carry her and causing her to fall forward. I reached out and grabbed her instinctively.

"Remember when we fucked at that company party? In the bathroom. I had worn this little black dress, which I knew would drive you crazy, and you dragged me away in the middle of the speeches and pinned me to a bathroom wall."

"You should sit down, Vicki," I said.

Her entire body weight was on me. She made no effort to move or straighten up. I had to half drag, half carry her to the nearest chair, where I sat her down as gently as I could.

"Or that time we did it in your car before walking into that client meeting," Vicki went on.

"You mean the client you didn't tell me you were trying to poach from us?"

"Ah, so you do remember," Vicki said, a note of triumph in her voice.

I tried to straighten up, but she grabbed me by the front of my shirt and held me fast.

"Why won't you admit it?" she asked. "We were great together."

Strange, I thought, how she remembered the crazy sex but not the crazy arguments after. She remembered the bathroom sex, but not the inappropriate speech she gave at the end of the night. When I thought about Vicki and me, it was impossible to look past the toxicity of our relationship.

"Okay. We were great together, Vicki. Until we weren't. If you want to go down memory lane, go all the way down the street."

"You're right," she said. "We were toxic." The words came out in a sigh, both tired and defeated. Her whole body slumped, and for the first time in all my years of knowing Vicki, she looked like she was about to cry.

"What's going on?" I asked her. "Talk to me."

Vicki dropped her eyes to the floor. She swiped at her face

with an unsteady hand, and I thought I saw her shoulders shake. I remained on my haunches beside her, at a loss on what to do.

She regained her composure fairly quickly. When she looked up, her eyes were moist, but she smiled weakly at me to let me know she was okay.

"Mike was going to propose to me," she finally said.

My eyebrows shot up, but I remained silent so she could continue.

"I found the ring in his sock drawer while putting away his clothes, and I just freaked out. I tried to forget about it; I told myself it probably meant nothing, and I was going to act as nothing had happened. But Mike has always been able to see right through my bullshit, so after he prodded, I confronted him about it. We had this huge fight. I don't even know why I was angry at him, but I was. I told him I wasn't sure marriage was something I was ready for, and then *he* got angry and said I was not being honest about why, and that the natural progression of any relationship should lead up to marriage..."

She trailed off. I could almost imagine how the rest of the fight had panned out. Vicki and I had had a very similar one years ago.

"He ended up giving me this ultimatum, telling me he wasn't going to stay in a relationship if we didn't want the same things, and then I snapped at him and made some snide comments about his ex and called his obsession with marriage Ross-like."

I let out a snort.

"You were lashing out," I commented.

"I was! But now everything is messed up, and he's moving out, and I don't know what to do..."

"I think you do," I said. I tried and failed to keep the smile off my face. I still couldn't believe I was having this conversation with Victoria Marsh.

"I get it now. This. You. Why you got nostalgic just now. I understand the compulsion to return to something that felt safe, even briefly. But Mike isn't me, Vicki. What you two had was healthy, beautiful. And you know I mean it because I hated admitting that to myself. Hell, I never even allowed the thought to cross my mind. But it's true. You're freaking out because you know it too. You're scared."

Vicki smiled too. "It sounded for a second there like you were admitting to being jealous."

I shrugged. "Only if you were being vulnerable for a second there."

She smiled again.

"Well, now that we're confessing things, I was a bit jealous too."

"Of Yvette?"

"Yeah. I might have said some unpleasant things to her outside."

"There's the Vicki I know and love."

"I'm sorry. I've been a bit unfair to you as well. Of course, you can see Emma more. I just never believed that you would follow through this time. And if I'm being honest, I hated that you could just waltz in and out of her life like that and she still loved you so fiercely."

"I never wanted to be that dad," I said. "I know I never wanted to be a dad at first, and I've been a dick about it, and I know there's no universe where I deserve a daughter as incredible as Emma. But I want to be there for her. I'm done missing out on her life."

Vicki shook her head. "How did two people this fucked up create something so wonderful?"

"Beats me, to be fucking honest."

"Okay," she said, punching me playfully on the arm. "I guess we'll work out the custody details later?"

I nodded. It was like meeting her for the first time all over again.

"Call him," I said as I straightened up.

Vicki stood up as well. She opened her arms wide, and I stepped into the hug with a feeling of immense relief. It was a warm, friendly hug, and I realized the relief was from letting go of years' worth of anger and resentment.

A creaking sound from behind us caused us to separate. I pulled away from Vicki and swiveled around, my arm still around her waist.

I saw movement out of the corner of my eye, and I froze.

There was a familiar female outline standing in the doorway.

Dread settled into the pit of my stomach. I knew who it was even before she came into focus.

Yvette looked from Vicki to me, and I watched her face go through the full range of emotions. Confusion. Disbelief. Disappointment. And, finally, anger. Her mouth fell open, forming a perfect O. I realized we were still holding each other and let go quickly.

But Yvette was already on the move. Without a word, she turned and walked away.

I cursed and took off after her. She had already disappeared when I got to the end of the hall. I looked left and right, catching a glimpse of a foot going around a corner into the main dining room where everyone was gathered.

I broke into a brisk run, turning the corner so fast I almost walked into someone.

"Cam?"

Meredith blinked up at me, holding out her hands to steady me. "Thank God, I've been looking for you everywhere. I need your help with something. It's urgent."

She slipped her hand around me and started to lead me away. I thought I saw Yvette step out the front door, and I knew I wouldn't be able to go after her.

Chapter 26

Yvette

As soon as I walked out of the house, I looked back. I wasn't sure why, but I hated myself for it. Because I wanted to see if he would come after me. I hoped he would. It's what they did in the movies, the big, romantic gesture, ideally through an airport or across a busy highway. The man would brave speeding cars and angry pedestrians just to get to her, and she would be forced to stop because she realized he wouldn't stop chasing her.

There was not going to be a movie moment for me. And I was okay with that, even though it made me all the more certain that I had misread this whole situation with Cam.

Vicki had been right. They deserved each other. It had taken every ounce of pride I had to brush aside what she had said to me and go looking for Cam. It's the hope that kills. Somehow, despite all that, I had allowed myself to hope. Maybe she was toying with me. But it was hard to discredit her words when they were that close together in a locked room away from everyone else. I shuddered to think about what else they might have been doing.

I didn't think about where I was going until I was out of the building and walking down the long driveway. Only then did I remember I had come with Cam in his car. The very person I was trying to get away from.

I pulled my phone out, stared at the screen for a long moment while my mind worked. Where was I going? Home? But where exactly was that? Cam's place? My own apartment? Did I have a third option?

I thought about just walking around, letting the day come to me. It could be the chance I had been waiting for to explore the city finally. I never really got around to it, what with work and the whole business with Cam. It would give me a chance to think, too. Clear my head.

Still, it would be impossible to clear my head without creating distance. Once I got back home, it would be impossible to keep Cam away, but it was important that I did. I knew exactly what happened when I let that man within touching distance. It was what had been happening ever since I met him.

And just like that, I knew what I had to do.

The wait for my cab took longer than I expected. Wyatt's estate was apparently quite some distance from the central business district, something I had not noticed on the drive up with Cam. I had been distracted the entire way there. I seemed to have been distracted ever since our first interaction.

People walked past me, going in and out of the estate, throwing me curious looks as they went by. I was still on edge. I kept looking behind me, expecting the tall figure of Cam to spring up from the direction of the house and run to me. Each time, my heart sank with disappointment, and my self-esteem took another little shot. Every time I heard a voice or footsteps and it wasn't him, Vicki's words played in my head, and I got more and more agitated.

Eventually, though, a car pulled up just outside the gate, and a red-haired woman with glasses popped her head out and smiled at me.

"Yvette, right?" she asked.

I nodded, sighing in relief. I walked around and got into the passenger side of the car.

"Funeral?" she asked me as we got on our way.

I wondered for a second how she could tell, and then I noticed I was in all black.

"Oh. Yes. My boss, actually."

"I'm sorry to hear that."

I nodded.

It wasn't rude that I had left early, was it? I hoped
Meredith wouldn't be offended that I had. I doubted she would
even notice; it seemed like half the city had shown up to pay their
respects to Wyatt. In between juggling guests and keeping the
function going, she would have her hands full. But I did feel a bit
guilty for not saying goodbye to Sheila, Cam's mom. We had only
interacted briefly, but she had been really nice to me.

"Do you mind…?" I asked, reaching for the radio. The
driver shook her head, and long red hair flapped about her face.

The music swelled in the car, something sad and beautiful.
It reminded me of my first night at Cam's place. My 'wedding
night,' as it were. It had all seemed so simple back then. Just the
two of us, dancing and running around in the living room while
classical music played in the background.

"Sorry," I said, my hand flashing out and switching the
radio off mid-song. "Silence works, too."

The driver smiled, glancing at me for a second before
turning back to the road. She was actually very pretty; her hair fell
around her face in a perfect halo, and she had flawless, glowing
skin. I was tempted to ask her how she got her hair to be so
lustrous, but she didn't strike me as the conversational type. So I
fell silent, and after a few minutes, I found that I actually preferred
it. There was something about being on the road, the wind
whipping through the windows and over you, with nothing but the
sound of the highway breaking through. It was strangely peaceful.

I had the rough outline of a plan by the time we got home.
There was a lot I would have to do, though, before I could put it
into action.

I thanked my driver, and she beamed at me as she drove
away. There I stood, in the middle of the street, still unsure which
way to go. Cam's apartment? Mine?

I turned, as I seemed to have been doing since I moved to
the damn city and walked toward Cam's apartment building. Like
all the times before, my heart was beating fast. Unlike those other
times, it wasn't out of excitement.

I unlocked the door and was hit right away by that familiar smell, that intangible scent of home. I hadn't even realized how much I loved that about the apartment; the combined fragrance of our brief life together. Our fake life together that existed only because he wanted to hurt his ex. The very same ex I found him fumbling around with.

I shook my head and ventured in. There was a lot to do, but I knew I had a little time. Even if Cam were able to get out of the rest of the service, he wouldn't drive back right away. I had at least an hour before I needed to worry about him.

I started with the bedroom. I tried to be as clinical as possible, going through the closets without throwing everything to the floor, removing my things without messing with the state of the room. It was almost unbelievable how much stuff I had accumulated over the weeks.

The bathroom was filled with my products; there was way pinker than there was before I moved in. I was forced to rush to my own house to get some bags because I had vastly underestimated how much I would have to ferry back. The clothes alone accounted for most of the trips. It was almost therapeutic, the feeling that I was finally removing myself from Cam's house, and, more importantly, his life. It was cowardly, doing it while he wasn't there, but I wasn't ready to face him just yet. The anger was bubbling just beneath the surface; beyond that, I didn't trust myself to be around him. Not yet.

It took a little over an hour, but I was finally done. I stood outside his door for several minutes, staring at the knocker, thinking back to our very first night together, when I had snuck out of my apartment in a nightgown to be with him. My God, what had happened to me?

I slipped the key from my keychain and slid it back under the flowerpot. Everything back to normal. As I made my way out of the building, it hit me, the finality of it all. I glanced at the pool, and then at the spot where we met, and it was all bittersweet.

I started to feel faint when I was walking up the steps to my own building. Dizzy. I grabbed the railing and shook my head to ward off a spell of nausea that came completely out of the blue. For a terrifying moment, the world swam in front of my eyes, and I couldn't tell up from down or left from right. I held on to the railing as tightly as I could. When the dizziness didn't pass immediately, I sank slowly to my haunches and, feeling around for something solid, sat down on the closest step.

I could hear my heartbeat thrumming in my ears. I could taste something salty on my tongue. I tried to think back, wondering if I had eaten something to upset my stomach. But I hadn't eaten at the wake. Or maybe that was it. I was weak from dehydration and starvation. I hoped that was the case, and that I would feel better as soon as I had something to eat.

After a while, my head started to clear. The haze lifted, and I was able to get up and make my way up the rest of the stairs, bags in tow. I made my way to the fridge and pulled it open. There wasn't any fresh food, as I'd been spending practically every night at Cam's. I briefly debated making another trip; there was leftover lasagna in his freezer. It felt weird, though, considering I had already 'said my goodbyes.'

I collapsed onto the couch, defeated. I would have to go to the store and get something to cook. Or, better still, order takeout so I wouldn't have to cook. I groaned as I got up. I knew myself well enough; if I got comfortable, I wouldn't be able to leave that couch. I went into the bedroom to grab a coat. I paused at the bags strewn around my bed. Then, shrugging, I grabbed one of the bags with my clothes and threw them onto the bed. I stepped out of the lace dress I had donned for the funeral service and stood in my underwear beside the bed.

I remembered packing my sweatpants at the very bottom of the bag. Rather than go through the clothes one at a time, I simply upended it and let its contents spill onto the bed. I gave it one final shake to dislodge any stragglers, and then I swept through the pile to spread it out.

Something hard nudged my finger. Hard but soft, and I didn't immediately realize why my heart suddenly lurched and started to beat. I pulled the clothes aside and reached for the box, my mind already racing to keep up with what my body already knew.

I held out my hand and tried to do the math. Time had practically flown by while I was at Cam's. Days had bled into each other, and then into weeks until I was barely aware of how long it had been. I had been reckless, too. Far too reckless. I stared at the box of tampons, and I felt the floor turn into jelly underneath me.

My body went limp, and I slid slowly to the floor. Or I may have dropped like a rock. All I knew was that the next moment I was curled up naked on the floor, nausea pushing at the backs of my eyes, panic beginning to eat at me.

It couldn't be. I didn't even want to think about it.

But even while my brain actively rejected the possibility, my body was contradicting it. It made sense if I thought about it. The heightened sense of smell. The wild swings of emotion, from giddy ecstasy to soul-crushing sadness. The tears that wouldn't let up earlier today at the funeral. And, just now, the sudden loss of balance, nausea, the dizziness. The truth dawned, slowly, like a distant light slowly growing brighter until it was impossible to ignore.

Chapter 27

Cameron

It had been more than 24 hours since I saw Yvette. Even beyond the fact that she was probably mad at me, it was the longest we had gone without speaking in a very long time. Twenty-four hours seemed like such a short time, and I was aware that for normal friendships, that wouldn't be cause for alarm. People had lives, right? Even if the people in question had been joined at the hip for over two months.

The service for Wyatt ran long. And even after everyone was gone, Meredith insisted I stay over to help her with the cleanup, and to discuss the company's next step. It was a credit to her that Penguin was still in excellent shape, and barring any major miracle, we could continue work as we had before. She had done a good enough job behind the scenes that the transition was going to be seamless. But even with that knowledge, she still wanted us to go over everything with a fine-tooth comb. She was giving everyone a few days off, but afterward, she wanted work to resume as usual.

All through that meeting, I thought of nothing else. Yvette's horrified expression kept springing into my mind and mortifying me all over again. She must have been furious. Worse, she was disappointed. I needed to find her. I needed...

"Cam? Are you paying attention?"

"Of course, Meredith."

Only barely, though. And it stayed on my mind for most of the night, carrying over into the next morning when I finally left Wyatt's estate. I had to make a quick stop by the office to collect some documents, and I half-hoped I would find Yvette there. But it was a faint hope at best. Indeed, when I got to the office, I knew she wasn't there. There was only a handful of staff present, those too getting a final batch of work done before taking a break, and those who preferred to work to keep their minds away from events.

I was in the latter group. From the moment Meredith had told me about Wyatt's death, I had thrown myself into work, planning, and fixing, and running things. It was the only thing I knew how to do, really. It helped, gave me a sense of purpose, and that was much better than sitting around moping, which Meredith admitted having been doing.

I asked around, just to be sure, but no one had seen Yvette since the service. Resigned, I grabbed the documents and left.

It was well past midday when I finally got home. I rushed upstairs, fumbling with the keys as I opened the door, and shouting her name as I entered the house. My voice echoed back to me, strangely loud and hollow.

She definitely wasn't in; there was none of the lived-in quality she imbued the place with. I was used to the smell of something cooking when she was around, coupled with slightly feminine energy I couldn't quite describe. Her scent was in the air, but it was faint.

I threw my coat down and reached for my phone. I had been sorely tempted to call her, but I had been putting off. Not least because I was scared of her reaction. I didn't think I could deal with her being angry at me; I had been convincing myself that the more I waited before speaking with her, the calmer she would be.

Now, though, I threw all caution to the wind.

But even as I felt my breathing come faster and my heart starts to patter, Yvette's voice thrilled that I had reached her voicemail. I hung up right before the beep. Whatever it was I would say to her it wasn't going to be via voicemail.

Something hit the corner of my eye as I walked to the couch. Something small and shiny. I stopped, crouched, and picked it up; a single glass earring. I recognized it right away; Yvette had worn it to the funeral. I knew because I had spent an unhealthy amount of time staring at her as she got dressed, then all through the drive, and for the most part of the initial ceremony.

Her earring on the living room floor could only mean one thing; she had been here.

I rushed into the bedroom in a mounting state of panic. At first glance, everything was where it was supposed to be. But when I walked to the closet, I noticed it was emptier than it had been before. All her clothes were gone. Her shoes, too, and the entirety of her make-up kits. There was further evidence in the bathroom; it had gone right back to looking like a bachelor's bathroom. The female touch was gone.

She had left me.

I walked back out and grabbed my coat, my brain churning. I doubted she would be in her place, but it was the first place to go.

I should have called her immediately she left. I should have shrugged Meredith off and chased after her. Who knows what she was thinking, and where that thought process would lead her?

I ran across the street and bounded up the stairs. I knocked on her door a few times, growing increasingly sure that she wasn't in. I tried to listen through the door, but it was eerily quiet inside. No sound of movement, or anything that would suggest there was someone in the house. I waited for almost ten minutes before giving up.

This couldn't be it, surely? She couldn't have just left like that. Granted, she was angry, and rightly so. But would she leave me completely in the dark?

I got to the foot of the stairs, and then, on a whim, I turned and went up instead of down. I don't know why, but I wanted to see the rooftop again. Nostalgia, perhaps. I wanted to see that old couch on which we made love. I wanted to feel the wind slapping against me, as it did while I stood on that ledge with her.

It was less windy today than it had been when Yvette and I went up there. Sunnier, too. The sun struck me right in the eyes as

I emerged, blinding me for a moment. This was it, then, where it all began. Our marriage. The third act in our story. Up to that point, we had been dancing around each other, always at arm's length; it was here that we crashed into each other with finality.

The couch was still intact. Still old and battered. I approached it from behind, shaking my head at the memory of Yvette sitting on it, her eyes filling with lust, my own arousal sudden and urgent. I grinned. Our attraction had always been so raw and passionate.

Just as I got close enough, I heard for the first time a low murmur, and, a few seconds later, the unmistakable sound of a woman giggling.

I stopped, the realization dawning on me that there was someone else there. I froze, perking my ears up. Seconds later, I heard the murmuring again, but this time it was from a deeper, gruffer voice. As I watched, a dark elbow poked out from behind the couch, and then a flash of dark hair.

I started to back away. Hopefully, I could do it without making a sound. The giggling continued, and the hushed yet excited voices. Then, without warning, the woman squealed in apparent delight. I saw a torso straighten up from behind the couch, and my plan to leave without alerting them went up in smoke.

She came up slowly, fluidly, like a dancer. Her hair was instantly striking; it was like a large halo of dark curls, an afro that bobbed and swayed slightly in the wind. She had fine ebony skin, and a beautiful oval face that transformed completely when she saw me standing a few feet away, foot raised in the air as I tried to leave.

Her hands immediately shot up to her chest. I hadn't even noticed, but she was topless.

The man's head popped up next; he was young, handsome, with straw-colored hair and a strong jaw. His thick eyebrows knitted together as he turned to see what had spooked his partner, and the frown only got deeper when he saw me.

"I'm so sorry," I said, deciding to get ahead of the situation. It wouldn't do to have them think I was spying on them. "I didn't mean to interrupt. I had no idea there was someone up here."

The man looked at his partner, his expression softening. "I thought you locked it?" he asked in a low, deep voice.

The woman shrugged, her hands still plastered to her chest as she tried to cover up her breasts. "I thought I did," she said to him.

"Please," I said. "Don't mind me; I was just leaving."

I raised my hands in apology, then turned and started to walk away. I was at the door when the thought popped into my head. I swiveled back around to face the couple. The woman had located her top, a bright yellow tank top, and she was now standing next to her partner. They were whispering urgently to each other in hushed voices.

"So sorry to bother you again," I said, teeth gritted. "But do you guys live in the building?"

"I do," the man said. He did look vaguely familiar. I must have seen him around while visiting Yvette.

"Do you know Yvette Matthews? She lives in 23."

The man laughed, to my surprise. He exchanged a knowing look with his partner. There was definitely a story there. "You mean the fed?" he asked.

"I beg your pardon?"

"Jen and I have a theory about her. She's rarely at home, only pops in once or twice a week, never has any visitors. And one time, there was this guy in a suit watching the building for like two hours. We think she's a federal agent of some sort."

I couldn't help grinning at that.

"It's nowhere near as exciting as that, I'm afraid. She works in the editorial department of a publishing firm."

The head of it, in fact. A flicker of hope sprang up in my

chest. I hadn't thought about that; Yvette had just been promoted at work. That meant she had to come back, right?

"But you know her, right?" I asked again.

"Sure," the man said. "As well as you can know a neighbor you never see, I guess."

"Have you seen her today? This morning, maybe?"

"I don't think so…" the man started to say, and then his voice trailed off.

"Actually, we did," the woman said, speaking up for the first time.

Two pairs of eyes turned simultaneously to her.

"When we were coming up here?" she said, frowning at her partner.

"Oh, yes!" he said, slapping his forehead lightly. "She was heading out, I think. Big bag and everything. We passed her on our way up here."

My heart leaped. "What time was that?"

"About 40 minutes ago? Yeah. An hour tops."

"Wait, did you say she had a bag with her?"

"Yeah. Looked like she was traveling."

My heart sank. "Okay," I said slowly. "Thanks, man. Sorry again for interrupting." And I turned and made my way off the rooftop and back down the building.

Where would she go? Clearly, the plan was to get away from me, but she didn't have any friends in the city that I knew of. Unless…

I stopped, the realization hit me like a slap across the face. Of course. She did have a friend, just not in the city. I had met him, too. What was his name…? The gentleman who had helped her move in. But that meant she was going back home!

I glanced at my watch, a feeling of urgency settling over me. It was just after one. With any hope, her flight hadn't boarded, and I could still catch her.

I raced down the stairs, taking them three at a time. I rushed to my car and jumped in. The airport was about 20minutes away. Less, if I flouted some traffic rules.

As soon as I got on the highway, though, I realized I had not accounted for traffic. It wasn't exactly gridlocked; there was a seemingly endless stream of cars in front of me, but they were moving. Even so, it felt like I sat there, bouncing in my seat, for hours. I kept looking at my watch. I kept muttering, 'Come on, come on' under my breath. I kept checking my phone in the wild hope that Yvette had called me back.

When the snarl-up cleared, I floored the gas pedal. I heard the angry hoots of other drivers as I shot past them, and the curse words flung at me, most of them snatched by the wind. I resigned myself to the fact that I was probably going to get a ticket, and once that caution was out the window, I could finally make it to the airport in good time.

I started the search right outside. It was weird because I had no idea what I was looking for. It would be impossible to pick Yvette out of a crowd like that. I went in and made my way to the nearest service desk.

"Hi…" My eyes darted down to the name on the lapel of the lady behind the desk. "Margaret. How are you doing today?"

Margaret smiled. "I'm very well, thank you. How can I help you?"

"What time does the flight to Rockford leave?"

"Are you traveling?"

"Me? No. But my… uh… someone I know is, and I was kind of hoping to speak with her before she does."

Margaret nodded, her slight smile telling me she knew exactly what I meant. She must have seen a few airport chase scenes, working here. She clacked away at her computer and looked back up at me with a frown.

"I'm afraid the flight is just about to board."

"But it hasn't boarded yet, right?" I asked hopefully.

"It will, in the next few minutes. I don't think you can..."

"Margaret?" I interrupted, leaning forward and treating her to my most charming smile. She blushed slightly, and her eyes were wide as she met my gaze. "I know you understand what I'm trying to do here. The love of my life is about to get on that plane, and I'm afraid if I don't tell her how I feel before she does, then I could lose her forever. Please."

The love of my life. It was the first time I was saying it out loud, admitting it to myself. But I realized as I said it, that I had known all along. Mother had been right. I was never going to get there without a little push. But here I was, terrified and vulnerable, yet the conviction I felt was incredibly strong.

"I think that's beautiful," Margaret said. "And I really wish I could help you out, but no one is allowed past the gate before boarding. I'm sorry."

"What do I need to do, buy a ticket?"

"That wouldn't help, as the flight is already boarding."

What if I made a run for it? I didn't ask that one out loud, but Margaret was watching me, and it's almost like she read my mind.

"You can't get past the guards over there," she pointed at a couple of beefy, menacing-looking gentlemen a few feet away.

I sighed, finally defeated. No big, romantic gesture, it appeared. No sprinting through the airport, dodging guards, and shouting Yvette's name as I ran. I was going to miss her by mere seconds, just like the day before. And I only had myself to blame. Why did I wait so long?

"Well, thanks anyway."

"I'm sorry," Margaret said, and she looked like she meant it. "For what it's worth, I'm sure she knows."

If only.

Chapter 28

Yvette

"Have you read the book, Miss Matthews?" Cavill asked, sitting back in his chair and turning his piercing gaze on me.

He looked nothing like I thought he would. When I thought of a fantasy novelist, I pictured a mousy, nerdy guy in his thirties; skinny, with glasses and a wild mane of hair. Cavill was the exact opposite. He was large, with a shiny scalp but a thick beard, and he was closer to polished intelligence than geekiness.

He looked like a Literature professor with tenure. Calm, confident, and assured, quietly assessing everything around him and listening raptly before speaking himself. He was decidedly impressive.

"I have, yes," I said. I grabbed my glass of lemonade and took a sip. "I kinda had to, seeing as I was editing it."

"Oh, I thought you were simply digitizing it?" Cavill asked.

"I am. We are, I should say. But it's not just about changing it from one medium to another. It's about making sure the message translates. I had to go over it from an editorial perspective, see if there was anything that needed updating."

"I'm not sure how I feel about that," Cavill said. He stroked his beard thoughtfully, but his eyes remained on me. "Maintaining the integrity of the work and all that."

"How do you mean?"

"Obviously, the book as it is now... that's not 100 percent the way I wrote it. As every writer knows, the finished product is a marriage between author and editor. The author's job is to bring forth his vision, and the editor's to amplify it, clarify. When I finished the manuscript for *King and Country,* I was worried it would get streamlined into this standard text, that editorial intervention would interfere with my voice. I don't think you would know the team that worked on my manuscript; it was a long time ago. Editors want to edit, as you can imagine. My point is, I barely survived that editing process. I'm not sure I can go through another one."

"I get it," I told him. "Of course, the most important thing is the writer's voice. I didn't mean I was going to edit it afresh. Only touching it up here and there, where necessary. And I won't be doing it on my own, of course. I want to create a dialogue with you. It's why I called this meeting. You'll have final say over everything I do."

Cavill nodded, seemingly satisfied. "Have you done this for all the writers whose books you're digitizing?" he asked.

"Only the stubborn ones," I said. That got a laugh out of him.

I finished my lemonade and looked at my watch.

"Would you excuse me, Mr. Cavill?"

"Of course."

I grabbed my bag and ducked out of the main seating area of the restaurant. One of the waiters gave me a funny look as I walked past her in the direction of the bathroom. I didn't blame him. It was my third trip there in the time I had been there.

I got into the farthest stall from the door and locked it. I was so pressed my bladder was threatening to burst open. I hurriedly opened my bag and rummaged in it for the kit. I fumbled with some wipes, cleaned the seat, and plopped heavily onto it. I got the little bottle I had thrown into the bag as well, and when I was almost done, I shifted and positioned it between my legs.

It was the third time I was doing this. I didn't feel any less nervous; if anything, it made me more anxious each time. Even though I already knew what to expect.

The waiting was the worst. It was agonizing, that lull, the deafening silence between taking the test and waiting to see the result. I knew it was only five minutes, but it felt much, much longer. Each of those seconds was an endless passage of time, during which I found myself drawing up scenarios in my head for how this would work out. If it would work out. The pacing didn't help. Deep breaths didn't do anything. There was apparently nothing to do but stare at that strip and wait. Even when I looked away, I found myself still looking at it.

Finally, I saw the screen start to change color. The tiny plus sign morphed slowly into view, as I had known it would, and it was still disappointing and shocking.

You can't deny it anymore, Vee.

Three out of three tests. Three of three positive results. At this point, I was deluding myself. There was no chance all three were faulty. Hell, there was very little chance even one was faulty.

I stared at the test until my vision started to blur. A single tear dropped onto my hand. I hadn't even realized I was crying. I wiped it away with an angry swipe of my arm. No, I was done crying. It was about time I thought about the next step.

But not just yet. First, I had a meeting to finish. And then I could contemplate my life falling apart.

I hurriedly retouched my make-up and patted down my hair. There wasn't much I could do about my eyes, though, which were slightly bloodshot from crying.

The waiter gave me another suspicious look as I walked out. Out of the corner of my eye, I saw him walk into the restroom. What did he think I had been doing, I wondered?

"Is everything okay?" Cavill asked me as I settled back into my seat. Somehow, he managed to walk the line between aloof and concerned quite well. Or maybe he was just being civil.

"Yes. Sorry to keep you." I had to. I had tried taking the test when I got to the restaurant, thirty minutes before he did, and then again fifteen minutes later, but my bladder had either been empty or uncooperative on both occasions.

"It's not a problem," he said.

"Are we in agreement, then?" I asked him. "About the

book?"

"One question," he said, putting up a long finger. "I understand the idea of digitizing books. I get the purpose. But tell me, honestly. Does this benefit me at all, or is this purely about your publishing company?"

"It's a bit of both, Mr. Cavill. And that's the truth. We get to modernize our library, maybe push sales a bit with the rereleased material. But we also put your book in the hands of new readers. At the very least, we introduce the world of *King and Country* to someone who wasn't around fifteen years ago when it was first released. I'm no writer myself, but I know one thing about all writers. You want to be heard. No matter what happens with the book, this gives you a second chance at doing just that."

Cavill grinned. I suddenly got the sense that there was more to the meeting than I had initially assumed.

"You know, Miss Matthews, you're a very impressive young woman," he said after a thoughtful pause. I couldn't say for sure, but I thought his eyes were smiling, too. "I don't say that about a lot of people, so in a way, it's high praise indeed."

"Uh, thank you, sir."

"How would you like to come work for me?"

"What?"

"As I said earlier, I care a great deal about the integrity of the author's work. In all the years I've dealt with publishing companies, I have learned that the business is always the priority. Even when they say it's not. Now, I'll give your firm credit; Penguin is better than most at the personal aspect. They at least try to understand their writers, instead of squeezing them into a box. And you're proof of that. Any other editor would have gone ahead with the digitizing without bothering to contact me. But you did. You made the effort to get me on board. You wanted it to be a conversation.

"I have a confession to make, Miss Matthews. I wasn't completely honest with you about my intentions. You see, this is a meeting, yes. But it was also an interview of sorts. I wanted to meet the woman who insisted on a sit down because she wanted to stay true to the spirit of a book written over a decade ago."

"I still don't understand," I said, shaking my head.

Cavill grinned again. "And I thought you were so sharp."

He reached into his breast pocket and pulled out a small case, from which he drew a card and slipped it across the table to me. It was a business card with his name and the words REAL written across in long, slanting letters.

"I'm starting a little publishing firm. Well, I *have* started a publishing firm. It's still very young. I'm actually in the process of recruiting similar-minded individuals. The good news is, I think I just found the first."

"You want me to work for you?" I asked, stunned.

"I'm glad you finally caught on. Yes, I do. But not for me. With me."

"But… I work for Penguin."

"Indeed. And you've been doing an excellent job there, from what I can see. I know the company is going through a bit of a shake-up, what with the tragic demise of the inimitable Mr. Banks. I have no doubt Penguin will remain in very good hands. What I'm offering you is a chance to start over, to be part of something new, to build something up from the ground."

I slunk back in my chair, completely at a loss for words.

I was so close to canceling this meeting like I had been doing since Wyatt died. It had been the one thing stopping me from leaving right away, that last post-it on the corner of the computer at the end of the day. And now this?

There was some appeal to his offer now that I thought about it. A lot of appeals, actually, primarily the chance to get away from Cam. In a way, the job at Penguin had always been doomed, especially after I slept with him before I even reported. This could be a chance to start over, as Cavill was saying. The prospect of not having to work in constant proximity with Cam was a temptation I could not overlook.

He had a point about the work, too. I had always wanted to work with artists. The appeal of editorial work was just as he had described it, amplifying. Figuring out what the author was trying to say and helping them do exactly that. If he saw that in me, it meant he understood who I was, who I wanted to be professionally. The more I thought about it, the more I realized it was a gift, a golden opportunity.

There was only one problem. Well, two problems, but one migraine at a time.

"The thing is, Mr. Cavill," I said. "I am sort of dealing with something personal, and I'm heading out of town for a while."

"Ah, so that comically large bag would be yours?" He pointed to the corner closest to us, where I had stashed my bag. The plan had been to leave the meeting and then the city.

"I don't know about 'comically large.' That one only has my make-up."

Cavill threw his head back and laughed. "A sharp tongue, too? You must come and work with me." He held up a hand as I started to speak again. "It's okay, Miss Matthews. I think I understand what you mean. Here's what we're going to do. I'm going to make this an open offer. You can take your time; think about it. Go on your trip, fight your demons. Then, when you get back, give me a call, and we'll sit down again. Does that sound good?"

"Yes. That would be wonderful, thank you."

"I hope you say yes, for what it's worth. I think we could be part of something great, you and me."

"You flatter me, Mr. Cavill."

"Excellent. To the next meeting, then." He held up his coffee cup, and I picked up my empty lemonade glass and clinked it against his.

"There is a gentleman over there who has been staring at you for a few minutes now," Cavill said suddenly. "Do you know him?"

My stomach did its now-customary wobble whenever I thought about Cam. He couldn't have found me here, surely? I looked in the direction Cavill indicated, and to my enormous relief, it was Tyler, sitting a few tables over.

"Oh!" I said, the relief oozing out of my voice. "Yes. That's my best friend, Tyler. He's here for me."

Cavill nodded, got up, and gave me a final wink. Then he straightened his coat and walked briskly from the restaurant.

Tyler came rushing over. I got up and threw myself into his arms. I was so happy to see him; I didn't even understand it.

"Whoa, whoa," he protested, setting me back down. "I'm not used to this much affection from you. Calm down."

I punched him on the arm instead.

"Much better," he said, dropping into the seat across from me.

"What took you so long?" I asked him, frowning slightly.

"Mad traffic just outside town. No idea why. Anyway. You ready for this road trip?"

"Oh, I thought you'd never ask."

"Let's go then. You can tell me what happened with your boyfriend on the way."

Chapter 29

Yvette

As soon as we got to the club, I knew this had been a bad idea.

Right at the door, the energy of it hit me in the face. The noise was oppressive. It seemed like I was standing next to a speaker wherever I stood. The very floor was vibrating, and the walls bounced along with the deep bass of the music. I wanted to turn to Tyler and tell him this was a bad idea, but I would have had to shout, and even then, I knew he wouldn't have heard me.

Then there was the lighting, which was problematic on a different scale. The club was dimly lit but not dark. There were strobe lights everywhere you looked, thin strips of multicolored beams that crisscrossed the whole room and flashing LEDs on the walls and ceilings. It felt like being in a dungeon one second, and the next, the inside of a kaleidoscope.

All of which combined to make stepping into that club a near-hellish experience. Even before Tyler dragged me to an open booth and nudged me into a seat, I felt sick. There wasn't a chance I was going to enjoy myself, but I didn't want to hurt his feelings by telling him I wanted to leave.

"What do you think?" he asked as he slid into the seat next to me.

Tyler was happier than I had seen him in a long time. I knew a lot of that had to do with the fact that I was back. I could sense his anxiety, though; he still wasn't sure if I was all the way back, so he seemed to be keeping one eye out for the moment I would repack my bags. I had only told him about the confrontation with Vicki; that it turned out Cam had been using me, and it wasn't at all what I had assumed it was. I left out the pregnancy. I couldn't figure out how to tell him that part. I had also omitted the job offer from Cavill.

Still, Tyler correctly deduced that I was restless. He was my best friend after all, and even with the time spent apart, he could still read me pretty well. His conclusion wasn't wrong; I did need to get away from it all, forget everything for a while. But he mistook the reason for me being in a funk; he assumed it was all about Cam.

And so, he had insisted on taking me out. He blew past my protests, shook his head when I suggested a nice night indoors. No, we had been doing that since I got back, he said. Four days in a row of staying in. I needed a change of scene, he pressed. He practically marched me into the shower and laid out an outfit.

"It's... interesting," I told him, forcing myself to smile, even though it felt stiff and dishonest. I had to lean into him and speak right into his ear. My eyes were finally getting used to the flashing lights, but the blaring sound remained a challenge.

"It's new," Tyler said. "I know you don't remember, but there used to be a dance studio here. The company that owned it folded, and the next thing we knew, this cool new club was opening up. I've always wanted to come here."

"Oh, you haven't been to before?"

"No, I was waiting for a special occasion."

"Like catching up with your best friend?"

Tyler grinned. "Exactly like that. I'll be right back." He gave me a customary punch on the leg, then got to his feet and walked off. I wrapped my arms around myself and checked the place out properly for the first time.

All around, people were drifting around in groups, swaying to the music, or even outright dancing. Everyone seemed at home, comfortable, having fun. I stuck out like a sore thumb, and that was just on the outside. I couldn't remember the last time I had been that carefree, that unbothered. It may have been just before I left this town, actually. Before I dove boldly into what was supposed to be my dream job.

But if that were true, then I would be happy to be home, right? Content, and not fidgety?

Tyler came back moments later, balancing two tall drinks in his hands. He slid back into the booth and set one of the drinks down in front of me. It was bright pink, with a single lemon wedge, and a long straw hanging out from the side.

"Uh, I don't know who you are, but my best friend is a man," I said. "A man who drinks manly drinks."

Tyler laughed. "Uh, wait till you're passed out under the table from just two of these, then we can talk about manly drinks."

I brought the drink all the way to my lips before it hit me. I gave myself a mental kick and brought the glass back down. Tyler was watching me, and his confusion was evident.

There it was, another reason why this night out was a bad idea. It was the one thing you did when you went out; drink. My mind had been in such a tangle I didn't even think about that part.

I looked at Tyler, and I knew I would have to tell him. I couldn't keep it from him anymore.

I realized, too, that it was the first conscious decision I had made about the pregnancy. I wasn't even sure how deliberate it was. Up until that point, I had managed not to think of it as an actual baby. It was just easier that way because saying 'baby' would make it a bit too real. But it couldn't get much more real than remembering I wasn't supposed to be drinking and then realizing it meant I was starting to think about what was best for the pregnancy. And the baby.

"What's going on, Vee?" Tyler asked me. It was subtle, but I noticed the shift in his expression, from playful and jocular to serious.

I shrugged if only to buy time. This was the worst possible time for this. I wished we were back at Tyler's, where I could figure out how to broach the topic. I wished I had already. I wished none of this had happened, that I hadn't met Cam in the first place.

Unwelcome tears stung my eyes, completely out of the blue. It was one of the more annoying symptoms that reared their heads early in the pregnancy; my hormones were all over the place. I was increasingly emotional, and it was erratic. I looked down quickly. Any longer and the tears would have spilled out, and I would just start weeping.

In a flash, Tyler had sidled up closer to me and put his arms around me. It was a simple gesture, one he intended to be comforting, and it undid me completely. The first sob burst from my lips, and I buried my head in the crook of his neck as the emotion welled up.

I don't know how long I cried. Silently, my body rocking slightly as Tyler held me. He didn't say a word; he didn't move. He just embraced me and let me cry it out. I was so grateful to him for his presence alone, for being there, and I was nearly overwhelmed by the wave of nostalgia I felt for simpler times.

Gradually, slowly, my shoulders stopped heaving, and my body grew still. I was so ashamed I didn't think I could look at Tyler after that. I felt him tap me gently on the arm, and when I peeked, I saw a white handkerchief being waved close to my face.

It took me some time to regain my composure. It helped that Tyler didn't rush me. I knew I looked like a complete mess, but I was past caring.

"I'm sorry I didn't listen," Tyler said, his lips close enough to my ear that he almost seemed to be whispering. His fingers were tangling in my hair, stroking, soothing. "You didn't want to come out, and I didn't listen."

"It's okay," I said, and I was surprised at how steady my voice was. "You were just trying to cheer me up."

I felt him shake his head. I lifted my head from the embrace and looked him in the eye.

"I was," he said. "But it was more than that. Come on, let's get out of here."

He didn't need to tell me twice.

I was surprised my little breakdown hadn't attracted more attention. People were still milling about in their packs, balancing frilly drinks as they navigated the floor, swaying and dancing to the music. Tyler led the way, using his long, bulkier frame to chart a path through the crowd. I clung to his hand, and we made our way out of the club.

An immense feeling of relief swept me up as soon as we got to his car.

"Home?" he asked, and I nodded, managing to even crack a smile.

"I think I know something that will actually cheer you up," he added, putting the car in gear, and driving out of the lot.

"What did you mean," I asked him. "Back there, when you said it was about more than just cheering me up."

Tyler shrugged. "I don't know, Vee. It hasn't felt like we're best friends at some time. I know it sounds silly, probably because it is. But ever since you went to the big city, I feel like you outgrew this place a bit. And me." He glanced at me as if to see whether I understood what he was saying. I wasn't sure, but I suspected the look on my face was incredulous.

"I mean, you've been here one week, Vee. We used to have all these hangouts, these places we would go, things we would do. We haven't done any of them. I thought, maybe this isn't what she's into anymore. So, this night out was supposed to be a chance for us to reconnect. I thought, you know, hip new club. Maybe we can check it out together, give you a taste of the city once more."

He shrugged again, and I knew he was embarrassed at the admission.

"You were right. It's silly. It's more than silly, man. It's dumb."

Tyler laughed. "Right. But forget all that. Are you going to tell me what's going on or what?"

"Can't a girl randomly burst into tears anymore?"

"Not you. You're a warrior. Come on, Vee. Talk to me.

I'm worried about you."

I sighed."This isn't exactly how I imagined myself breaking this news, but okay. Here goes. I kinda lied to you about the reason I left."

"Okay…"

"Well, not completely. Let's just say I was a bit liberal with the details. Cam's ex-girlfriend did corner me at a funeral and basically tell me what he was doing with me was just his MO. That definitely happened. And I walked in on them half an hour later, alone in a locked room. Also happened. But all of that isn't why I left. God, this is nerve-wracking."

Tyler was staring so intently at me I was worried he would run us off the road. At the last second, he glanced at the road and then turned back to me.

"I'm pregnant," I said on an exhale.

It was the first time I was saying it out loud, and it felt strangely therapeutic, like a weight lifting off my shoulders.

"Cam's?" Tyler asked.

"Yeah."

"Have you told him?"

"Um, I don't know if you noticed, Tyler, but I ran away."

"Oh, so that's what this is about?"

"More or less."

"You didn't speak to him before you left?"

"Not even to deliver my leave notice. I sent it in via email, called you to come to get me and wrapped up my last meeting. I didn't want to see him; I didn't think I could handle it. I'm still not sure I can."

Tyler pulled into a small convenience store off the highway. He smiled back when I raised my eyebrows in question."As I said, I know just the thing to cheer you up."

It was a simple store, clearly meant to serve as an

emergency stop. Tyler made straight for the refrigerator, with me in tow. He scanned the shelves, squinting, then his eyes lit up, and he punched the air. "Yes!"

He reached for a large tub of ice cream and presented it to me like a trophy.

"Oh, you beautiful son of a bitch," I told him, grabbing the ice cream and hugging it. "You *do* know me better than anyone."

Rather than risk crashing the car and, as Tyler pointed out, risking all three lives, we sat outside the store on the parking lot.

I opened the ice cream tub and dug in right away. As the first spoonful melted on my tongue, I threw my head back and let out a content sigh that was almost sexual. Catharsis. Why hadn't I thought of this before?

"Do you know what you're going to do?" Tyler asked me. "About the baby? I think I know what you're going to do to the tub of ice cream."

"I haven't even had time to think about it, to be honest. I also forgot to tell you I got another job offer."

"Uh, what?"

"The guy at the restaurant? Stoic, scholarly type? He wants me to work for him at a publishing company he's starting up."

"That's huge, Vee. Right?" I loved that he wasn't sure.

"I think so. It's an opportunity to get away from Cam, so there's that."

"Is that what you want? To get away from him?"

I shrugged. "I'm not sure what I want." And that was an honest response. The whole point of this trip had been to give me some time and space to think, figure things out. Instead, it had succeeded only in helping me overthink things, and therefore, not figure anything out.

"Do you love him?"

I looked over at Tyler, my mouth full of ice cream. "What are you, a shrink?" I mouthed.

"If I were I'd tell you to stop dodging the question."

"You'd be a terrible shrink. You're supposed to be gentle and reassuring, not callous and aggressive."

"I guess it's a good thing I'm just your friend, then."

"Just a friend? You break my heart, Tyler."

Tyler reached out and held my arm, which had been scooping yet another helping of ice cream. "Do you love him?" he asked me again, his eyes like lasers, boring right through me.

"I don't think it matters," I said with a small shrug. I couldn't bear to look into Tyler's eyes, so I dropped my gaze into the ice cream tub. "I'm kinda busy worrying about this pregnancy and what I'm going to do about it. I don't know if I also have time to think about the asshole responsible for it."

"Some would say the two are intricately linked."

"Some would be wrong. Look, Tyler. I appreciate all this. I love you for trying to cheer me up, and I'm sorry I didn't tell you about what really happened with Cam. But I'm not ready to deal with all this. Not just yet. It's still a bit raw. I'm getting there, but I'll need some time. So, you know, can we talk about something else?"

He looked at me for a long time as if he was trying to read my mind. Eventually, he nodded, as if he was accepting that he wouldn't be getting anything more out of me.

"Restaurant's done," he said. I thought it was an excellent choice of topic. "We should be ready to open in a few days."

"No way, really?"

"Yup. All thanks to you, of course."

"Oh, it was nothing. Can I come and see?"

"Sure. You can come with me tomorrow to make some final checks."

"Sweet. It's a date. But on one condition."

Tyler rolled his eyes. He already knew where I was going.

"Promise you won't badger me with Cam questions."

"I will make no such promises," he declared. But he gave me a playful shove with his shoulder. "Come on, let's get you home."

Chapter 30

Cameron

I had always known I would go after her. It was never in doubt. The only question was when.

I knew she had gone back home, so that was a good starting point. I had made a point of trying her phone every morning but had long given up hope that she would answer any of my calls. So, the only way I was going to see her, speak to her, was in person. But when? How?

It was the absolute worst time to leave; the company was in rebuilding mode, everyone was still adjusting to the news of Wyatt's death, and things hadn't returned to normal yet. As Meredith repeatedly told me, it was leadership time.

And I would have been all for that role if I wasn't met the morning after by that email from Yvette, requesting a few days off. It was very smartly done on her part; I couldn't exactly say no, because she said she needed time to refocus after the recent events, which I initially understood to be a reference to Wyatt's funeral, but later realized might just as well have meant the stuff with us. She timed it a day after leaving, too, so that even if I said no, I would still have to give her some time to plan a return trip. Very smart, efficient thinking. But that was Yvette for you.

After that, I couldn't focus on anything at work. I was effectively a zombie, dragging myself from one meeting to another, nodding mindlessly at the charts and documents put in front of me, and responding with "What?" whenever someone nudged me or asked me something more than once.

It was Gabriel who snapped me out of it. Gabriel, of all people.

He showed up unannounced to my office, where he found me staring absently out the window and informed me that he had been calling my name for the last five minutes.

"You are out of it, man," he commented, sitting down and sliding a thick folder across the desk to me.

"What's this?" I asked him.

"Good news," he said. "But I'm guessing it's not the good news you're hoping for."

"Just tell me, jeez!"

"Shared custody agreement. Vicki's lawyers sent this to me this morning. Something about a verbal agreement you two had, that this was just to formalize things?"

"Oh, yeah."

I had forgotten about my little moment with Vicki back at the funeral.

"This *is* good news, right?" Gabriel asked. He was studying me closely with his eyes narrowed in suspicion.

"Yeah, of course."

"I have to say, buddy. It doesn't look like it. Unless you didn't actually want this whole thing to be over?"

"This back and forth with Vicki. You want it to be done, right? You're not using it as some twisted scheme to keep her close, are you?"

"Don't be ridiculous, Gabriel. This is about Emma. This was always about Emma."

"Okay, then we should celebrate, right? Go out for a drink after work?"

"I don't know… It's kinda crazy here at the moment."

"What the hell is going on with you? You never say no to drinks."

"I'm not saying no. I'm saying some other time."

Gabriel looked at me like I had just insulted him.

"Okay, man. Enough of this bullshit. This is about Yvette, isn't it?"

I tried to remember if I had ever talked about Yvette to him, with him, but I came up blank.

"I don't see what that has to do with—"

"And yet here you are, so distracted you didn't even notice your shirt is buttoned up wrong."

"What?"I looked down in panic. It was almost two in the afternoon. If it was true, then I had been going around looking like a madman all day. But my shirt was buttoned up just fine. Gabriel was grinning when I looked back at him.

"And that's my point exactly. You didn't even know."

"What do you want, Gabriel?" I said, a little exasperated. I wasn't in the mood for his games.

"Just go after her and stop torturing yourself."

Once again, I tried to think, but I couldn't remember a single instance where I had shared what happened between Yvette and me with him.

"You know what? Fine." He got up and straightened his coat. He pointed a long finger at the document and then at me. "Don't forget to go over this and sign it. I know you two made up and everything, but you can never be too safe."He turned and walked to the door. He stood there for a moment, then turned and looked at me."Go after her," he said, then he gave me a little salute and was gone.

I told myself I was already thinking about it, that Gabriel had simply voiced a thought I had been toying with in the first place. But something about his prompt spurred me into action. There was no real reason for me not to go; it was affecting my ability to work. Among other things. I was almost sure I would be able to let it go if only I could speak to Yvette and hear it directly from her. If she told me to my face that it was over. Not that it had ever really begun. Maybe then I could move on.

Two days. I would drive to Rockford and be back in two days. I would seek her out and speak to her, get things sorted out, and then drive back. I could finalize the work I had today, carry whatever I didn't, and work on it at the hotel. Or, and a smile snaked across my face when I realized this, I could delegate. It was one of the perks of being a boss.

Once I made up my mind, I found everything falling into place. It was like waking from a stupor, like being reanimated after a long period on ice. I could get the urgent work out of the way and focus on planning the trip.

The drive up to Rockford was more scenic than I had expected. It was a reminder that I didn't get out as much as I should. But I already knew that. Even before taking over from Wyatt officially, I had been working way too much, so there was never any time for a trip like this.

I loved being out on the road. The wind and the open road were surprisingly pleasant, and I made a mental note to myself to do this more often. I imagined doing this with Yvette, and another pang hit me. I couldn't really blame myself for it, but the two of us hadn't gotten out much either in our brief time together. Work and the complicated situation of our fake marriage. And then Wyatt's death, and that unfortunate incident with Vicki. We had almost run the full course of an entire relationship in a few months. If she would have me, maybe we could drive back together, make a road trip of it. I would love that.

I made an excellent time. It was unusual, having the road almost entirely to myself. But even then, time seemed to fly. I was rushing toward something, someone, so the time seemed to dilate. I was pulling into the city a little over four hours later.

I knew exactly what sort of town Rockford was, even before getting properly acquainted with it. It was one of those tightly knit communities where everyone knew everyone else, and every building looked like it had been around for ages. I had no trouble locating the hotel I had booked online, and I wasn't surprised in the least to discover that it looked nothing like the ad. Not in a bad way, though. The Bedrock Hotel was billed as a modern-day inn, with sleek, high walls and an open floor plan in the reception area. But its real charm was in the way it managed to retain some of the vintage feels.

I was hoping I could track Yvette down soon, but not so hopeful as to forego booking a room for the night. The portly lady behind the counter peered at me curiously as she asked me how long I was staying, and I shrugged and told her two days. To begin with. Less, ideally, I wanted to add. But she didn't seem the type for small talk.

I went up to my room and threw my suitcase onto the bed. Then, changing into less restricting clothing, I locked my room and headed out once more. I stopped at the reception desk, figuring I might as well start asking from there.

"Hi, excuse me? I'm looking for a lady by the name Yvette Matthews. I know it's presumptuous to assume that everyone in town knows everyone else, but…"

The lady shook her head. "I don't know a Matthews, but you should ask our security guard over by the door. He is good with names and sometimes with faces."

It turned out he was more than just good. With minimal description, he immediately knew who I was talking about, and even correctly pointed out that 'Miz Matthews' had left for the big city a few months ago. He didn't know much more than that, but he did tell me to try asking at a local restaurant over in the center of town.

"I know she used to hang out with Nancy's boy. The best shot you have is to look for him."

I was pleasantly surprised by how easy it had been. Nancy's boy was definitely Tyler, Yvette's best friend, and I already had an address for his restaurant.

I decided to forego the car and just walk. It would be more fun seeing the town that way, and there was the slightest chance I could run into Yvette on the street. It was a small town, after all.

Rockford was beautiful. Small, slightly claustrophobic, but it was a perfect place to settle down. It wasn't too much of a stretch picturing myself buying a house with a large yard, starting a family, living a simple life. I hadn't even noticed how quiet it was, how peaceful it seemed without the bustle of endless traffic, and people yelling at each other in the streets. From what little Yvette had said of Rockford, she had always sounded slightly ashamed of it, like she couldn't wait to get out. I didn't understand that. But then again, my world must have seen just as strange to her at first.

Finding the restaurant wasn't hard. It was right in the middle of the busiest part of town. The sign blinked up at me from a distance, but once I got up close, I realized the neon lights were off. And, closer still, I saw that the doors were closed. I glared at the sign on the door that read 'Closed for Renovation,' and my heart sank like a lead weight.

I was just about to turn and head back when I saw a flash of movement through the glass on the front. I was sure I had imagined it, but I cupped my hands on the glass and squinted into the store all the same. I was just in time to catch a heel as it disappeared into the back. There was someone inside.

I hurriedly walked around the building, looking for the back door. I had to jump over a pile of what appeared to be building materials, navigating past an over-full garbage dumpster, and finally emerging into a narrow street with a small black door.

I walked up to it and gave it a sharp rap.

Maybe I had imagined it, I thought. Maybe the foot I had seen was a trick of the light. Maybe…

I heard the sound of footsteps, and after a loud clink, the heavy metallic door swung toward me, and out stepped the tall, skinny guy I remembered from that fateful day when Yvette moved in across from me. His eyes popped when he saw me. He definitely recognized me. He almost looked frozen like I was the last thing he expected to see at his door. Which was a fair point, actually. Holy shit, I was actually doing this.

"Hi. Tyler, right?"

I extended my hand, and after a brief moment when he continued to stare, I let it fall limp to my side. I thought I heard something thud to the ground behind Tyler. My eyes flitted over his head, but he stepped up and outside the building quickly, closing the door behind him.

"Um, I don't know if you remember me…"

"Of course, I remember you," Tyler said, suddenly finding his voice. "You're Vee's… boss."

He couldn't have been less subtle about it. I saw it in the way he looked at me, in the slight curl of his lip. He knew about Yvette and me. And, apparently, it wasn't all good things.

"Uh, right. Cameron. Anyway, I was… well, I am… looking for Yvette. I wonder if you might know where she is?"

I saw the hesitation in his eyes. I could almost hear the gears turning in his head as his mind worked. It told me two things; he knew exactly where Yvette was, and he was trying to figure out how not to tell me.

"I haven't seen Vee since last month," he eventually declared, throwing a hand to his hip to back up his defiance.

"Well, she left work, so I assumed she would come home."

Tyler shrugged. "I don't know anything about that. Last I heard from her she was excited about this huge promotion at work, so I doubt she would leave right in the middle of all that."

"Right."

"Even if she did, I'm assuming she would want to be left alone." There was no mistaking the hostility there.

"You're assuming?"

"Yeah."

I wasn't going to get anything from him. That much was clear. "Okay. Thank you, Tyler. If you do hear from her, please tell her to call me. Please."

Tyler opened his mouth, no doubt to say something scathing and unhelpful. He didn't get to, though. From behind him came the loud buzzing of a phone, and even though it was immediately silenced, it had definitely happened.

"Looks like my phone is going off again," Tyler said quickly. "Good luck with Vee."

He swung the door open and disappeared behind it. I stepped closer and pinned my ear to it, trying to listen in. After about a minute of airy silence, I shrugged and shook my head. Maybe finding Yvette wasn't going to be as easy as I thought.

Chapter 31

Yvette

Tyler found me under a table when he came back.

I had managed to crawl out of the kitchen and back to the dining area, where, for whatever reason, I decided the safest course of action was to get under a table. I kept expecting Cam to barge in and find me there, bent over in a ridiculous position, my dress riding up and exposing my thighs. Not that that would match my embarrassment at being in this position in the first place.

"Well, well, well," Tyler started to say, but I held a finger up to my lips, indicating that he should shut up. I pointed to the door behind him and then made the shushing gesture again. *Don't speak; he could still be out there.*

Tyler nodded, his grin clearly an amused one. He glanced dramatically at his watch and then yawned. After about a minute, he dropped to his knees and slowly crawled under the table to me.

"Do you really think this is necessary?" he whispered.

I shushed him again, but he plowed on nonetheless.

"He's gone, woman. For Christ's sake."

But I didn't come out. Not until five minutes later, when I was completely sure.

"Surely, this is a bit too much work just to avoid someone," Tyler said, dusting off his pants as he straightened up. "Isn't it easier to just tell him to fuck off?"

"Hey, the deal was, no discussing Cam. Remember?"

"Actually, the deal was that I wouldn't ask questions about him. And I specifically refused to agree to that deal. Besides, it's not my fault the man just showed up."

"How did he look?" I asked before I could stop myself.

What was he wearing? What did he smell like? Had he shaved? Was he in casual wear? Khakis? Shorts? Oh my God, Cam in shorts.

"Nope, never mind," I said quickly, shaking my head.

Tyler's eyes went wide, as they usually did when juicy gossip was involved. "Oh, he looked wonderful," he said. "Polo shirt. Fit him like a glove. It was just muscle city up in there, just cords of taut muscle stretching that poor shirt out. Sweatpants. Loose. Comfortable…"

"Stop it," I said, but my mind was already picturing it. "I meant, what did he want?"

"From the looks of it, you. I mean, you've got to hand it to him, Vee. He came all the way out there looking for you. Imagine him running around town, asking people if they knew you. And didn't you say he took over from your old boss? So he would have had to take a couple of days off work just to make the trip…"

"What is this?" I asked, cutting across him. "What exactly are you trying to do?"

"Just processing. Anyway, I'm sure you heard. He asked about you; I told him I had no idea. Although I don't think he believed me. I'll tell you what, that phone almost gave us away. Was that you?"

"Oh, shit. Yeah. Sorry. That was Cavill. I'm supposed to call him back, give me a minute."

I grabbed my phone and redialed Cavill's number. I paced the length of the dining room as the phone rang, my fingers dancing along the edges of the brand new mahogany tables.

"Already busy, eh, Miss Matthews?" Cavill boomed into the phone. I could tell he was smiling.

"I'm so sorry about that. I was just crossing a particularly busy street, and I couldn't answer the phone."

"Of course. Safety first. Smart."

"How are you doing, Mr. Cavill?"

"Oh, I would be much happier if a certain elusive editor were on my team."

"Patience, sir. All good things and all that."

"On a serious note. Have you given my offer any more thought?"

I had given it a lot of thought. "I have," I said. I didn't mean to be elusive, but I didn't have a concrete answer for him just yet.

"I'm not trying to put undue pressure on you, Miss Matthews. Far from it. However, I do have a small task for you. Call it a favor. I think it might help you decide."

"Decide whether to come and work with you or not?"

"Precisely."

"Okay…?"

"Now, I have been in contact with a very young writer, a woman from Africa who writes wonderfully. I was hoping to convince her to let me publish her manuscript, something she has resisted quite strongly, and for the very reasons I wasn't completely sold on your pitch to me. Just this morning, however, she agreed to work with me, but on condition that we send back an honest review of her manuscript. Now, I've already gone through the work. I won't sully your experience of it by telling you what I thought of it. But I would very much like to hear your thoughts on it."

"I'm not sure I have the time, Mr. Cavill. To be completely honest. I'm juggling a few things…"

"Just take a look, okay? That's all I ask. Read the first page, and if it doesn't immediately drag you in, then that in itself will be feedback. Read it. That's all."

"I'm guessing this is time-sensitive?"

"Well, yes and no. Yes, I would like to have sent something back by the end of the week. No, you're not to rush, under any circumstances."

"Hmm." It was a thoughtful pause, a cross between a sigh and a verbal protest. Cavill seemed to take it as tacit agreement.

"Excellent, Miss Matthews. I'll send the manuscript over to you right away. Happy reading." He hung up before I could say anything else.

Not that I knew what that would have been. I trooped back to Tyler, only then remembering that Cam had just come all the way to Rockford and that I still had to deal with that.

"Was that your new boss?" Tyler asked.

"Not my new boss yet," I said. I sank into the nearest chair and buried my head in my hands. "Yet somehow he's given me homework."

"Oh, come on, Vee. This pregnancy has made you slow. How come I know everything you're going to do, but you don't seem to?"

"What are you going on about now?"

"You're stalling, but it can't be because you don't know what you want. You know exactly what you should do, what you're going to do."

"And what's that?"

"The job? Of course, you're going to take it. It's what you've always wanted to do. And you'd have the autonomy, unlike this headless behemoth you've been slaving for."

"Okay, and what about Cam?"

"Hmm. I'm afraid in order to answer that, I have to ask *you* a question about Cam, and I've just been informed that I'm not allowed to do that."

"You're right. I don't want to know. Moving on quickly, do you know anywhere with good WIFI around here? I need to do this thing for Cavill before I get home; otherwise, I'll have to deal with it in the morning."

"Oh, because MY restaurant doesn't have good WIFI?"

"The renovation is great, Ty, really. But your WIFIis trash, and you know it."

Tyler scoffed. "You could try this new coffee shop downtown. It's quiet. Secluded. Perfect place for you."

"Thanks, buddy."

I got up and scanned the room for my handbag. It was a good thing I'd brought my laptop. I felt Tyler's hand on my forearm and looked back down at him.

"Stop stalling," he said, his expression suddenly serious. "Call him."

He was right about the restaurant, as Tyler tended to be about these things. It was in a corner of the last street in the downtown area before heading out into the ritzier area of town. It was almost out of place among the bland, all-purpose stores that lined the block; a bright blue splash of color in an otherwise dull street. It stood out without being obnoxious, though. It had a simple sign that read'Coffee Shop', and a small blackboard advertising the day's special (blueberry muffins).

Inside, it was nearly deserted, which somehow increased its appeal for me. I located the most isolated spot in the corner farthest from the door and sat down as a beaming woman danced over to me.

I started to order a coffee, had my periodic reminder that I was pregnant, then asked for lemonade instead. I smiled back at her when she brought it and asked her to keep them coming. Then I pulled out my laptop and logged on to my email.

It had been a while. My inbox was teeming with unread messages, all of them apparently urgent, most of them from work. And one from Cam that I pretended not to see.

At the top was the manuscript from Cavill. I clicked on the document and leaned back, already skeptical. I had never been one for fantastical fiction, and this looked every bit like the next Lord of the Rings.

And then something curious happened. Just as Cavill had said, I found myself smiling at the writer's choices in her writing, nodding appreciatively at the way she expressed herself. Without even realizing it, I flipped a page, and in the back of my head, I knew I wasn't going to be able to put it down. It happened with the best books. It was rare, but when it did, it was beautiful.

I got so lost in the story I didn't even notice I had already started editing it. The glasses of lemonade piled up around me… people walked past me, the music around me swelled and then changed and then died down altogether, and still, I didn't look up from the book. Whoever she was, this writer was incredible.

Maybe Tyler was right. Maybe I had always known I couldn't turn down Cavill. Was I ever really going to say no to him? Even if I was, would it be based on professional considerations, or would it have been entirely about Cam?

Ah, Cam. I must have thought about it so hard that I was hearing his voice in my head. Strange. It sounded so lifelike, so… close?

My eyes flashed up, my fingers froze above the keyboard, my other senses slowly coming into focus. I had to blink to confirm what I was seeing, and when the man in front of me didn't disappear as I expected him too, I gave a little gasp of horror.

"You've been avoiding me," Cam said, smiling that irritating smile of his, and it made my heartache and swell and flutter like I hadn't known it could.

He was here. Impossibly, he was here, in the coffee shop, looming above me as he always did. Had he followed me here? No, that couldn't be possible. I had left the restaurant for almost two hours after his appearance. This was…

"This is absolutely remarkable!" Cam exclaimed, shaking his head in disbelief. "I've looked for you all day, and here I was, about to give up, and the first café I walk into, there you are."

It took a minute, but I finally found my voice again. "Did you follow me?" I knew he hadn't, but it was the only thought of playing in my head. Over and over.

"Follow you?" Cam asked. And then realization dawned on his face. "Ah, so you were with young Tyler at the restaurant. I thought I detected a whiff of your perfume. And heard your phone vibrate."

"What… what are you doing here?"

Cam looked around like I had just asked him what year it was. "Uh, getting coffee."

"Here? Now?"

"Yeah. I saw it from the other side of the street. Nifty little design, don't you think? Understated, yet it somehow pulls you in. Subtle."

"What are you doing here, Cam?" I asked again, a touch more forcefully.

Cam's face fell. It was heartbreaking to see.

"I'm sorry," he said. "You don't want to see me. I get it. I just wanted to talk to you. Explain what happened. If you'll let me. Because the thing you walked in on, with Vicki and me … nothing was going on. I know people always say this, but it wasn't what it looked like…"

"Cameron. Please. I don't want to do this with you right now."

There it was again, that momentary flash of hurt across his face, almost enough to snap my resolve. Eventually, his shoulders slumped, and I realized with a sinking feeling that he had really given up this time.

"Okay," he said. "I'm sorry, Yvette. I really am."

I felt the pool of tears gather behind my eyelids, so fast I barely had time to react. I made a desperate swipe at my cheeks, hoping to catch the errant drop before it tumbled down my cheek. Damn those hormones. Damn me for being weak and emotional and a total mess.

When the tears didn't stop threatening to fall, I let my head drop. I felt rather than saw motion in front of me, and I half-hoped that Cam had left because I couldn't bear the thought of breaking down in front of a man for the second day in a row.

But he wasn't gone.

I felt his hand touch my chin, impossibly gentle. His fingers brushed the skin of my cheeks, slow and soft and tender, and he tipped my head up to look at him.

My vision was blurry from the film of unrelenting tears. I only saw his vague outline, only felt his proximity from the heat pouring off him. But I smelled him alright. Male, and him, and the closest thing to home I knew.

I blinked, letting the tears drop. I never got to open my eyes, though. Cam's lips descended on mine, catching me by surprise and prompting a stunned "Oh!" from me.

The shock of it rendered me immobile for some time. Enough time for him to pull in closer and increase the pressure with his lips. Before I knew it, my own lips were parting to let him in, and the soft gasps from me were suddenly moans as my body lit up.

God, how I had missed this.

Everything about him turned me on. His scent, the feel of his hands on me, the taste of him. I had never been able to lie about that, not to myself, and certainly not to him. It was why I had fought so hard to get away from him. Even subconsciously, my body knew it could never say no to him. Not when he could turn me into mush with just the brush of his lips.

He kissed me softly, yet with passion and intent. He was letting me know how he felt about me, asking with his lips, demanding that I acknowledge it. His hand roamed my face, tangled in my hair, grabbed the back of my neck, and pulled me in firmly but never forcefully. My own hands remained planted firmly on the desk, unable to move, incapable of moving, terrified of moving lest I reach for his clothes.

It was heaven and hell. I wanted this; I needed this. I had denied myself this for so long. Why?

The memory came back, the image flashing across my retinas so hard I blinked, and my eyes flew open. I lifted my right arm and hit out, catching him across the face, striking him soundly across his cheek and drawing a pleasant smacking sound that echoed around the room.

If there was anyone who wasn't looking at us, they were now.

"I'm sorry," I said, reaching up and trying to rub Cam's face. "I'm so sorry; that was involuntary."

"It's okay. I deserved it. And I missed you too." His eyes were alive with passion and lust and affection as he looked at me. I tried to remember what I had been mad about just then, but all I could think about was that kiss and how damp my panties felt.

"Now, please, Yvette. I know you're mad at me. But for the love of God, would you please give me a second to speak to you."

"Oh!" I gasped, another, different memory occurring to me.

"What?" Cam said, clearly confused.

"This is it!" I said, looking around us to indicate the coffee shop. "The story of how we met."

It took him a second. It was beautiful to watch the comprehension sneak into his features and transform his face. "Oh yeah! The story we told to Gloria and Wyatt. Holy shit, this is exactly it!"

"Totally. Now you're supposed to sit down and wait for me to finish working."

"True. But I have a better idea. Will you come with me?"

I could still feel the eyes of the patrons in the coffee shop on us. They kept slipping in and out of my line of vision whenever I focused on Cam. Or I kept forgetting that it wasn't just the two of us.

Stop stalling, Yvette.

I nodded, well aware of what I was really agreeing to and not caring. But for the first time in days, I was sure of something: I was done running.

Chapter 32

Cameron

I had been to many beautiful places, but the most beautiful by far was the Annie Memorial Gardens in Rockford. This trip had provided a wealth of surprises. But the gardens were my favorite so far. They were lush. Green everywhere you looked, serene and stunning, it gave new meaning to the expression 'the great outdoors.'

It was Yvette's idea. She didn't want to wander aimlessly around town as I did. She wanted to show me 'her favorite place in the whole world,' and once we walked in, it immediately became my favorite place in the whole world too.

She wanted to check out the pool first, so I nodded meekly and followed in her wake. This was it, I thought, the moment I would look back on for all my life and remember as the happiest, the most profound.

I grabbed Yvette's hand and stopped her.

"Listen, I need to get this out because I'm afraid it will ruin this beautiful moment, and I can't have that."

Yvette swallowed hard but didn't say a word.

"What you saw back at Wyatt's house, that wasn't what it looked like. Vicki was upset about her relationship with Mike, and she was drunk. She stumbled, I caught her. That was it. Nothing happened. I swear."

To my surprise, Yvette nodded. "I know," she said. "She had a few things to say to me too."

"Ah. What did she say?" I asked, my teeth gritted.

"She said that you were using me all along like you used her and others before. She said that the two of you only connected because you're the same horrible person in two separate bodies.

She said something about you helping her steal clients from Penguin. She said a lot of things…"

I shook my head."My attraction to Vicki was almost entirely sexual, to be perfectly honest. I was young and hungry in the industry, and I was attracted to that ruthless quality she possessed, believing it was what I needed to make it in the industry. It's something I felt I had as well, or needed to, which was why we got along so well. But our relationship was never going to work. We were just not right for each other. I've spent a long time being angry at her for that, and I realized she has, too. But it was just that simple. We weren't a good match. I just wish I had realized it before I got her pregnant."

Yvette shuddered visibly.

"I didn't help her steal clients. She stole my client portfolios and used my intel to target the ones she thought were weakest. She was the one who used me.

"As to using you, I'm sorry, Yvette. The thought of her taking Emma away scared me so much. I hate that Vicki and I let our conflicted feelings for each other affect our relationship with our daughter, that we were using her to get back at each other. I shouldn't have dragged you into this mess, and I'm sorry for that. I know we haven't had the most straightforward journey. But I thought you knew how I felt about you all along. My feelings for you were real. Are real."

Yvette shrugged.

"I should have told you this weeks ago when I first felt it. But I was scared. It's a bad habit, genetic, in fact. But I'm not scared anymore. Not of this. Yvette Matthews, you floored me the moment I set eyes on you, and I have been completely in your thrall ever since. I love you, with every fiber of my being, with every thought and every emotion in my body, and with the fiercest conviction. I have loved you since you snuck into my house and charmed your way into my heart. Ours was a fake marriage but only in name. I love you."

Yvette buried her head in her hands, and then she stepped

forward and dropped her head onto my chest. I held her, grateful that she wasn't looking directly into my eyes because I wasn't so sure I would have held my resolve.

I had expected to feel nervous, embarrassed, even. But I only felt relief. It was so good to finally get that out there. Admitting it to myself had been the hard part; this was easy.

When Yvette looked back up, her eyes were moist again."I'm sorry," she said, her voice slightly shaky. "I've been an emotional wreck these past weeks. Don't mind me."

I shook my head. "You're allowed to feel, Yvette."

"You're right. And what I feel, what I have always felt, is raw, and inexplicable, and terrifying. Because it makes no sense to feel that way about someone you just met. But I did. And I do. And I can't run from it anymore; I don't want to. I love you, Cameron Palmer."

I grabbed her once more and crushed my lips onto hers. The momentum swung her backward, and when it swung back the other way, I lifted her and twirled her around while kissing her. She squealed happily, and it was perfect.

"Wait, wait," she said, tapping me on the arm so that I could put her back down. I did, frowning slightly.

"There's something I need to tell you. Oh. Two things, actually. First, I got a job offer from one of our writers, and I'm actually really excited about where that takes me. I realize what this means for Penguin, and Meredith's wishes that I take over Editorial, but I think we could benefit from working apart, don't you think?"

"What was the other thing?" I asked nervously.

Yvette stared at me, her expression suddenly vulnerable, as if she was trying to see from my face how I would take whatever it was she was going to say."I'm pregnant," she finally said, her voice barely a whisper.

It was like a ton of bricks had just been dropped on my head.

"What?"

But she remained silent, letting the weight of her words slowly sink in, watching me with cautious, tentative eyes.

I reached down and grabbed her again, this time around the neck and just behind the knees. I scooped her up like a child and squeezed her tight as she laughed. When I put her down, she lashed out and punched me on the arm, but her face was radiant, and I realized how wrong I had been earlier. The gardens were beautiful. Serene. One of a kind. But they had nothing on Yvette. She was the most beautiful creature in the entire universe, and I was lucky to even be in her presence.

On a whim, I dropped to my knees and grabbed her hand. "Yvette Matthews," I said. "I don't have a ring, but I promise to get you the largest one I can find. I have no speech, but I'll write to you about the grandest one. All I know is that at this moment, you've made me the happiest man in the world, and I would be honored if you let me try to do the same for you. Will you marry me? For real this time?"

I couldn't hear her response. She was weeping again, openly, and her words were incoherent even before they were snatched away by the wind. But she nodded, and when I stood up, she threw her hands around me, and it hit me that I was indeed going to have a family. It was the happiest moment of my life, bar none.

Epilogue

"Are you ready?"

Cam poked his head in the bedroom and caught me staring at the baby cot.

"I don't think I'll ever be ready," I said. "Look at that face; just look at it!"

Cam walked into the room and slid his hands around my waist from behind. We swayed in silence as we both watched James sleep. He looked so peaceful, so beautiful and precious.

"You're going to be late," Cam whispered.

"You're going to make me late if you don't put that thing away," I joked, pushing my ass back into his swelling groin.

Cam flipped me around and caught me with his mouth. His tongue parted my lips and found mine ready. It was a heavy, dirty kiss, and it immediately filled me with lust. Two years and the man could still turn me on with a single look or a wayward touch.

"Ew!" The voice came from the door.

Cam and I broke apart, and he had a similarly sheepish expression to mine.

Emma was standing in the doorway with her hand perched dramatically on her hip.

"You two need to get a room," she announced, rolling her eyes for good measure.

"We do have a room," I said. "We have all the rooms in this house."

"Well, we need to get going, Mom. Or we'll both be late. I'll be waiting in the car."

She twirled gracefully and floated out of the room.

"She really should be a ballerina, that one," Cam commented, reaching once more for my waist before I slapped his hand away. "She's too graceful for a football player."

"Did you hear? She called me 'Mom.'"

"She's been calling you Mom for days now."

"True. And it kills me every single time."

Cam grabbed my face and brought it right up to his. "Yvette Matthews Palmer. You're stalling. I must insist that you leave before I run out of self-restraint."

"Oh, I wouldn't mind that at all," I trilled, reaching down and giving his bulge a good squeeze.

"Tell Cavill hi for me, yeah? And tell him to be nice to you. It's only your first day back."

"Oh, I'll be fine. It's you I'm worried about. Are you sure you can handle the demands of being a working, stay-at-home dad?"

"I think we'll manage just fine. Now go. There's an angsty prepubescent girl hooting rather aggressively in my driveway."

I leaned up and pecked Cam lightly on the lips. "I love you," I whispered. "You have one job—keep our son alive."

He patted me playfully on the butt. "I'm sure we can figure out how to make another one."

I waved at him as I walked out. I knew he had been joking, but the idea had started to hold more and more appeal to me. Why not have another baby?

"You two did it, didn't you?" Emma asked me when I got into the car.

"How could...? It's only been two minutes!"

"Rabbits do it in seconds," Emma countered.

I reached over and gave her hair a ruffle, which ignited instant protests. "Mom!" she yelled, combing it through with her fingers.

It made me smile, the warmth suffusing every part of me until I felt like I was going to burst. This was it, I thought. This was what it meant to be happy.

THE END

Dear reader,

thank you so much for reading my book, it really means the world to me! If you liked it and want to do me a little favor, please leave a short review on Amazon – that would be too wonderful!

XOXO
Mia

Made in the USA
Monee, IL
15 April 2021